STROKES OF DESPERATION

Vicki Milikan's Story

A Cook's Cove Mystery

JUDY LESLIE

Judy Leslie

Copyright © 2024 by Judy Leslie

All rights reserved.

No part of this book may be reproduced in any form or by any electronic or mechanical means, including information storage and retrieval systems, without written permission from the author, except for the use of brief quotations in a book review.

ISBN: 979-8-9890819-6-7

Cover by: CoveredbyMelinda

https://www.coveredbymelinda.com/

Also by Judy Leslie

Cook's Cove Women's Fiction Mysteries

THE HOUSE AT THE COVE - #1 OF DUET

NO PLACE TO HIDE - #2 OF DUET

Related Stand-alones

STROKES OF DESPERATION

TAKEN FROM THE SEA

THE SHADOWS FROM THE PAST

Women's Fiction Small Town Romances

The Love in Leavenworth, WA Books Series

RENOVATING HEARTS

HEART STRINGS

RESCUING YOU FOR CHRISTMAS

LOVE AMONG THE FLAMES

HEARTS UNCORKED

Check out the release dates for Judy's upcoming books at www.judy-leslie.com

Author Notes

Please note this is not a cozy mystery. This book contains scenes that may be uncomfortable to for some readers.

Strokes of Desperation
VICKI MILIKAN'S STORY

A Cook's Cove Mystery Novel

Mystery, Suspense, Romance

Prologue

Catori

They were coming for her.

 She ran through the woods, jumping over logs across the path. Branches whacked her legs, and ferns slapped her ankles. Pushing herself, not daring to look back, she had no idea how far behind her they were. The beat of her heart was pounding in her ears. Dodging tree limbs to the left and right, she ran as fast as her feet would carry her.

 Leaping over a fallen log in her path, she lost her balance and stumbled into the opening of a dead tree trunk. Head over heels, she tumbled, dropping onto a bed of leaves as a sharp spike of wood pierced her back and slid through her body. Yet, she dared not even scream.

 The air that had jumped from her lungs was not returning. One leg lay twisted next to her as warm blood pooled like sap all around. As she lifted her arm, touching the splintery point that now protruded through her chest, flashes of her life whirled around her: her father, her boyfriend, the people who had betrayed her—those who tried to hold on to her when all she wanted was to escape to a better place.

Above, through an opening in the tree, the sky was now rippling with pricks of light scattered like ambers on coal. On the shore nearby, water pulsated to the rhythm of her slowing heartbeat, and in the distance, the voices of coyotes called to one another. Tears mixed with dewdrops fed the moss beneath her head. The sound of a woodpecker faded into the dull rapping in her mind.

Her spirit rose, leaving her body, not knowing what to do and where to go. It flew up into the trees and looked around. Her life was not supposed to end this way. It would not end this way.

Fragments of herself were fading fast—her childhood was now gone. Frantically, the spirit flew, retracing the girl's path, searching for a place that was safe. Looking around at the moss-covered limbs and dead branches of the old ones, her spirit recalled each footstep she had taken earlier. Going backward over logs, following her muddy steps until it found something that had once belonged to her. Then it dissolved into the wooden necklace she had lost while running, her token from the boy she once loved, dangling from a lichen-covered limb. It swung back and forth when the wind blew, waiting, the memory of her last few years alive now safely locked inside.

Her memory hibernated in that tiny piece of wood through the different seasons. Leaves dropped, and the snow came. Birds left and returned, building nests and laying eggs. The young ones flew off and found their own mates. An occasional stranger passed through the woods, but none found the necklace. There were whispers in the breeze, secrets passed along, a buzzing in the silence.

One day, the necklace caught the eye of a curious crow who swooped down and inspected the piece. After realizing the wooden pendant wasn't something to eat, the crow carried it off. Leaving the woods with the necklace in its beak, the bird followed the shoreline, then circled above Cook's Cove.

It dove down and landed. Perching on a porch roof, the black bird cocked its head at the red-haired woman who often fed crows that came by, setting out a plate of leftover crumbs. The crow ruffled his feathers, dropping the necklace on the railing, where it bounced and landed on the welcome mat.

The woman discovered the crow's gift lying on the ground. Picking up the necklace and examining it, she noticed how unique it was; a slice of wood with a phosphorous-looking design ran through the coin like a vein. It didn't appear old, only a bit dusty—not something that would fit in with the antiques in her shop. The woman carried the wooden piece inside, removing its leather string. But rather than toss the medallion in the garbage, the woman decided to add the bauble to the jewelry box sitting on her kitchen counter.

The woman went over and switched on the light in the basement. Then, taking one stair at a time, she brought the useless stuff into the dim, musty room. Shelves that once held jams and jellies were now homes to things she would need to revisit later and decide what to do with. After placing the jewelry box on a shelf, she returned upstairs and turned off the light.

Chapter One

Vicki

Vicki looked out the window facing the water. Off in the distance, above the horizon, a bluish-gray line was forming. A storm was expected to hit later tonight. She'd heard on the radio earlier that it was going to be windy, along with a torrential downpour. However, the sun hadn't moved far enough west to be swallowed up by the clouds just yet. There were still people out on the beach, enjoying the afternoon sunshine like the bad weather would hit somewhere else, not in Cook's Cove. Vicki shivered at the thought of a storm. After living through several bad ones in this house over the years, she wasn't looking forward to another one. She hated the sound of the wind as it whistled through the cracks of her hundred-year-old Victorian house and the pounding rain on the roof. There would be missing shingles and puddles on the floor to deal with the next day. She let out a breath. *I hope this one doesn't cause a lot of damage to the town.*

The sound of the bell above the door turned her attention back to the gallery, letting her know she had a customer. She shed her thoughts on the weather as she trotted back into the retail area of the house to see who was there.

Inside her boutique gallery was a collection of art pieces made by local artists that she sold on consignment—jewelry, woven sweaters and scarves, pottery, sculptures, and, of course, her paintings. She was proud of all the beautiful things they made and was glad to have a place to show off and hopefully sell them.

Vicki entered the room to find a sandy-haired man in his late twenties looking up, admiring her paintings. The wall held several. One showed a seagull in flight, its white wings stretched out over the ripple of blue water. Another was of a weathered rowboat with peeling gray paint lying in the sand. Next to that picture was a fleet of colorful boats tied up at the marina.

"I'd like to buy one of the paintings you have on display." The man pointed to a white boat with its red, yellow, and blue-striped spinnaker puffed out by the wind. The boat appeared to be racing across blue-green water. White strands of clouds filled the sky overhead. "I hope to have a boat just like that someday. I want to sail around the world," he said, standing back.

"That is a nice goal to have. When you get one, you'll have to sail the boat up to Cook's Cove and show me." Vicki winked. She flirted with all her male customers, regardless of their age.

He walked over to the counter with her. "I'd love to do

that. Do you have a dream you're shooting for?" He pulled out his wallet, searching for his credit card.

"Oh, I don't know. I did once." She had pushed those thoughts away a long time ago.

He set his hand on the glass counter, cocking his head at her. "We all have dreams. What was yours?"

"You won't laugh?" She ran his card.

"Not unless you were planning on being a stand-up comedian." He grinned.

"No. I wanted to be a famous artist once. But that didn't work out." She handed back his card.

"It didn't work out? I'm buying one of your paintings today, aren't I?"

"Thanks. However, my dream extended beyond Cook's Cove. It included doing shows in famous galleries in big cities."

"Your work is nice, and I like it. But, no offense, the stuff in those places needs to be unique, and your paintings are—"

"Yes, I paint boats and seagulls. I got that." She turned. "I'll get the ladder to take down your new painting." She went behind the curtain, returned with the ladder in her arms, lugged the thing over to where the painting was, and leaned the metal against the wall.

"You want me to help you?" he asked, hurrying behind her.

"That would be nice." She climbed up the steps, unhooked the picture, and gingerly handed the canvas to him. They both went to the counter, where Vicki wrapped the painting in a protective covering and brown paper. "Promise me you'll stop by and say hello when you sail your boat up here." She smiles, handing his new purchase over to him.

"That's a deal." He smiled.

After he left, Vicki sighed and returned to the counter, stumbling a little as her shoe hooked into a hole in the rug. She glanced at the floor. This part of the house could do with an update. The carpet was worn in front of the display case from all the tourists trampling in. A more modern one would be nice. *One can only dream,* she thought. Everything costs a lot of money these days.

Vicki tidied up the counter, picked up a magazine, and flipped it open randomly. It landed on an article about "sipping and painting." Offering something during the summer might bring in more money. She pictured women painting together, enjoying a bottle of Merlot while trying to recreate a still-life with shells, a net, and starfish.

The bell above the door rang, and Vicki looked up to see a little girl shuffling awkwardly in the doorway. A glance at the clock told Vicki she'd been staring blankly at the same article for thirty minutes.

The child trotted over with several papers in her hands, then set them down on the counter; they were crayon drawings. The one on top was a red cartoon crab with large claws and dark eyes with eyelashes.

"Would you be interested in selling these?" the little girl asked shyly, putting her hands behind her and swinging her body back and forth. She had a goofy grin on her face.

Vicki winked at the girl. "Let me see what you've brought me."

Vicki turned them over one by one. They had a wonderful quality about them that only a child could

Strokes of Desperation

capture—not accurate, but a crude interpretation. She knew her response would mean a lot to the girl.

"These are very good. Did you draw these?" Vicki set her elbow on the counter, cradling her cheek on one of her fists. She pointed to one. "I think the eyelashes are a nice touch."

"It's a girl crab."

Vicki nodded, then stood back up. "How much do you charge for your pictures?"

The girl's eyes widened. "Seventy-five cents apiece."

"Okay, it's a deal. How about I put them right here by the counter so people can see them?" Vicki pointed to the place she had in mind.

"Could you frame them for me so they look like I'm a real artist?"

"Well, let me see." Vicki went behind the curtain that hid the back room and returned with several small mat board samples held together by a metal loop. She laid different colored ones over the child's art.

"I like that color." The girl pointed when Vicki laid a yellow mat on top of the red crab.

"How about I buy all your drawings from you and then mount them on mat boards to create a little display next to the cash register?"

The girl's head bobbed up and down. "Wait until my mom sees this!" She ran out the door and dragged in a woman dressed in blue slacks and a sweater.

"I'm a real artist now, Mom. The lady is going to sell my pictures." The girl beamed.

"You don't have to do this. I just told her she could show you her drawings," the girl's mother said apologetically. She looked over at the girl with a smile. "Sara, you shouldn't ask people to do things like that."

"Oh, it's no problem. I'd love to sell your daughter's drawings. I was once a child making similar artwork," Vicki replied.

She took out a crisp five-dollar bill and handed the money to the grinning girl, who looked up at her mother and giggled. They both waved goodbye and left.

Vicki thought about when she was a child, thrilled to swirl colors together and create whatever popped into her mind. She would sit on the beach, make up stories about what she drew, and later show them to her father, though he never appreciated them. She remembered the first time she won an art contest and how excited she had been that people liked her picture. It was of a snarly piece of wood that had washed up on the shore with little shells hidden in its branches. The painting hung in the school lobby with a big blue ribbon draped over the top. After that, she became determined to enter as many contests as she could, and she won several.

Vicki sighed. She secretly still wanted the recognition that came from being a prize-winning artist.

Several hours later, after the last customer left, she heard a clattering outside. Her eyes flashed to the clock on the wall: five o'clock, closing time.

The door flew open, banging against the wall. "Sorry," David said as he closed the door behind him. "I've got a driftwood table I'd like to bring in. If that's okay."

Pausing from tallying her sales for the day, Vicki looked over at him. "Sure, you can put the table over in the corner."

Strokes of Desperation

David smoothed back his brown hair that the wind had tousled. He was wearing a gray T-shirt under a puffy green jacket. It was nice that someone closer to her age had moved into town. Most of the cute single guys only showed up in the summer on their boats, looking for a one-night stand. She had learned that David had taken a job in construction, working for her best friend Jenny's husband. He seemed less of a jerk than some of the guys she'd met who worked in that field and had only recently started bringing in his tables for her to sell. She was curious about him. He struck her as someone she'd like to get to know better.

He struggled at the door when he returned with a table in his arms. She dashed over and held it open for him as a gust of wind flew inside. He carefully maneuvered the twisted gray table to its spot and set it down. Then he stood back.

"What do you want to sell it for?" Vicki asked, going over to inspect his creation. The base was full of intertwined pieces, and the top was a sanded slice from a tree trunk that had bleached out in the sun. A light resin preserved the wood and made the table suitable for everyday use in someone's beach home. It was an interesting novel piece that fit perfectly in her gallery of handmade items.

David scratched his head while looking at his table. "Do you think three hundred dollars sounds fair?"

"Hey, I would sell it for more, but it's your piece. Just remember, I take forty percent commission."

"That's fine." He stood there like he wanted to say something, then cleared his throat. "There's a storm coming in tonight."

"Yes, I heard. I hope it isn't a bad one. I hate it when it howls."

"You might want to make sure you've got everything secure and flashlights handy in case the power goes out."

She was hoping that wouldn't be necessary. "I'll be fine, but thanks for your concern. If I need someone to protect me, I'll call you." She winked.

"Promise." He grinned, then took the receipt she wrote for him, folded it, and put it in his T-shirt pocket.

"Goodnight, David." Vicki shooed him out with her hands. She was suddenly hungry and wanted to close up.

"Goodnight, Vicki." He disappeared out the door.

She went to the window and watched him go down the steps to his truck. This time of year, the days were shorter, making her want to curl up and stay inside. Tonight, there was even less light. The sky was now growing dark, and the sun was obscured by the impending storm. A wind chime outside pounded out a high-pitched warning. Shivering at the thought, she turned the sign to *Closed*, drew the curtains, and then went over and locked the gallery and front doors. Remembering the little girl's drawings, she picked them up to take with her. Then, glancing around, content that everything was fine, she turned out the lights and headed upstairs for the night.

She retrieved a leftover salad and a beer from her small refrigerator in the kitchen, then went to her studio, setting little Sara's pictures on a table for matting later. Leaning against the wall, she took bites of vegetables, shoving them into her mouth as she looked at the pieces she had painted stacked around the room. There were various sizes of similar artwork—shells, seagulls on pilings, and assorted boats. They were all images of the local seaside community that the tourists loved to buy.

She spent most nights after closing the gallery in this room, creating the inventory for when the hordes of out-of-towners drifted in on vacation or for the weekend. After painting the same pieces for so many years, she could do them in her sleep.

On one side of the room, leaning against the wall behind her easel, sat two unfinished images she had painted just for herself. One was of a couple of women sitting at a table in an outdoor café by the water. They appeared to be in conversation about something she could only guess at. The other was the silhouette of her friends, Jenny and Shaun, walking down the beach and holding hands with the sunset in the background. She had plans to give it to them when it was finished.

Admiring the painting for a moment, a pang of jealousy hit her. It would be nice to someday be in a loving relationship like they had, instead of the meaningless flings she always found herself in. Well, she was content with her life as it was right now. No need to muck it up with wishful thinking.

She set her salad on the counter and then guzzled the beer. After selecting a small canvas for her easel, Vicki pulled out her painting supplies. *Might as well start working.*

Around ten-thirty, the howling outside started to become louder, and a draft from the wind skirted around her feet. Paints were put away, brushes cleaned, and then set out to dry.

She went to the closet, got an extra blanket, and laid it across the bed. Choosing flannel pajamas to keep her warm instead of her usual T-shirt, she got dressed and set her robe on the edge of the bed in case she needed it. She then crawled under the covers and got comfortable. The storm wasn't predicted to end until morning.

The clatter of rain on the roof made her worry that she might have a leak tonight. However, there wasn't anything she could do unless she knew where the drip was coming from, and she wasn't about to get up and go searching for one. Any puddles would have to wait.

A sound whistled through her house like a ghost. She felt the house sway. Pulling the blanket up around her neck and then over her head, she told herself everything was fine. She was safe. Eventually, she drifted off to sleep.

THE LANDSCAPE WAS SHIFTING *all around her. The space between the Earth and another world was cracking open, and she was lost in a room of mirrors. Trees were bent from the amount of water falling from the teardrops of a face hidden in the sky. Growls and screams from breaking limbs flew all around.*

Something was about to happen.

Chapter Two

David

David listened to the drumming of rain against his windshield as the wipers swished back and forth at high speed, allowing only a fraction of a second for a glimpse of the road in front of him. Tonight, he was driving on instinct. It was what brought him out in this shitty weather in the first place. David sensed that something awful was going to happen at Vicki's art gallery tonight. He didn't know exactly what, but the feeling was strong enough to get him out of bed and into his truck in the middle of this storm.

As he maneuvered through the torrential rain, he remembered how hard a time he'd had adjusting to the world back home after he left the military. His premonitions didn't earn him the recognition he once held. He tried working as a cop for a while but found that job frustrating because of his strong "intuition" telling him when people were in trouble. It was an asset when he was on the battlefield, but you can't arrest people on a hunch. He needed to catch them red-handed, doing the harm he could've prevented. So, after a couple of run-ins with the police chief, he ended up going back into construction, working for Shaun in Cook's Cove. Now, he could pick and choose when to follow up on his instincts—like tonight.

His tires splashed through streets, which were now small rivers, and he turned left onto a road lined with old Victorian houses with businesses occupying the first floor. He looked up through his splattered windshield. The distorted shadow of a large evergreen was swaying violently in the wind. Now he knew what was going to happen and was powerless to prevent it. He closed his eyes and took a deep breath, trying to send Vicki a telepathic message, "Get up and leave now!"

As David pulled up to the gallery, he could see that a large limb from the evergreen had already fallen and crashed through the roof and one of the upper windows. Shards of glass littered the sidewalk leading up to the entrance. He jumped out of his truck into the downpour and sprinted to the front door. Please let her be okay, he prayed silently. He yanked on the handle, but it was locked. Peering through the window, he could see that the gallery was dark inside.

"Vicki!" he shouted, panic rising in his voice. He banged his fist on the door, then pressed his face against the glass, trying to see deeper inside. A flash of lightning illuminated the interior for a brief moment. David caught a glimpse of fallen paintings and debris scattered across the floor. But no sign of Vicki.

Strokes of Desperation

Where was she? Was he too late? Fear and guilt washed over David as he kept shouting her name between thunderclaps. He had to find a way inside.

David kept yelling Vicki's name as he frantically searched for a way into the damaged gallery. Rain poured down his face, blurring his vision as he ran around to the back entrance. Just as he was about to kick down the door, a flash of intuition stopped him in his tracks.

He suddenly saw a clear image in his mind of Vicki running down the street, away from the collapsed tree and shattered storefront. She was soaked from the rain, her hair dripping as she fled in terror toward Jenny's shop down the road.

David blinked rain out of his eyes, trusting his instincts. He turned and sprinted down the empty sidewalk, his boots splashing through deep puddles. The wind whipped his face as he ran, scanning the dark storefronts for any sign of Vicki.

About halfway down the block, he spotted a figure darting beneath a streetlamp. It was Vicki! Despite his relief at seeing her alive, David's heart sank, knowing the fear she must be experiencing.

"Vicki!" he called out, waving his arms, but she didn't respond.

Chapter Three

Vicki

A few minutes earlier

"GET UP AND LEAVE NOW!" the voice in Vicki's head yelled.

Bolting upright from her sleep, Vicki grabbed her robe and ran downstairs as the thundering sound of a tree came crashing down through the roof. The fresh smell of wet pine permeated the air among the splintered wood and broken roof trusses on the floor. Her heart was pounding in her ears. She tried to make sense of what was happening. Was she still dreaming? Looking up from the bottom of the stairs, she saw a limb lying across the entrance to the upstairs hallway like a huge, dark green spider. A cold chill swept down the hole, following the rain that danced on her floor. This was no dream. A tree had fallen through the roof of her house.

Her cell phone was upstairs.

She took a deep breath, then forced herself to go up. Stepping around pine needles and chunks of wood, she slipped under pieces of plaster to the sound of buzzing wires from somewhere she couldn't place. Determined, she made her way back to her bedroom in the dark. Her phone had been knocked to the floor when the dresser fell over. Crawling on her stomach, feeling around through branches and pine needles until she found her phone, she slipped it into her pocket. Another creak and plaster broke off and crashed down, filling the air with dust.

The light of her phone was all she had. Shining it, looking around for a way out, she slid across the floor. Finding an opening in the branches, she poked her head out, then punched the number for her best friend, Jenny. It went to voicemail. Next, she tried Shaun.

"Hello?" a sleepy voice answered.

"A tree fell through the roof," Vicki told him, her voice cracking. Sitting on the floor, she could hear her house creaking from its wounds. A chill swept through the dwelling. Something was banging above in the wind.

"What?" Shaun's groggy voice asked.

"I was asleep, dreaming, when a giant tree came crashing through my roof. I don't know what to do."

"You had a bad dream?"

She took a couple of breaths, trying to focus, then slowly said, "Shaun. A tree just came down through my roof."

"Are you all right?"

"Yes, but branches are lying all over the floor, and the rain is coming in. Can you come and fix it?"

"I'm sorry, Vicki. Removing a tree is going to take more than just me. And looking out the window, it's really blowing out. I can come and get you, though. Oh, Jenny says you can stay at her house. Here, I'll put her on the phone."

"Hi, Vicki. Are you alright?" her friend asked.

She looked around at the broken twigs and arms from the tree. "I'm okay, but I have no idea about the damage to my house."

"My place is just down the street. Why don't you go there? You know where the secret key is, so just let yourself in. Shaun will have someone over to look as soon as the sun comes up."

"I'm just in my robe, and it's dark in here."

"You don't want to risk that structure caving in on you. Just get out of that house now. Make a run for it. Don't think about anything else but your safety. Take whatever you need from my closet to wear. You can stay at my house as long as you want. Just let Brooke know when she comes in tomorrow. I'll be by in the morning."

Using the light from her phone as a guide, Vicki made her way downstairs by feeling the wall. She ran to the front door and opened it. The wind immediately tore it from her grip and slammed it against the wall. It was pouring. She grabbed her umbrella from its stand, then went out, pulling the door closed behind her and locking it.

Sheets of rain were blowing in drifts down the street. Only in her bare feet and a thin robe, she went down the stairs to the sidewalk. She pushed through the torrential downpour and battled against angry gusts that threatened to turn her umbrella inside out. Water gushed around her toes as she splashed through little rivers while running in the direction of Jenny's house.

Shivering on the porch, she tried to remember where Jenny kept the key. As she set the umbrella down, the wind immediately pushed it across the floor. She grabbed its handle and closed it. The rain pelted her from the side. First, she searched the flowerpot. The key wasn't there. Next, under the welcome mat. *Damn it, where is it?*

Lightning flashed, and she jumped as the sky lit up. *It's okay*, she told herself and continued searching, trying not to relive the tree falling through her roof, though it kept playing over and over again in her mind.

"Vicki?" a deep voice asked.

She gasped and picked up her umbrella, swinging at the stranger. Afraid, her instinct was to protect herself.

"Whoa!" He raised his arms.

She continued hitting him, smacking it against a yellow raincoat, arms, and the top of a head. Beads of water flung through the air.

"Hey, calm down."

"Stay away from me!" Vicki jabbed the tip of the umbrella toward the figure's face.

He dodged the move, batting it away with a quick backhand. "Vicki, stop it!"

She paused for a moment as the familiarity of that voice eased through the fog of fear clouding her mind. She lowered the umbrella, which was now just broken wires and torn fabric. *Oh, shit.* It was David, the cute guy who made driftwood furniture, not some pervert out to get her.

"I'm sorry, but you startled me." She looked at him and the tiny drops of rain in his dark hair and beard. He wiped the wetness from his eyes with the back of his hand. He was as wet as her, only he had a coat on, and she was in a damp mop of a once-fluffy robe. Gathering her thoughts, she said, "I can't find where Jenny hid the damn key."

David pulled his phone from his coat pocket, punched in a number, then looked at her. "I'm here with Vicki, and she can't find the key." He then handed the phone to Vicki.

Why hadn't she thought of calling Jenny? "I feel like an idiot, but I forgot where you keep the key," Vicki said, pushing her wet hair back that kept blowing into her face like little strands of twisted rope. "Of course, I forgot. I guess I'm just a bit frazzled right now," she replied.

She uncovered the key, which was tucked into an opening on the back of a wooden chair sitting on the porch.

"You look like a drowned rat," David said, a sly smile forming on his face.

Tugging at her robe that stuck to her damp pajamas, she began to shiver. "What are you doing here?" She turned to David, searching his face for an answer.

He wiped the drips from his cheeks. "I'm sorry. I didn't mean to frighten you. Shaun called me and told me what had happened. He asked that I check on you, so here I am. Are you alright?"

There she stood in her soaking wet robe, her hair a dripping mess, and he was asking her if she was alright after what she had just been through. "I don't know," she replied, wiping the wetness from her nose.

"I know you've just been through a hell of a shock. I thought you might need a little support."

Support? What kind of support does he have in mind? She questioned his motive. Then again, no man in his right mind would show up in the middle of the night in this God-awful rain, thinking he could use that as a flimsy excuse to take her to bed. She debated if she should ask him to leave or invite him in. He probably wasn't a threat, and she could use some company until her nerves calmed down.

"Do you want to come in?" She opened the door, but the wind blew it wide open. He snatched the handle, stepped in, and pushed the door closed behind them.

When Vicki turned on the lights, the dark room lit up into a fantasy world. Jenny's shop was a menagerie of beach-themed merchandise. Glass items sparkled, and red and golden starfish lay on white, teal, and mint-green furniture, along with shells and an assortment of brass nautical pieces.

Vicki looked around to get her bearings. She stood in the entry, dripping wet, wondering if she would ruin the hardwood floor if she walked on it. Then she pranced to the base of the stairway in bare feet. "I'll be right back; I need to put on something dry and warm."

"I'll make some tea," David called, taking off his jacket and hanging it on the coat rack by the door, then tugging at his boots.

Upstairs in Jenny's room, Vicki pulled open the drawers until she found a pair of gray sweatpants and a sweatshirt. In the bathroom, she threw her wet robe and pajamas in the slipper tub, dried her damp skin with a guest towel, then slipped on the dry clothes. Taking another towel, she squeezed the wetness from her hair, then combed her fingers through, untangling the snarls.

Returning downstairs, she found that David had set two steaming mugs on Jenny's pristine white kitchen counter.

"Thanks," she mumbled, still trembling from the cold and the shock of what happened. Then, overcome with dizziness, the room began closing in on her. She grabbed onto the counter to keep from falling.

"Are you okay?" David came around next to her.

Her eyes filled with tears. She clapped a hand over her mouth and turned away. Her body shook, and she held up a finger, indicating that she needed a minute. "I'm fine."

"You don't look fine to me. You're shaking." He came closer, taking her arms and pulling them to him. Then he stepped forward, draping his body around her, hugging her. She tried pushing him away, but he held on.

"David, what the hell are you doing? Let go of me," she said, elbows flailing against him.

He tightened his grip. "Holding you until you relax."

She struggled again. "Why?"

"Because you need a hug, and I'm going to give it to you as soon as you stop thrashing around like a wild animal."

"I don't need a hug."

"Yes, you do."

Then she quit resisting, frozen at first, stiff in his arms. Now experiencing his warmth, she couldn't hold back her emotions. Holding on to him, resting her head on his shoulder, tears flowed down her cheeks; her world had come crashing down. He was grounding her from the shock of the tree falling. She snuggled him like a teddy bear. She needed that hug.

He stroked her hair. "It'll be okay," he whispered.

After a few minutes, she lifted her head and pulled back, looking at him. He peered into her eyes as if he was speaking to her soul. He quickly dropped his gaze, letting go of her. Then, acting somewhat embarrassed, he said,

"My little sister would often have night terrors. Holding her was the only thing that would calm her down."

"Oh." Having never grown up with a parent who gave her any physical comfort, Vicki was a bit confused by her reaction to his hug.

David reached over and handed her the mug of tea. "Drink this. It'll warm you up."

Vicki took a sip, wrapping both hands around the mug. She wondered about David and the kind of family he had. She had seen TV shows where family members freely hugged strangers and welcomed them into their homes—families that cared for one another. She put on a front and acted like it was no big deal when men hugged her, but this was different. David was sincerely trying to comfort her.

"That must have been a shock to have a tree come through your roof while you were sleeping," he said.

"It scared the hell out of me," she replied. "I was dreaming when a voice yelled at me to get up, and I woke up and just ran downstairs. When I went back up to get my phone, a huge branch was lying across my bed. I would've been crushed."

"Good thing you were able to get out in time."

"Yeah." Her mind was still reeling from what had taken place, but her nerves were calming down. "A good thing." She took a sip of warm tea.

David smiled, then tipped up his mug, finishing his tea in a gulp. "I should go and let you get some rest," he said, moving toward the door. He slipped on his boots and looked back at her, eyes twinkling in the light. He tilted his head, scratching his thin beard on one side as if he was thinking something. Then he slid his arms into his coat and opened the door, letting in a cold breeze.

A flash of lightning lit up the sky.

He turned back to her. "Will you be okay?"

She nodded. "Thank you, David." She felt awkward and exposed.

"I'll be at your place in the morning with a crew to get that tree down. Goodnight."

Vicki locked the door behind him. Sprinting up the stairs, she wondered where she should spend the rest of the night. She opened Jenny's bedroom door and noticed how much different the room looked now from her days of sleepovers with Jenny while growing up. There was now a modern, light wood dresser, not old oak, and a king-sized bed rather than a double bed. All the childhood toys and teenage posters were gone. Vicki smiled when she recognized several paintings she had done of seals and another of an orca hanging on the wall. After the house fire, Jenny had done a fair amount of remodeling, and Vicki hadn't been upstairs to see the changes. The room looked comfortable enough, but this was her best friend's bedroom, and she was unsure of adopting it while staying there.

She went across the hall and opened the door. Turning on the light, she saw pictures on the wall of Jenny when she was a kid. This had been Susan's old room. Leave it to Jenny to try to preserve her memories with her mother after she died. At least she had good memories to keep. Vicki shook her head. Tonight, she'd stay in this room.

Vicki pulled back the covers and climbed in, still wearing the sweats she had on, just in case she had to escape. There was a slight musty smell from the sheets not being used. The quilt would keep her warm as long as the power didn't go out.

Lying in this strange bed, she listened to the rain outside

tapping against the window, wanting to come in. Was she safe here? Mapping Jenny's yard in her brain, Vicki concluded that, yes, she was safe from trees.

A soft whooshing sound pushed inside from somewhere, repeating in a shallow rhythm with each sway of the storm. She sat up and looked around, then got up and checked the window. It was closed. She crawled back under the covers again. A thumping sound was pounding in her ears now. *Shit.* She flipped onto her side. How was she going to sleep?

Then she realized the thumping was coming from her. It was her heart beating. She needed to quit worrying about all the strange noises in this room and get some sleep.

She fluffed up her pillow and shoved one arm under it, facing the wall. Now, she found herself thinking about David, who had shown up on the porch earlier, providing her comfort when she needed it. His pretty blue eyes had stared into hers, filled with genuine concern and understanding. His nice, muscular arms wrapped around her, offering warmth and protection. He'd awaken something deep inside her, a pull that terrified her. It was more than just physical.

But she'd have to suppress any fantasies of being with a man like him. She'd learned the hard way that getting too close to anyone was a mistake. She couldn't risk anyone finding out the truth about her past. Those scars were to remain hidden forever.

Besides, there was no future in a guy like David. She wasn't going to fall for someone who couldn't give her the life she always dreamed of. She wanted a man with money who could take her places and show her things outside this little tourist town. Not a construction worker and not another artist. That's what she told herself, what she believed.

Once she dropped off to sleep, her mind filled with strange dreams that made no sense. Colors turned into shapes and then melted into swirls of watercolor that beamed down from the clouds like rainbow-colored hurricanes, tearing up the trees below and tossing leaves like sketchpad paper into the air.

IN THE MORNING, Vicki awoke to the sound of buzzing chainsaws. She had left her phone in the bathroom, and there was no clock in the room, so she had no idea what the time was. Dragging herself out of bed, she went to the bathroom to shower. She found a brush she had somehow missed the night before tucked behind a mirror in a drawer and used it to smooth out her long hair. Under the cabinet was a box of unopened toothbrushes, so she took one. After rummaging through the clothes Jenny had left in the closet, she found a sweater and a long skirt to wear. Shoes were another matter. Her choices were tennis shoes, a pair of boots, or flip-flops. Jenny's feet and hers were not the same size, so the flip-flops would have to do.

Stepping downstairs with the sound of slapping beneath her feet, she discovered she wasn't alone in the house.

"Hello?" Brooke, Jenny's assistant, walked over with a curious look on her face. The girl was nineteen and Native American. Vicki was aware that Jenny treated Brooke like a little sister, even helping to pay for Brooke to take evening business classes at the community college a couple of nights a week.

Strokes of Desperation

Vicki slipped a clip over a handful of hair she'd gathered at her neck as she sighed. "Good morning."

"What are you doing here?" Brooke took a bite of the pastry she held in her hand.

"Jenny told me it was okay to stay here. A tree fell on my house last night, and I had nowhere else to go."

"That sucks. I saw the trucks out back, and of course, you can't miss all the noise." Brooke put her hands to her ears.

Vicki rubbed her hand down the sides of her skirt. "Sorry. I'll be staying here for a while, but I'll try to keep out of your and Jenny's way when you're working." Vicki's eyes went from Brooke to the kitchen. There were mugs of tea from last night on the counter.

"Okay," Brooke replied and went back into the shop area, turning on more shop lights and shuffling things around.

Vicki rinsed out the mugs and set them on the dish rack to dry. She thought about David again and how nice she felt wrapped in his arms last night. "That was a fluke. He just happened to be there when I needed someone," she mumbled to herself, dismissing any more thoughts about him. She raised her eyes and voice to Brooke. "I'm off to see what's happening at my place. Catch you later."

Vicki passed through the shop area, went out the front door, then headed in the direction of her house. The grass in other people's yards appeared damp in spots, brown and muddy. At least the rain had stopped, and the sun was peeking out from behind a cloud.

Yellow tape was strung around her house and those of her neighbors on both sides. She lifted the tape, crawled under, and walked to the backyard. Pine needles and branches covered the grass. In the alley, she heard the racket of a noisy chipper chewing up limbs. A couple of tall ladders that reached the roof rested against the back of her house.

"Hey, look out below!"

She shielded her eyes, looking up to the roof. Someone suddenly grabbed her by the waist, threw her over their shoulder, and quickly carried her back to the alley. A large branch came down in a thump near where she had been standing.

"You can't be walking around here, damn it!" David scolded her as he set her on her feet. He was wearing a dust-covered white hard hat with goggles pushed up across the top. Sawdust and flecks of wood covered his shirt, and he smelled of fresh-cut pine.

She didn't know why, but tears filled her eyes. She wiped them away with her fingertips.

David stood there, watching her with a frown. "Oh, hell." He pulled off his hard hat, throwing it to the ground, then took her into his arms and hugged her, telling her softly in her ear, "I'm sorry I yelled at you. We're cutting up that big old tree and dropping branches. You could've gotten hurt."

"It's my fault. I should've known better." She was embarrassed to find herself in his arms again. She was behaving like a stupid, helpless child.

He released his grip and stood back. She wiped away more tears with the back of her hand, then looked down at the sawdust stuck to her sweater. David gazed at where the dust had collected on her, too. Throwing up his hands, he muttered, "I just —" His face softened, and he reached over and brushed some wood from her hair. "Are you going to be okay, Vicki?"

"I suppose so. I guess I'll have to figure things out." She shrugged, blowing out a deep breath.

He took her hand, leading her down the alleyway and around to the front of her house. "You're a strong woman. We'll get your roof covered until it can be repaired. Call your insurance company so they can start processing your claim."

They stood at the bottom of the stairs leading to her house's front door. Vicki kissed him on the cheek. "Thanks, David." She backed up and put her hand to her mouth, surprised by her own action.

A smile widened on his face. "You probably don't have anything to eat at Jenny's house. Can I buy you dinner tonight?"

Was he asking her out? She looked at what she was wearing. "All my clothes are upstairs in my room." She glanced up at the windows. "Is it safe to go in there?"

"No, I don't want you going in there until after we've evaluated the damage."

At the sound of footsteps, Vicki turned to find Jenny walking toward her with little Jamie on her hip. Jenny was glancing up at the roof of Vicki's house; Jamie was sucking on a cookie that left a circle of brown mush around his lips.

"Oh, Vicki, what can I do to help you?" Jenny set Jamie down, crouching to wipe his mouth with a tissue.

Vicki clasped her hands together. "I don't know. I don't even know what *I* can do."

David smiled at Jenny. "I was just inviting Vicki out for dinner, but she told me she has nothing to wear."

Jenny looked over at Vicki. "She can wear some of my

clothes." She picked up Jamie again, hoisting him onto her hip. The boy laid his head on his mother's chest, shyly giggling. Jenny smoothed his hair as she glanced at David. "I have an idea. Why don't you both come to our place for dinner tonight?"

"Sounds great." David gave Jenny a salute and Vicki a bow, then headed to the back of the house.

Jenny turned to Vicki. "David is a great guy. Shaun thinks highly of him."

"I wouldn't know." Vicki could see that Jenny was trying to play matchmaker.

They started walking back toward Jenny's house.

"Maybe you can get to know him a little better tonight."

Vicki stopped, facing her friend. "Jenny, I'm warning you, he's not my type."

"Why's that?" Jenny prodded.

"Trust me. He just isn't."

They arrived on Susan's porch; Brooke was already chatting with customers inside, which they both noticed as they slipped in the door. Jenny put Jamie down, and he scampered inside to play with the basket of stuffed toys in the corner.

Jenny turned to Vicki and sighed, placing her hand on Vicki's arm. "You just ask if you need something, okay?"

Vicki shook her head with a sad smile. "I'll be fine. But I should go make a few phone calls."

"Okay, head up to the den if you like. I'll leave you to it."

Vicki pulled out her phone as she wandered up the stairs and was already punching in the number for the insurance agent by the time she closed the door.

"Eight thousand dollars?" Vicki paced back and forth across the Persian carpet in front of the fireplace.

"Yes, it's one percent of the value of your house. According to your contract, you chose to go with smaller payments, so you have a high deductible," the insurance representative said. "You'll have to pay that before the insurance kicks in."

She brought her hand to her forehead. "So, when will that be?"

"We'll send an adjuster out to look at the damage, and then we'll need to get a quote for the repairs. Our records show that your house is at least one hundred years old, so if the damage goes beyond just the roof, it will have to be brought up to code. Was there water damage, too?"

"I think so." Heck, she had no idea to what extent her house was damaged. "How long is this going to take?"

"We will need to review the damage, and if we okay the cost of repairs based on the estimate, then we can cut you a check for half the amount, minus the deductible, as soon as next week. That money will need to go to the construction company so they can start work based on their schedule. However, you won't receive the other half until the house is restored."

"So, what are we looking at timewise?" She held her breath.

"It depends. Some claims can take six months to a year to settle."

"Six months?" She let herself breathe. "I can't wait that long. Do I have to pay for everything if I want it done sooner?" Vicki's stomach knotted.

"That depends on your contractor."

"What about my loss of income? Will you cover that?" She closed one hand, digging her nails into her palm.

"Well, it looks like you chose not to go with the business coverage plan."

"Jeez. Thanks." Vicki hung up. She'd have to transfer funds from her meager savings for the insurance deductible. Her business was seasonal, and she'd spent all winter drawing down her finances. Money around here was like the tide going out in the winter and coming back in during the summer.

Shoot. Her mortgage and car payments were going to be deducted from her checking soon. Where was she going to get the money? Without an income, there was no way the bank would loan her any money. She brought her fists to her mouth and blew out.

Reluctantly, Vicki called the artists who had items on consignment in her shop, telling them what had happened. She paced back and forth across the rug some more.

"Oh, that's too bad, Vicki."

"I don't think any of your items were damaged, but we'll have to wait until it's safe to enter the gallery. I'll have David retrieve your stuff, and you can come get your jewelry and sell it somewhere else if you want. I know we're all working on a tight budget, and I can't expect you to wait until I'm open again."

"Sure. Thanks for letting me know."

One artist wasn't very happy.

"Okay, Ted, if you don't want your pottery items and just want me to pay you, I'll do that. How much would you say everything is worth?" She was hoping for a discount.

"Five hundred dollars after your commission."

"Fine. I'll send you a check." She ended the call.

"Thanks for your support," she grumbled. She was pretty sure his pottery went for less than that.

Vicki plopped down on the couch. This really sucked. How was she going to paint when all her supplies were up in her studio? She could get a job as a waitress or work at a bar.

No. She wasn't going to give up yet.

Then it hit her, and she frowned. She'd taken that little girl's crayon drawings upstairs to mount on the yellow mat board. Those pictures were probably ruined. *Oh, no!* It had meant so much to the little girl to be able to see her art on display in the gallery. Now, that wasn't going to happen.

Chapter Four

Vicki

Vicki looked out Jenny's car window as they rolled past her house, her eyes widening at the sight. A huge blue tarp now covered the gaping hole in the roof, flapping in the wind like a wounded bird. She bit her lip.

The tree had destroyed more than just the roof. It had torn through the very fabric of her life, ripping apart the sanctuary she had built for herself.

Jenny glanced over at Vicki, her eyes filled with concern. "You okay?" she asked in a gentle voice.

Vicki forced a smile, nodding, but her mind was elsewhere. The house was more than just a building; it was a symbol of her independence, her strength, and her resilience. And now, it was a broken mess.

"I will be," she whispered, more to herself than to

Jenny. "I have to be." She replied, her eyes still fixed on the house as it disappeared in the distance.

Jenny reached over and gave Vicki's hand a reassuring squeeze before turning her attention back to the road.

They stopped by the daycare to pick up Jenny's little boy, Jamie. After he was buckled into his car seat, he began chattering excitedly about his day.

As they drove out of town, Vicki leaned her head against the window, her thoughts drifting, knowing that she'd have to stay strong.

As they traveled the coastal road, plenty of fallen trees sat in pieces next to the road. The destruction was widespread, evidence of nature's fury and indifference.

Once they turned down the gravel driveway and parked, Vicki got out and looked around at the evergreens skirting the shore.

Vicki followed Jenny and her son to the home's entrance and went inside. Every time she came here, she was amazed. This was a beautiful custom house built by Shaun before he met Jenny.

The ceiling in the main area went up twenty feet and was covered in pine. Two huge windows facing the view flanked the stone fireplace. The whole area was open—the living room, dining room, and kitchen. It was like living in a modern lodge with all the natural touches. She spotted one of David's driftwood tables in a corner next to where Shaun practiced playing his fiddle. The bookshelves lining one wall always impressed her. There must have been several hundred books on everything from house designs and cooking to folklore.

Jenny set Jamie down on the hardwood floor, and he took off running for the basket where his toys were kept.

Vicki followed Jenny to an extra bedroom that had a closet full of clothes.

"Pick out whatever you want. I know my stuff isn't your style, but you might find something to wear tonight. So, help yourself. I need to get dinner started."

Going through Jenny's wardrobe, Vicki pulled out various dresses from their hangers, but each one was more suitable for Jenny rather than her.

She finally decided on a soft blue slouch sweater dress. Vicki slid the dress over her head and pulled it down. She noticed in the mirror that the dress didn't look so slouchy on her body. It wasn't like she was overweight, but who was a size zero other than Jenny these days?

Vicki studied herself in the mirror, turning to the side. The dress was shorter on her, and it hugged her curves. She bit her lip with a mix of satisfaction and uncertainty. This would have to do for tonight. Her intent wasn't to look like she was dressed for a date, just a relaxed evening with friends. Unfortunately, she happened to be cursed with one of those bodies that could make a garbage sack look sexy. She smoothed out her hair and wondered what David would think of her outfit. Would he still look at her as a friend, or would he decide to cross that line? She grinned. She'd just have to find out.

Returning to the living room, she found little Jamie playing with a truck on the floor, pushing it around while Jenny's dog, Salty, watched.

Vicki strolled into the kitchen area where Jenny was chopping vegetables. "I still can't believe you're a mother."

Jenny stopped with the knife in her hand and turned toward Vicki. "Neither can I, but I can't imagine my life now without Shaun and Jamie."

"You and Shaun were meant for each other."

"Well, we went through a hell of a lot before either of us was ready to admit it."

"I guess you did. Maybe that's the secret to love—it's a test. You have to find out if that person will stick around and support you when bad stuff happens." She'd never found anyone who did that. Of course, it wasn't something she expected either. A long time ago, she realized she was no princess, and Mr. Prince Charming wasn't coming to rescue her. Life can be cruel sometimes, so she damn well better figure things out on her own if she wanted to survive.

Vicki leaned her elbows on the counter, grabbed a piece of carrot, and bit into it. "Is there anything I can do to help?"

Jenny tossed her head. "You can set the table. I've already fed Jamie, so just set it for four."

Shaun walked in through the front door as Vicki laid out the silverware.

"Daddy!" Jamie ran over to greet his father.

Shaun picked up his son, whirled him around, then chased him through the house to the sound of giggles. When they reached the kitchen, Shaun kissed his wife on the cheek and then turned to Vicki.

"That tree was destined to fall. It wasn't smart of the guy who owns the property behind you to remove the surrounding trees and leave that one. Those evergreens have shallow roots and need other trees to help block the wind. A single tree can only take so much pressure on its own before it topples over, and that was a bad storm."

Vicki frowned as she laid the last fork and knife. "Shouldn't he be responsible for paying for the damage, then?"

"It doesn't matter whose property the tree fell from. Your insurance is supposed to cover it."

She crossed her arms in front of her and kicked at the floor. "They want me to do all sorts of things I can't afford to do to the house. Why do I pay for insurance if they don't cover everything?"

Shaun put up his hands. "I'll meet with your insurance adjuster and provide the estimate."

Jamie tugged at Shaun's leg, so he squatted down and cradled him in his arms, making faces at the boy.

"Sorry," Vicki replied, blowing out a breath. She didn't need to take out her frustration on him.

Shaun smiled up at her from the floor. "Hey, I'll do everything I can to get your house repaired for you. But I have several projects I'm working on now and no men to spare."

"Well, thanks for taking the tree off my roof."

"You bet."

Shaun disappeared with Jamie to bathe him and tuck him into bed.

A little while later, the sound of the knock on the front door sent Shaun over to it. Vicki's heart leaped in her chest as she turned to see David wearing a blue shirt that matched his eyes and accentuated his muscular frame. He looked effortlessly handsome, but she noticed that he seemed awkward and unsure how to greet her. His eyes met hers, and for a moment, time seemed to stand still.

She returned his smile with heated cheeks, a rush of memories from their interaction last night flooding her mind. The way he had held her, how safe she felt in his arms—it all came rushing back, leaving her off-balance.

With a sudden need to escape, she trotted into the

kitchen, her confidence having flown out the window. She was embarrassed, confused by her attraction to him.

Jenny looked up, her eyes narrowing as she looked at Vicki's flushed face. "Everything okay?" she asked.

Vicki waved her hand dismissively. "I'm fine. Just a little warm in here, that's all."

Jenny's eyes flicked to the doorway where David had entered, and a smile tugged at her lips. "I bet," she teased.

Vicki rolled her eyes but couldn't suppress a smile. "Stop it. I'm here to help, not be interrogated."

Jenny laughed, handing her a bowl of salad to toss. "Alright, alright. But you know you can talk to me about anything, right?"

Vicki's smile softened, "I know."

Vicki helped Jenny get everything ready and put food on the table while the two men talked about an upcoming construction project they would be working on.

"Hey, dinner is ready," Jenny called, and the men came over.

"This looks delicious, Jenny," David said, rubbing his hands together.

The casserole was passed around along with the salad. A large jug of water sat in the middle of the table. Vicki stared at it. No alcohol. Boy, she could use a drink tonight.

Vicki turned. "I want to thank you again for letting me stay at your place, Jenny."

"As I said before, you can stay there as long as you want. I rarely sleep there anymore now that I'm married."

Shaun sheepishly interjected, "She stays there to get away occasionally."

Jenny's eyebrow went up, and she reached over and playfully slapped his arm.

"Well, you do." Shaun winked, grinning at David and Vicki.

Vicki sighed. "Now I need to find a new place to paint since my studio got trashed."

"Oh, you can use one of the spare rooms upstairs at my place," Jenny said. "I have several to choose from."

"Are you sure?"

"Any except for Susan's," Jenny said as she took some bread and held out the basket to Shaun to take a piece and pass it on.

"I slept in there last night. I wasn't sure about sleeping in your room, so I stayed in hers. Is that okay?"

Jenny's wince didn't go unnoticed. "I would prefer it if you left that room alone. I don't know how Susan would feel about you sleeping in her bedroom."

"Susan's dead, Jenny. Why would she care?" Vicki chuckled and rolled her eyes, shooting David an amused look.

Jenny scowled. "Just stay in my room, okay?"

"Jenny thinks the house is haunted. That Susan's room is a sacred space," Shaun said after a mouthful of casserole.

Vicki leaned forward. "Really? You never told me that before. Does she rattle chains and make things float?" She wiggled her fingers in the air, giggling.

"No," Jenny replied softly. "But don't be surprised if you hear voices and have some weird dreams."

A memory flashed into Vicki's head. "Oh, now I remember! When we were kids, she used to dance around with bundles of sage, telling us she was chasing away evil spirits."

"It is a strange house. And well, sometimes evil spirits

come inside at night," Jenny said as if that was a well-known fact.

Ridiculous, Vicki thought. "I remember Susan believed all that old stuff she sold in her shop had magical memories attached to them, too." By the grins on their faces, Vicki could see that the men were enjoying the banter.

"They do," Jenny replied. "They act like magnets, collecting the experiences of their owners. When I was a kid, Susan would tell me about the different things in her shop and the stories attached to them."

"Oh, come on." Vicki laughed. "I didn't know you were so superstitious, Jenny."

Jenny looked to Shaun, and he added, "As my Aunt Aoife would say, 'There is more going on in the world than we can see or even understand.'"

"Well, what do you think of all this, David?" Vicki asked, putting him on the spot while looking directly at him with a grin.

David wiped his mouth with a napkin. "I don't know. But I've had unexplainable things happen in my life."

"Like what?" Vicki asked with a smirk, pretending to be interested.

"Strong intuition about some things before they happen," he said.

She held a forkful of salad in the air. "Care to elaborate?"

"Sometimes, when someone I know is in danger or hurting, I get a strong urge to go find them. Sort of like I did last night with you, Vicki."

"Me?" She jolted upright in her chair, almost choking on her salad. "I thought you said Shaun called you."

"He did, but I was already in the neighborhood. I saw

the tree fall, and by the time I found a parking spot, you were running down the street."

"That's creepy," Vicki replied, recalling how he had suddenly appeared on Jenny's porch in the middle of the night during the storm, seemingly out of nowhere.

"I just wanted to make sure you were safe." He blushed. "Speaking of magical objects, all the wood I gather has a history connected to each piece. So, in a way, my furniture contains hidden stories, just like the antiques in the old shop you were talking about."

Vicki giggled. "So, you're telling me your furniture is haunted? You guys are funny."

Shaun looked at David and shook his head. "Never thought of it like that before. But you're right. Those old trees have probably seen a lot of changes over the years."

"You guys are pulling my leg, right? Trees with memories." Vicki looked at them over her water glass.

Shaun and David glanced at each other, and then both started chuckling. "There's no use in talking about this stuff. Vicki is a nonbeliever in the spirit world," Shaun said.

"Okay, I get that there's another world or dimension out there that we don't understand. I'm a painter, remember? I paint what I see and add my interpretation to it. But that's not voodoo or magic."

"You're very talented, Vicki," Jenny said. "I love the painting of the orca you did for me. I get a lot of compliments on it. In fact, I think you should put the stuff you paint in my shop until you can open your gallery again." Jenny turned to David. "Why don't you bring in your tables too? My customers would certainly be interested in those."

Vicki could tell Jenny was trying to change the subject.

Strokes of Desperation

Then she thought about her house. "I need to start painting again. Shoot, I bet all my paints and canvases were ruined." She pinched the bridge of her nose.

Jenny reached over and squeezed Vicki's other hand. "I'll support you any way I can."

"I'll be okay," Vicki sighed. "But thanks for the offer."

When the time came to leave, David volunteered to drive Vicki to Jenny's house.

They rode in his truck in silence until the lights of a mini mart pierced the darkness from around a corner. Vicki sat up a little straighter at the sight.

"I know Shaun and Jenny don't drink, but I do, and I've been dying for a glass of wine all night. Can you stop so I can pick up a couple of bottles at the mini mart?"

David obliged and pulled into the lot. Vicki headed inside the small, dimly lit store and made her way to the aisle to pick out a bottle of wine. The selection was modest, but she quickly found a bottle of red that she knew would be perfect to top off her evening.

When she met David back at the counter, he had a container of chocolate ice cream tucked into his elbow and a mischievous grin on his face.

"Are you going to eat all that yourself?" Vicki asked playfully, getting out the cash Jenny had tucked in her pocket while they were cleaning up after dinner.

"I am unless a certain young woman invites me in to share her wine," he said, his eyes twinkling as he shoved her cash back at her and handed the clerk his credit card.

Vicki's heart skipped a beat at his words, a thrill of anticipation running through her. She knew that this evening was about more than just wine and ice cream; it was a chance to explore the connection that had been growing between them to see where it might lead. She wasn't looking for a relationship, but a casual fling might be nice.

Soon after they walked into the kitchen, she passed him the bottle opener and wine and set out a pair of wine glasses, bowls, and spoons. He popped the cork and poured them both a glass.

Vicki snatched hers from the counter, her nerves suddenly getting the better of her. "I've been dying for this all evening." She took a large gulp and smiled.

David pulled up a stool and sat next to her. She found his presence both comforting and exciting. He took a sip from his glass, then dished up a bowl of ice cream and slid it over to her. He then made one for himself, his eyes never leaving hers.

"Did you really have a premonition that a tree was going to fall on my house?" she asked.

He nodded. "Yes, and when I saw you struggling with what had happened, I wanted to help you. I know I may have overstepped my bounds, but I felt you needed comforting at the time."

Vicki's found herself touched by his concern and understanding. "I wasn't expecting you to do that."

She took another, larger swig of wine, then faced him, a glow coming over her as she remembered how good she felt in his arms. She let her thoughts wander, wondering what kind of lover he would be. "I'm not used to being held under those kinds of circumstances. I'm usually undressed when I'm in someone's arms." She flipped her hair over her shoulder, looked at him, and laughed.

"Oh." He blushed and looked down, clearly caught off guard by her statement.

When he didn't reply with a flirtatious remark, she quickly added, "Not that I couldn't get used to being held fully dressed." A pang of uncertainty was now gnawing at her. "It's rare. And well, no one ever hugs me except my gal friends."

He still didn't raise his eyes, and Vicki pouted. She was saying all the wrong things. Then she lashed out with, "I don't need codling when bad things happen. I am capable of dealing with my emotions on my own. It's not like I'm a child, you know."

Finally, he brought his eyes up, his look cutting right through her BS. "I know you put on a strong face for everyone, but it's okay to show your emotions to me. I won't judge you. Hell, we've all struggled to figure out what to do when we're faced with a crisis."

"Thanks." She tried to make light of it, but his words had touched something deep inside her. Showing her feelings was a big deal, and she rarely let anyone see who she was beneath her carefully crafted façade.

"What are friends for if they can't support one another?" David added.

"Friends? Is that what we are?" She twisted her hair with her finger, her eyes searching his, looking for an answer to a question she wasn't quite sure how to ask. Men didn't want to be friends with her. They didn't care about how she felt inside about things. They had an entirely different agenda.

He reached out and took her hand, his touch sending a jolt of electricity through her. "At the moment, yes."

Her mind was buzzing. She wasn't planning on buddying up with him. She had Jenny for that.

David lifted his glass and took a swallow. "I should go."

He set his drink down and stood up, taking a card from his pocket. He set it on the counter as he said, "I don't want you sneaking into your house. Here's my number. I'll retrieve whatever you want and drop it off." He headed for the door.

Having a male friend like David was a new concept for her. She didn't know what that meant.

"Bye." He raised a hand and was gone.

Chapter Five

Vicki

Vicki pulled open the drawers in the dresser, looking for something to wear. Everything of Jenny's was either too small or impractical. She picked up her phone and called David. He didn't answer, so she left a message on his voicemail.

"Hi, David, about last night," she paused, remembering their conversation. She wasn't sure about this 'friend' thing and hated being dependent on anyone. "Umm. I—I need my clothes from my bedroom closet and from my dresser on the floor and whatever else you can salvage. Okay, thanks, bye!"

Eventually deciding upon the outfit she had worn the night before, she headed downstairs and found Jenny and Brooke discussing clients. Jenny immediately smiled at Vicki, grabbing something from a nearby counter.

"Shaun thought you might need this," she said, passing Vicki's purse to her.

"Thanks, I certainly do." Vicki wandered over to a display and picked up a starfish. "I was wondering if I could borrow some of your small items to use for a still-life painting. Shells, sea glass, starfish—things like that."

"I've got boxes in the basement. You can go through those and pick out whatever you want. There's also some of Susan's old stuff down there. Things like old jewelry and odds and ends. Take whatever you want."

"That's helpful, thank you." She replaced the starfish and approached the door, stopping before leaving. "I'm about to head into Bellingham. Is there anything you'd like me to pick up?"

"No, we're fine," Jenny replied, going over to her computer and sitting down. "Oh, I think your car is blocked—the guys have their trucks in the alley. You can take mine instead. It is out front." Jenny dug through her purse and tossed Vicki her keys.

TWO HOURS LATER, Vicki returned with Jenny's mini van full of different-sized canvases, sketchpads, brushes, drawing pencils, and boxes containing tubes of assorted paint colors, as well as a couple of easels.

She parked behind Jenny's house so she could come in through the back door and not disturb any customers. Stopping to say hello before carrying things in, she spotted two of David's driftwood tables sitting among Jenny's furniture. *So, he came by while I was gone.*

After carting her supplies upstairs, she went to Jenny's

old bedroom and found her own clothes stacked on the bed. Her lacy underwear was sitting on the dresser. *How embarrassing.* Well, she *had* asked David to bring everything.

One of the rooms down the hall turned out to be the perfect place for her to paint. It had a window facing the back of the house that let light in during the day and was spacious enough to set up all her supplies. She couldn't wait to get started.

First, she set her paints out in a row on a shelf according to color. Next, her brushes—different-sized round and flat ones—then the filbert, angular, comb, and wisp-shaped ones. The ones she'd use most often were gathered up and placed in a cup for easy access. She had forgotten how expensive those little bristles could be.

There were palettes for mixing colors and cups for soaking used brushes. She hung up a couple of smocks and aprons on a rack and set down a plastic tub to toss the dirty ones in. Along the wall were dozens of stretched, primed canvases in various sizes. In a pile were sketchpads and drawing pencils. And finally—and most importantly—she spread a tarp on the floor so she didn't accidentally ruin Jenny's hardwood.

Smiling, she admired the space. Now, this room looked like a studio she could work in.

Running downstairs to the main floor, she retrieved the key to the basement door. Flicking on the light, she peeked down the stairs. Taking one step at a time into the dim room, she waited for her eyes to adjust. It was part of the old house and smelled musty, like the basement in her own house. An old, dead water heater leaned against one wall. The old pipes that ran beneath the new floor had been replaced with updated plumbing, but the room still felt like part of the past.

Dusty wooden shelves once used for canning now held several tan cardboard boxes. Vicki moved them around, searching for what she needed. She pulled out one box and put it on the floor. Lifting the lid carefully, she discovered it was full of odd jewelry, old watches, broken necklaces, and brooches with missing stones. She poked through the items to see if something there might appeal to her. She was pretty sure Jenny wouldn't object to her salvaging whatever she found.

After a moment, she set the box to the side to explore further later and began looking for sea-themed items instead. One box was full of shells in an assortment of shapes. After picking out what to use, she carried everything back to her studio.

Feeling like a kid with new toys, she laid all the seashells and beach finds out on the floor. There was even a tan buckskin she'd retrieved from a box of Susan's junk. Dumping out the box of jewelry, she spread the pieces out on a cloth. One immediately caught her eye. It was a light-golden medallion made of wood encased in resin. She examined the piece more closely. The shape reminded her of a slice from a freshly cut branch with its small rings. There were phosphorus-looking fine lace threads running through a crack. She could tell the piece was handmade. There was a hole for hanging, but no string was attached. Finding several chains in the box, she picked a silver one with a twist fastener. Sliding the pendant onto the chain, she placed it around her neck, twisting the lock closed. Scooping up the other pieces, she put them back in the box and set them aside.

Vicki stood up and strolled around the room, looking at everything she'd picked out, watching the dimming daylight hit them from various angles. She chewed on the inside of her cheek. Why couldn't she figure out what to paint? Everything appeared so much blander than usual; nothing inspired an image in her head like it usually would. Her mind was not cooperating. Bored and frustrated, she decided to retire for the night.

In the bathroom, while getting ready for bed, she couldn't help but admire the necklace she'd found. The pendant lay nestled at the top of her breast. Reaching around to unclasp it, she found the closure wouldn't turn or come undone. *Oh, well.* The necklace wasn't heavy and probably wouldn't bother her. She'd sleep with it on.

Trotting to Jenny's room she pulled back the covers and crawled inside and turned out the light from the nearby table. Closing her eyes, she drifted off.

SHE WANDERED THE FOREST, *listening to the wind for clues to its history, searching for the necklace's origin. Above, light streamed down like small spotlights from heaven. A breeze rustled the leaves of the maples, and the evergreen branches swayed. A world of light and dark danced, full of shadows. A hundred shades of green and brown crowded around, watching her as she walked among them.*

A forgotten soul shaped a mist around her, causing leaves to shudder, and an illusion began to take form. A breath of air rushed by, inhaling and exhaling. A crow let out a cry.

Tree limbs shook, sharing secrets with one another as squirrels leaped from limb to limb and the night hawks cawed.

In the shadows, two golden eyes of a wolf watched her from its hiding place, then raised its head and howled, warning her of what happens to the vulnerable when they travel through the world alone.

This forest was both alive and yet steeped in death. Many disregarded items had been passed by but never found—a shoe, a water bottle, a love, and a life.

VICKI AWOKE SUDDENLY with her hand on her chest, the wooden object nestled under her palm. She absently closed her fingers into a fist, enveloping the pendant, and rubbed it between her fingers, looking up at the ceiling. *What a strange dream*, she thought.

Now wide awake, she got out of bed and went to her new studio. Retrieving a sketchbook from a shelf, she sat on the floor, intending to draw. The paper was empty, like her mind. She could do one of at least a hundred drawings she'd done in the past of seagulls sitting on posts or sailboats. Which one should she do?

Positioning her hand, she pushed the pencil across the toothy white paper. It was just a line—a line without an image. Setting the pad aside, she retrieved a dried starfish from the box of stuff she'd brought up from the basement. One of its limbs broke off in her hand. Positioning the broken piece in such a way that the break wasn't noticeable, she attempted to draw the creature. After copying the shape's outline, she found the starfish boring. She scribbled across her drawing.

Throwing the sketchpad to the side, she crawled to her feet and went back to bed.

VICKI TUCKED the necklace inside her yellow sweater as she went downstairs. Once in the kitchen, she poured herself a mug of hot coffee from a pot Jenny had made earlier.

"Would you like to walk into town for breakfast?" Jenny asked, walking into the kitchen and startling Vicki. "It's pretty quiet in the shop right now, and Brooke can handle things without me. I didn't get much to eat this morning, and my stomach has been growling since I got here."

Vicki perked up at the idea. "Sure, I *am* curious about my house. Maybe I could stop by and take a peek."

They went out on what looked like a beautiful day. The sky was clear, and the bay was sparkling under the sun. A slight breeze blew up from the water. Tulips were poking their heads out of the pots sitting on Jenny's neighbor's porch. Everything seemed normal until they got to Vicki's house. Stopping in front, Vicki gazed up at the Victorian structure with its large bay window. Yellow tape was still strung around the yard, and there was a big "Do Not Enter" sign on the front door.

She left Jenny on the sidewalk and ran up the stairs to try the door. It didn't budge. She put in her key, but even with it unlocked, the door wouldn't open. Something had been placed against it from the inside.

"What the heck?" Vicki turned and looked at Jenny, waiting at the bottom of the steps. "Something's blocking my front door." Vicki drummed on the door with her fists, then stomped back down to the sidewalk.

Jenny held up her hands defensively. "Shaun didn't have anything to do with that."

"I bet David's responsible," Vicki snarled through clenched teeth. "Just wait until I see that man again!"

"If it was, I'm sure he did it to keep you safe." Jenny touched Vicki's arm.

Vicki pushed it away and glared at Jenny. "It's my house, and he had no right to prevent me from entering."

"Maybe you should talk to him about that, then."

"Who does he think he is? My protector?"

"Vicki, don't get all worked up about it. He probably meant well."

Vicki grumbled all the way to the restaurant. She didn't like men trying to control her. She could take care of herself. She pulled out her phone and punched in David's number. Her call went to his voicemail—again.

"David, I tried to get into my house but couldn't open the front door. Something is blocking it. Please call me. I need to get in there."

"Vicki, it may not be safe inside yet," Jenny said. "Shaun wouldn't want you wandering around in there, either. Go easy on the guy."

Vicki sighed, slipping her phone back into her purse. "Okay, I won't ruin our meal complaining about it."

They sat at a table outside, behind a plastic barrier to protect them from the breeze that had picked up since they left for the restaurant. The shore was empty except for the gulls in the sky gliding in the wind. They held out their wings as though they were fearless against the pressure. They were in control, not the force pushing against them.

It was April, still early for most tourists. She had time to create a decent inventory if she put her mind to it. But something was holding her back.

Vicki looked over at her friend, who was rummaging through her purse. "Jenny, I just can't get motivated to pump out all those little pictures of shells and starfish now that I need real money to pay for everything."

Jenny looked up. "You know, Vicki, the people who come to my shop have plenty to spend to decorate their homes. Maybe you should try focusing on doing a few larger paintings and sell them for a lot more money."

Vicki pouted. "Like what?"

"I don't know, whatever comes to you. You've always been good with color and design. I love the big painting you did of the orca in my shop."

The waitress appeared, and they both ordered coffee to start.

Vicki set her hands down and tapped her fingernails on the table in frustration. "I need some inspiration."

Jenny opened her compact and finger-combed her bushy red hair, which the wind had made a mess of. "Go for a walk on the beach. Bring your camera and take some pictures. A lot of interesting things wash up on the shore. You never know. You might find something."

When the waitress returned, they both ordered quiche and a salad. Vicki stared out at the water again, wondering if the beach would inspire her or if she'd have to look somewhere else. She once had taken refuge in her imagination, spending hours gathering things from the shore to draw. Her art was a way to express herself and also a place to escape from what was going on in her life. She needed that to happen again before reality came crashing down on her.

After returning from brunch in town, Vicki headed to the den above Jenny's shop and looked through some old magazines Jenny had kept. They were just full of ads and items she'd never buy. Next, she turned on the TV and flicked through the channels until she got to the end, then turned the TV off. She was restless and desperate for ideas. Nothing was coming to her.

She called David, but he didn't pick up. *Why is he avoiding me?* Then she remembered the comment she'd made about hugging. "Oh God, what if he thinks I'm just a whore looking for a lay? Not that it matters what he thinks."

Goose pimples prickled at her arms and neck as an old memory tugged at her. She pushed it away. She wasn't that person.

Setting the phone down, she went downstairs and into the kitchen, where she pulled some cheese and fruit from the refrigerator and put them on a plate to nibble on.

Brooke came in and pulled up a stool. "Could I ask you a favor?"

"Sure," Vicki replied, shoving the plate over to share with Brooke.

"I want to get a tattoo. I've decided on a little crab and a starfish next to each other. Do you think you could make a drawing I can take to the parlor for them to duplicate?" Brooke picked up a grape and popped it into her mouth.

"Of course." Vicki smiled. "Where are you going to want your tattoo, and how large do you think you would like it to be?"

Brooke held out her arm. "I want it on my wrist, just about two inches long or wide."

"I'll have it to you before you leave today."

"Great. Thanks."

Briefly enthused by the prospect of creating something, even if it wasn't original, Vicki came up with three options that she gave Brooke. But after returning to the den, her motivation waned once again, and she was left staring at blank pages, surrounded by uninspiring clutter. She wasn't quite sure what to do with her time while she waited for ideas, and ultimately, none came to her, so she went to bed.

RUNNING, *leaping over fallen trees, pushing past branches. Something was pursuing her.*

SHE WOKE UP TIRED, like she'd run an endless marathon, and the dream faded into her mind. The details just washed away, along with any indication as to why she'd been running.

Sitting up and looking around, she realized she wasn't at home in her bed. Oh, right, she was staying at Jenny's. She looked up at the ceiling. *She was safe.* The effects of the incident must have been lingering in her subconscious.

Vicki lay there listening to the sounds of the house. The creaks and hums were loud in her head. The sound of pitter-patter from feet out in the hall grabbed her attention. Jenny had told her that any noise was Susan's ghost, but it was probably only a mouse. Cuddling the pillow, a sudden sadness cradled her. She wanted to go back home to her own bed.

Chapter Six

David

Early in the morning, David went out to his workshop to check his wood supply. There were only a few small branches left, so he put his sled in the back of his truck and left for the beach. He figured there would probably be several new chunks after that storm.

Once he'd found a place to park, he began combing the shore where the tide had receded. He pulled his sled behind him, occasionally stopping to examine a piece of wood, and dusted off the sand. He chose the ones he could use and left the others to be reclaimed by the water later in the day. He preferred older pieces that had been bleached by the sun. However, newer ones with lots of knots went into the pile, too.

He combed the beach, searching for driftwood as the morning sun began to burn off the remaining fog. He tried to focus his attention on the task at hand, but his mind kept wandering back to Vicki.

He felt a pang of guilt seeing her name repeatedly in his notifications. David knew he should have called her back already, but he just wasn't ready. There was too much swirling through his head after that night.

When he first met Vicki a couple of months ago while bringing his handcrafted tables into her gallery, it was purely a business relationship. But over time, something had shifted, and she piqued his interest.

This is why seeing her so vulnerable after the tree hit her house had rattled him. The tough, confident woman he knew was replaced by someone small and afraid. And the way his heart ached at the sight surprised him. Sure, he had always found Vicki attractive - her long blond hair, dark eyes, and radiant smile were hard to ignore. But he never let himself go there, never crossed that line from friends to more.

But holding her shivering body, feeling her nestle against his chest, seeking comfort - it awakened new feelings in him. A fierce need to protect her, to be the one she turns to. The one she...

David shook his head, trying to dislodge where his thoughts were headed. This was dangerous territory. He had been careful to keep relationships casual after his wife's behavior. The risk of letting someone in so deeply again terrified him.

He'd felt his phone vibrating several times the previous day, but he ignored Vicki's calls. He'd planned on her being upset about him blocking the entrance. Just the same, he didn't want her messing around inside her house while they cleaned things up. With Shaun's schedule, he knew that it would be a while before they could begin repairing the damage. She was lucky to have a free place to stay until then. He was waiting for her to calm down before he explained why he'd blocked the door. He knew by putting this off, he wouldn't be gaining any friendship points with her. However, that was a risk he was willing to take.

David crouched, using his legs to lift a particularly heavy log onto a space he had made on the sled, then straightened, dusting sand from his hands.

He was worried about Vicki. His intuition was nagging him again. Something was going to happen to her, and he didn't know what it was. Right now, he'd keep their relationship casual. There was no point in letting it progress to where he'd get pulled into her problems. She was a strong woman and could take care of herself. Still, that little bell was going off, and darn it, if he could only figure out why!

Chapter Seven

Vicki

Sun streamed in through the window, interrupting Vicki from her restless doze. With a sigh, she pushed herself up from the mattress and stretched her arms in the air. She dreaded the prospect of another unproductive day in the den, so she got dressed, pulled on her rubber boots, and retrieved a bucket and camera before heading out.

She slipped on her sunglasses as she reached the beach. Occasionally, she squatted down, flipped her glasses to the top of her head, and adjusted her camera's lens to focus on creatures in tide pools, kelp curled around dead trees, and odd shells and strands caught in the roots of old logs.

"Hi, Vicki!"

She looked up to see David collecting driftwood fifteen feet away. She'd been so focused on what was on the ground that she hadn't noticed him. He had his pant legs rolled up and was pulling a sled with gnarly wood piled on top. His shirt was unbuttoned, flapping in the breeze, exposing the fine hair on his chest. He appeared comfortable in the cool weather. She bit her lip. He looked pretty darn cute like that.

"Collecting wood for your haunted furniture?" she called.

"You got that right." He walked over and flashed her a big grin.

He was the last person she expected to run into at the beach today. She backed up and tripped over a log, landing on her behind in the sand.

David reached down to give her a hand, but she ignored him, pushed herself up to her feet, and then dusted herself off. The wind whipped up her hair, tossing her sunglasses. She fought back the wild strands, intentionally trying to annoy her by slapping her in the face.

David looked amused, which made things worse. She brought her hands down from trying to smooth her hair and turned at an angle so the wind wouldn't blow strands in her face. Stiff-legged, she slowly reached down to pick up her sunglasses and retrieve something from her bag to secure her hair. Then she toppled over again.

David tried to hide a laugh, but she heard his snort.

She pulled her hair back but wasn't able to capture all of it in the scrunchie and now had a lopsided tail. David stood there with his arms crossed as she struggled to get up. She tried to act like she was fine but felt like a strawman losing its stuffing. She dusted the sand off her backside and faced him, then remembered that she was unable to get into her house.

"Why did you block my front door? You have no right to do that."

He put a hand on his face, rubbing the stubble, looking right at her. "I knew you would try to go back in, and the house just isn't safe yet."

"*You* went inside," she threw back at him.

"Well, I know how to maneuver around broken pieces of wood."

"Was that supposed to be a joke?"

"I didn't want you falling through the floor."

She glared at him. "It's my house."

His blue eyes glared back at her. "Yes, and right now, it's too dangerous to go inside."

She looked away. "Is there anything salvageable in my studio?"

"No, I'm afraid not. Between the tree and the rain, the room was completely destroyed. The floor will need to be replaced, along with the interior wall."

She bit her lip. "Everything?"

"Yes. Everything. The rain washed away your paintings, and the floor was a rainbow of needles and sludge."

"Maybe it's good that I didn't see that." Her voice cracked, and she plopped down on the log she had tripped over, staring at the sand. She had been hoping things were different. That something could have been saved. It felt like part of her had been stripped away. All the hours she'd spent drawing and painting had been wasted.

David sat down next to her. "I'm sorry."

She looked out at the horizon. "I don't know what to do. There's no way I can make enough art before tourist season to pay my mortgage. Jenny says I should focus on just painting a few big pieces to sell in her shop, but I don't know what to paint. I don't have any inspiration."

"Maybe you need to take your mind off what happened. Give the muse time to return."

"I thought I was by taking pictures of stuff on the beach. I'm trying, but it doesn't seem to be working. Nothing is calling to me."

After a short pause, David said, "Well, why don't you come with me to my house? I'll make you dinner tonight."

She looked at him; his face wore a gentle smile. He was trying to cheer her up. Her other choice was a microwave dinner at Jenny's house.

She returned his smile with a halfhearted one of her own. "Okay."

"Follow me." He jumped to his feet and pulled his sled across the sand to his truck. He tossed wood on the bed, then closed it up. Vicki climbed onto the front seat with her bucket, bag, and camera, not knowing what to expect. She groaned when she pulled the visor down to look at herself in the mirror. Pulling out her scrunchie, she regathered her hair, but it still didn't look right. She slammed the visor back up.

David glanced over at her. "You look fine. Don't worry about it."

He followed the road out of town, past Shaun's, then turned down a gravel road toward the water. As they got closer, a huge barn with a metal roof came into view next to an A-frame house.

"Is that your workshop?" Vicki asked, getting out of the truck and slamming the door. The shop had two large doors and looked like you could keep a big camper or a boat inside.

"Yes, would you like to see it?" He unlocked the side door and went in. Vicki followed.

David flicked on the lights. The temperature was different from the outside, a little warmer. In the middle of the room sat metal tables with huge saws. There was no sawdust on the floor; it had been swept clean. Leaning up along a wall were tall slabs of different types of wood. The smell was wonderful.

Vicki went over for a better look at the wood lining the wall. She ran her hands over them, feeling the grain, carefully inspecting how the lines came together, then moved away like ripples after tossing a pebble in the water. She felt the dark knots that dotted the surfaces where branches had once extended.

"How interesting," she said. "These look like veins. I never thought of trees as having veins before. But they have arms. That's what those knots are, right?"

David nodded his head in agreement.

"Do they have hearts too?"

"Maybe hidden in their cores. I don't know. They have memories, too—in their rings. You can tell by the thickness if there was a harsh winter or a mild one."

Vicki noticed in one piece how several dark lines came together like streams flowing into a river. "I've never seen trees with wood like this before. Where did you find these?"

"Those pieces aren't from trees that grow around here. I have to special order them. After they're delivered, I cut them to the thickness I want and then prepare them. The ones you're looking at are black walnut, maple, acacia, and elm."

She would've never guessed David had all of this in his shop building.

"Come look at these." He motioned her over to another area, pulling back a cloth to reveal a finished table. He removed the coverings from several others around for her to see. One was the size of a conference room table, and several were dining tables, all with natural irregular edges along the sides. The tops had a low-luster polish and, depending on the wood used, went from amber to a deep red and caramel, then dark brown. They all sat on black metal legs.

Vicki wandered around, examining the tables. "These are beautiful. I thought you just made driftwood furniture. I didn't know you made tables like this."

"Most of the tourists in Cook's Cove are only interested in the beach look. I sell these other tables to high-end furniture stores in Seattle and Portland."

"Well, I'm impressed," she said, placing her hands at her waist.

His cheeks turned pink. He motioned her to follow him. "Come, I'll pour you a glass of wine."

Inside, the house was a traditional A-frame with a big, open room and stairs that led to a loft bedroom above. Huge windows faced the water. Handmade light-colored wooden furniture filled the area. The overall design had a natural, modern look and with a uniqueness to it. On the surfaces sat hand-blown glass lamps and bowls that looked like something from beneath the sea.

"Did you make these?" she asked, lifting one of the bowls and turning the glass over, admiring its beauty.

"Yes, I took a class in glass blowing a few years back." He pulled out a couple of steaks from his refrigerator and set them on the counter to season.

"You make me look like an amateur." Vicki frowned. "I

Strokes of Desperation

once thought my art was pretty good. After college, I went to New York with dreams of becoming a famous artist—" She stopped suddenly. She hadn't meant to say that. It just slipped out.

David seemed not to notice her silence and handed her a glass of wine. "What was that like? New York, I mean."

"It sucked." Her throat suddenly tightened at the thought, and she found it difficult to talk. She took a long gulp of her drink as she waited to shut the feeling back down. "I wasn't there very long. It was—not what I expected." There was no way in hell she was going to tell him what happened in New York. "Anyway, I came back and decided to paint tourist pictures. I had to pay the bills, and no one cares about fine art around here." She swirled her glass, then took a smaller sip.

"Well, New York is a pretty tough market to try to break into. I admire your ambition. It takes guts to venture out like that."

"I was naïve at the time. I had no clue what I was doing."

"Well, I'm glad you came back to Cook's Cove." He smiled. "Have you thought about doing any shows in Seattle?" He put the steaks in the oven to broil and set the timer.

"No, I haven't tried to paint anything but birds, boats, docks, and sea life for quite a while." She began opening drawers, looking for silverware.

He pointed to where to find them, then took out a couple of plates. "Maybe now is the time."

"If I could only figure out something to paint."

She finished setting the table while David cut some bread and put slices in a basket. He took out two potatoes and popped them in the microwave. After the buzzer went off, he retrieved them with his hands and juggled the burning things in the air until he could release them onto a serving dish.

The steaks were now ready, so he brought one hanging from a fork and dropped it on her plate. Then he brought the other one for himself and sat across from her. After refilling her glass with wine, he raised his and said, "To art. The muse."

She poked out her lower lip. "My muse has been hiding."

"You can't force it. Maybe she's just waiting for the right time." He took a sip, then set his glass down.

"I hope she doesn't wait too long," Vicki replied halfheartedly.

After dinner, David lit a fire in the fireplace and sat down next to her, bringing the bottle of wine with him. She had misjudged him. He made more money off his art than she thought. In fact, she bet that those tables sold for several thousand dollars apiece.

She noticed a frame that was sitting on a table next to her. It appeared to contain a medal of some sort. It was a gold cross with an eagle in the middle. She turned toward him, looking for a response.

His face flushed pink. "It's a Distinguished Service Cross. I received that for rescuing some men under fire in Afghanistan."

"You're a war hero?" Vicki asked.

"Sometimes life forces you to choose between taking a risk or living with the result of not trying. You try to do the right thing and not think about yourself. Sometimes you win, and other times you lose."

Emotions rippled inside her. Who was this man? David apparently thought deeply about things. He was so different from the men she had known—cowards and manipulators.

Next to the medal was a photo of several men in uniform. "Are these your friends?"

"They were part of my squadron."

"Did you ever have to kill anyone?" *Is he capable of doing awful things?* she wondered.

He looked at her. "I don't want to talk about war right now. I want to hear more about you."

To him, this was probably polite conversation. To her, however, he was probing into her past. "What do you want to know?"

"Did you grow up around here?"

"Yes." An image of her house outside of town came to her mind. She willed herself not to see it, but she failed, and the memory showed up just the same. The house was a dump, a one-story wooden rambler with three small bedrooms and one bathroom with a mineral-green stain in the bathtub and the toilet. Susan had better furniture in her antique shop than Vicki had in the living room. Her father didn't care about where or how he lived. He worked assembling parts at an aircraft manufacturing company— mostly on the swing shift at night. The commute was long, but he needed the money and couldn't find a job that paid as well, considering his lack of education and limited skills.

Pivoting away from the question, she knew the answer she usually provided, "In beautiful Cook's Cove," wasn't going to cut it today. David would see right through her. She suddenly had the urge to tell him her secrets. The things she had never told anyone before.

But that would be the worst possible thing she could do

right now. That door was to remain forever shut. No one would ever be trusted with her story, especially someone like him.

Struggling with what to come up with, the words tumbled out. "My childhood wasn't very pretty. My parents divorced when I was young, and my dad raised me. My mom ran off with some guy when I was eight, and I never saw her again. After that, my sister died, then it was just my dad and me. But he didn't give a shit about me, so I pretty much raised myself."

"That's a lot to carry." He took her hand. It felt warm, and she found herself vulnerable around him again.

"I don't know why I'm telling you this. It's not like anyone cares about other people's shitty childhoods." She slipped her hand out of his.

Her secrets were her own, a part of her she had hidden away, a dark and painful reminder of the choices she had made and the price she had paid. To let someone in, to allow them to see the real her, to know her fears and her shame—it was unthinkable. The walls she had built were her protection, her shield against the world, and she couldn't let them crumble, not for anyone.

His sapphire blue eyes peered into hers. "I told you once before it's okay not to always be strong. Sometimes, you just need to lean on someone."

David was different than any man she'd ever met before. He saw her, really saw her, in a way that no one else ever had.

She looked into his eyes; one side of his mouth went up in a grin, and she knew his compassion was genuine. She was drawn to him and wanted more. She stared at his lips. They looked soft and inviting. Leaning over, she was about to kiss him, then quickly pulled back. *She couldn't let this happen. She couldn't risk it.* If she let him reach past her defenses and touch the part of her that was hidden away, then he could hurt her.

His smile got wider.

She wiped the tears that now stung her eyes. "I don't know why I did that. I'm sorry." She was blabbering.

He squeezed her knee again. "I should get you home—or back to Jenny's, I mean."

"Yes, right now, I don't have a home."

"Does your father still live nearby?"

"Heck no. If he did, I wouldn't be here. After I went to New York, he left. I don't know where he is. I guess he had no reason to stay here anymore."

David got up and held out his hand to help her up. This time, she took it.

He drove her to Jenny's place. When she got out of the truck, she found him standing there. "I'll walk you to the door."

After putting the key in the lock, she turned around and hugged him. "Thank you, David."

He smiled, looking into her eyes. "Thank you, Vicki."

"For what?"

"For telling me about your family. Trusting me."

"Oh," she said. "I don't usually do that."

"I could tell."

She watched his eyes go to her mouth. He looked like he wanted to kiss her but didn't. Instead, he turned and left.

She locked the door and went upstairs. Jeez, now she was confused. This was not good. She was letting her guard down. She needed to be more careful, or he'd find out too much about her.

But the image of David's smile, the sound of his laugh, and the warmth of his touch lingered in her mind, a haunting reminder of what could never be.

Holding the wooden necklace between her thumb and forefinger, she rubbed it. She needed to focus on painting.

Chapter Eight

David

After David dropped Vicki off, he couldn't quit thinking about her. She was gorgeous and sexy as hell. At times, he caught her eyes sparkling with mischief, her smile a tantalizing promise of something more. Still, it was more than just physical attraction that intrigued him. There was a depth to her, a complexity that drew him in that she was hesitant to share, which made him want to know more. But. It was the "but" that was the obstacle, the nagging doubt that kept him from giving in to what he was feeling.

Driving down the tree-lined road to his house, he wondered why he even cared. He'd been burned by a woman before, stupidly marrying his high school sweetheart before he enlisted in the army, only to discover that she was sleeping around while he was gone. He should have known better. She was a hottie and knew it, always flirting, never happy unless all the men's eyes were on her. Boy, she knew how to work it, too. Men acted like bees to honey around her.

Sort of like Vicki. He knew she put on a flirtatious act, yet he sensed she was insecure, wanting romance but scared to death of real love. There was a vulnerability in her eyes, a longing that went beyond mere physical attraction. She was searching for something but was afraid.

David understood that fear all too well. After what his ex-wife Kelly had done, cheating on him while he was deployed, he found it hard to make himself vulnerable again either. The betrayal had cut deep, leaving scars that still ached.

Kelly acted flirtatiously to get back at him for enlisting. It was her way of punishing him for being away from her, jerking his chain.

David knew his marriage was over when he came home on leave to surprise Kelly and found her in bed with another guy. He threw both of their naked bodies out of the house and locked the door. Bet they had to scramble that night. Maybe that was what propelled him to take the risks he did in Afghanistan. There was no one at home waiting for him. He had nothing to lose.

Deep down, he knew his marriage to Kelly would end like that. He just didn't want it to be true. Hell, when had any of his hunches turned out wrong? Was this a gift or a curse?

After his marriage ended, he went on a binge of seeing how many women he could bed. Maybe he was trying to prove something by playing the stud. But after too many nights of meaningless sex, he decided he wanted something more. He wanted a woman that he could have a relationship with on a deeper level, like his parents had before his mom passed.

As he pulled into this driveway, he shook his head. Unlocking the door and going into his empty house, he looked around. A sudden loneliness came over him. He longed for a woman he could hold, that he could share his life with. Someone who loved him as much as he loved them.

Taking a beer from the refrigerator, he sat down on the couch. He put his head back and looked up at the ceiling. So why did he have feelings for Vicki? She was stubborn and independent, but her flirtatious nature disturbed him. Why would he want to fall into the same trap with another flirt? He didn't want to play games. *Damn it.* All he knew was that Vicki had touched something deep inside him, and he couldn't shake it.

He tossed a pillow in the air, then caught it. Something about Vicki drew him to her, something he couldn't quite put his finger on. She was strong and independent, yet there was a softness to her, a tenderness that called to him, that made him want to protect her and take care of her.

His intuition told him she was a loving, caring person. *That* was the girl he was curious about—the one hidden inside. But would she let her guard down enough to let him see who she really was?

He sensed Vicki had lived a hard life, which caused her to put up that barrier in the first place. Sure, she pretended she didn't need to lean on anyone, but all he wanted to do was hold her when she did lean on him. Yeah, she was struggling right now, but she could get back on her feet again with a little help—if she'd only ask for it.

But she was stubborn, thinking she needed to do it all on her own.

He tossed the pillow again. He was definitely attracted to her, and he was pretty sure she was attracted to him, too, and not just on a superficial level, though she tried to pretend she wasn't.

Chapter Nine

Vicki

After tossing and turning to a fitful dream of running through the woods, Vicki woke in the middle of the night with an image of a young woman in her mind.
 Stepping over to the room across the hall, she went to a drawer and pulled out a fresh sketchpad and pencils. She sat on the floor cross-legged, then just let her hand flow, drawing lines that turned into whips of hair tumbling down. Like a blind person searching, she scribbled, looking for something, anything. All Vicki could come up with was the back of a head. She tore the page out and set it aside, then attempted another.
 This next drawing revealed more, but of what? Just when she thought she had an idea, the image floated out of focus in her mind. *Damn it. Don't leave me.* She let out a breath of frustration.

Her third attempt was a sketch of a girl's face hidden beneath her hair that flowed over her closed eyes like she was sleeping. Disappointed, Vicki ripped the new sketch out of the book and set it on the table. Then she had an idea.

She carefully dragged the full-length antique dressing mirror from Jenny's room to the studio, hoping not to scratch the wooden floor. The mirror flopped around, but Vicki managed to steady it before banging into the open door. Mirrors helped reveal angles that weren't obvious when doing still-life drawings, uncovering details often missed.

Inside the room, the mirror now seemed quite large, but she liked the tilt feature, moving it back and forth. Vicki stood in front, gazing at her own image. She adjusted her hair so that one side covered half of her face. Reaching for some paper and a pencil, she sat on her stool and captured her reflection. The drawing was just a rough self-portrait, but she needed to keep drawing until she hit on an idea she could run with.

Satisfied with what she had sketched, she surveyed the room. A few other mirrors in different sizes would help, too. Ones she could place all around the studio, like a carnival funhouse.

But additional mirrors meant more stuff to buy. Vicki let out a sigh. She'd been charging her supplies, and the bills were adding up. She tried to push the stress out of her mind, certain the pressure to produce was blocking her from coming up with anything worthwhile to paint.

Physically and artistically drained, she headed for bed.

Strokes of Desperation

THE SOUND of pounding on the door got her up.

Jenny poked her head in. "Are you going to sleep all day?"

Vicki rolled over and looked at the clock—ten a.m. She moaned. "I was up late last night."

"The stuff you ordered has arrived."

Vicki placed her feet on the floor and stretched. "I need coffee."

"I've got a pot on downstairs." Jenny leaned over. "Where did you get this cool necklace?" She reached out, taking it in her hand to examine it more closely.

"I found it in one of the boxes in the basement. I was hoping you'd let me keep it."

Jenny let go of the wooden coin. "Sure. Did you find anything else like this?"

"No, mostly junk."

"Well, coffee and your stuff are downstairs." Jenny left, closing the door behind her.

Vicki yawned, got up, and pulled the curtains back. Another day at Jenny's. She looked out at the water, wanting to just sail off into another life.

In the kitchen, Vicki poured herself some coffee, inhaling its fresh scent. The taste was strong and bitter, so she added some vanilla coffee creamer, turning the drink a rich mocha color. Vicki preferred her coffee to taste like toffee. Next, she cut an avocado in half. After smashing the green fiber into a thick paste, she squeezed in a bit of lemon, salt, and pepper, then spread it on toast.

Breakfast in hand and already crunching through a mouthful, she trudged back upstairs and into her studio in hopes of some new inspiration. She slipped her painter's smock over her head, then set out drawing pencils and tubes of paint.

Now, whenever she tried sketching a boat or seagull, images of the same girl popped into her mind. The pull was so strong that she finally surrendered and began drawing what it revealed in her mind's eye. At first, there was only a girl's face, but gradually her body appeared. The girl was a teenager with long, dark hair. Her body, though slim, had curves like Vicki's at that age.

Once she was confident as to what the girl looked like, Vicki decided to try painting the girl's image. She squeezed different colors onto her palette, experimenting with golden ochres, deep purples, ultramarine blue, and greens. Confused about the skin tone—if it should be warm or cool red, blueish, cool or warm yellow, golden ochre, or what?—she finally decided to go with a mysterious, exotic look, with pigment a tone darker than her own skin.

Drawing her hand across the canvas, she outlined a face. Next, she picked up a different brush, pushing color into the image. In the beginning, what appeared to be a mask became a nose and high cheekbones. The hollows she outlined for eyes, dabbing in a light gray. The pupils were a layer of several greens and golds, crystallizing into a sphere containing a dark iris, like a pinhole into another world. When Vicki carefully added in the white, the painting's eyes came alive and twinkled back at her.

She smiled, pleased with her work, and set aside the painting to dry. Positioning another canvas in its place, she began to paint another portrait of the same girl. Soon, she lost track of time, and the day disappeared. Now, it was after midnight.

Despite the stiffness in her back and legs, she pushed

herself to continue painting. It was a cramp in her leg that finally got her off the stool. Reaching down to rub her calf, she tipped over her palette. "Shoot!"

She sighed with relief as the thing landed on the tarp and not the hardwood. Retrieving the palette, she set it upright on the small table. The colors were now mushed together, reminding her now was the time to stop.

As she slipped her dried-paint-encrusted smock over her head and tossed it to the side, her stomach growled. Twisting the lid off her water bottle, she tilted the liquid up and drank the whole thing down in long swallows. The day and night had gone by, and now she could see the faint light of dawn in the sky beyond the window. She dropped the empty bottle in the garbage on the way out of the room, flicking the light off as she left.

Blurry-eyed from staring at her work for hours, she rubbed the bridge of her nose while taking the stairs down to the main floor one step at a time. Should she make coffee or just eat something first?

Opening the cupboard, she took out a box of flax flakes and shook the contents into a bowl. The milk was sour, though, so she dumped it in the sink and grabbed some coffee creamer instead to pour on her cereal.

Sitting on a stool, spooning the dry flakes in her mouth, she stopped and heard the sounds of birds singing in the background. Her internal clock was messed up.

At the sink, she rinsed the bowl, then picked up a banana and peeled the skin back to take a bite. She pulled back the curtain on the window and peered out. A garbage truck was picking up trash. People would just be waking up to start their day. Maybe if she went upstairs, she could nap for a few hours.

Overcome with sudden drowsiness, she zombie-walked up to the bedroom and dropped into bed, exhausted.

It was noon when she awoke to the sound of voices. Someone was laughing. Remembering she was at Jenny's and there was a shop below her, she put the pillow over her head to block out the noise. But it was no use; she was awake now, so she got up and trotted into the bathroom to clean up. After putting on some clean clothes, she slipped out the back door without Jenny noticing her.

Walking along the back alley, she looked up at the damage to her house, noticing a tarp flapping in the breeze where the plastic hadn't been tacked down all the way. Her foot kicked a small pine branch covered in needles, and she reached down to pick it up. She brought it across her nose, inhaling its scent. *Damn, tree.*

A breeze was blowing, and she wrapped her arms around her sweater, pulling it tighter to her body. She felt lost. This house had been the first place she'd felt connected to. She'd purchased it with some of the money her grandmother had left her years ago. This was where she'd grown her business. And now it was all for nothing.

She let out a sigh, staring at the gaping hole in the upper floor where the tree hit. What if things weren't as bad as David had said? Maybe he just didn't want her in the house, period. She wanted to see the damage with her own eyes.

Going over to the back door, she twisted the handle. It was unlocked but stuck. She shoved the door with her shoulder, causing a slight movement, then put her back to it, pressing her weight against it as she walked backward, forcing the door open.

Inside, it was dark except for the light from the open

door. She made her way to the curtain and then out into the shop area. A dull light filtered down from the split where the curtains met. Everything was gray with dust. She sneezed from the tree spores and plaster that tickled her nose. Above were several cracks in the ceiling, and a light fixture dangled down from exposed wires. Her glass display counter was empty of its contents; there were no shiny pieces of jewelry inside. In fact, peering around, she could see that all her gallery's merchandise had been removed. David's name came to her mind.

Strolling over to the gallery door, she opened it to see the outside entryway. The exterior door had a chair wedged against it. *He thought that would prevent me from coming inside.*

Standing at the base of the stairs that led to her upper floor, she took a breath. Pine needles had gathered in the corners of some of the steps. Other than being dirty, the steps looked fine to her. She gingerly placed her feet on them one at a time and went up.

Once she could peek into the hallway, she glanced around. A small pile of wood and branches sat at the far end. The entrance to her studio was just fifteen feet away. The door was hanging from its top hinge, and some of the floorboards were uneven.

There must be something I can salvage—at least the little girl's crayon drawings! They suddenly became important, symbolizing saving her childhood dream from destruction. She visualized her father's attempts to persuade her to give up on her dream to be an artist. But instead, his malicious attempts only made her more determined.

Vicki slid a foot forward, cautiously moving toward the door. She was doing this for that little girl she had once been. Taking another step resulted in a loud creak. *Be brave.*

As she placed her foot down again, it made no sound. She smiled and relaxed and took three more steps. She was getting closer. More confident that she would make it to the studio, she took a couple more steps.

A harsh crack tore through the quiet. She froze. In an instant, the floor gave out underneath her. A splintery board sliced her pants and the skin of her leg as she fell. Throwing her elbows out to the sides, she caught what solid floor was left. Now supporting her weight by her arms, she dangled, caught between floors. She gritted her teeth, trying to pull herself up, but it was no use; she didn't have the strength. The surrounding boards creaked and groaned under her weight, and with them, so did she. Her arms began to burn; how much longer could she hold on?

Chapter Ten

David

David was inspecting the foundation of a house, with his mind focused on the task at hand, when he got the flash. A sudden feeling that something was wrong. He knew immediately that it had to do with Vicki.

Damn it. He told Vicki not to go into her house. He'd warned her to stay away. But Vicki was headstrong, independent, and stubborn. She never listened.

He couldn't just leave right now; he was waiting for a delivery that he couldn't miss. The materials for the new project were due any minute, and he had to be there to sign for them.

But he couldn't stay and let her suffer. *Shit.* He pulled out his phone and called Shaun, who was working at another site miles away.

"Shaun, I need to leave."

"What's up? You sound like this is urgent."

"It's Vicki. I have a gut feeling that she's in her house and about to have an accident."

Shaun was silent for a moment. "Trust your intuition, David. I'll send someone over to be there for the delivery."

"Thanks for understanding."

"Just keep her safe, David."

"I wish I could, but she is one stubborn woman."

"Aye, that she is."

David hung up. He knew he had to get to Vicki to make sure she was okay. But he also knew that he was leaving his team in a lurch, disrupting the schedule, and potentially delaying the project. He looked around the site. Well, he needed to go. This woman was taking over his damn life.

He jumped into his truck and took off. He knew he shouldn't be driving so fast, but the feeling was gnawing at him to get there soon.

Not thirty minutes later, he went inside the house and found Vicki lying on the floor in her gallery. God, she was stubborn!

He immediately went to her. "Vicki? How are you feeling? Is anything broken?"

He looked at her pale face. Blood was seeping from a rip in her pants. David took off his work shirt and removed his undershirt, which he wrapped around her lower leg.

"Put your arm around my neck. Do you think you can walk?"

"I don't know, it hurts."

He scooped her up against his bare chest, leaving his work shirt on the floor, and carried her over to his truck parked out front.

She tried standing but winced. He helped her in and drove her to the nearby clinic.

He knew it wasn't serious but wanted her checked out just the same.

"It's just a twisted ankle, David," she said. "I'll be fine."

"We'll see," he replied, "I told you not to go into the house, didn't I?"

She rolled her eyes, a smile tugging at her lips. "Yes, you did."

They arrived at the clinic, and David helped her out of the truck, then scooped her up in his arms.

The receptionist looked up, her eyes widening at the sight of David's bare chest with Vicki in his arms.

"It's her ankle," he explained, his cheeks reddening. "Can we see a doctor?"

"Of course," she replied, her eyes still lingering on his chest. "Right this way."

"That's one nasty cut," he said, setting her down on the examining table. His shirt around her leg was now soaked in blood. A nurse came in and gave him a gown to cover his bare chest. David watched as the doctor cleaned the gash and pulled out the splinters embedded in Vicki's leg.

"I'm sorry," Vicki said, wincing; the local anesthetic obviously hadn't kicked in yet.

David just stared at her. Now was not the time to give her an extended lecture about how stupid she was for going into her house. She was like a stubborn child, determined to go against what was good for her. She should have been grateful that she didn't have to spend hours waiting for someone else to find her.

"You'll be fine in a few days," the doctor assured Vicki. "Just stay off it as much as possible."

Vicki remained quiet after that, most likely embarrassed by her actions. The doctor stitched her up, gave her some pills, and then released her with instructions on when and how often to clean her wound.

They remained silent as David drove her back to Jenny's. After parking, he reached behind his seat and pulled out a spare T-shirt, slipping it on before opening the door to get out.

"I can manage by myself," Vicki said.

"Can you?" One eyebrow went up as he looked at her. It was a loaded question. He had his doubts about her stubborn determination.

She opened the door to his truck, put one foot down, swung the other around, and collapsed onto the ground, yelping in pain.

David hopped out and ran around. She glared at him as he slid his arms around her bottom and picked her up. He carried her to the door and then went inside.

"What happened?" Jenny came running over. "Is she alright?"

Curious customers looked over with concerned faces.

"I'll let her tell you," David replied. "Where shall I put her?" he asked, swinging her toward the back of the shop.

"Upstairs in the den, I guess."

Jenny followed him as he carried Vicki to the room she indicated. He set Vicki down on the couch, then helped put her leg on an ottoman.

He turned to Jenny. "You'll need to help her. Nothing's broken, just scraped and bruised. But the doctor gave her pain pills, and she'll need to rest so she doesn't hurt herself again."

He looked back at Vicki. She held out her hand for him to take and squeezed it when he did. She looked up at him with her sweet, soulful hazel eyes and said, "Thank you," which made taking off work to help her worthwhile.

Chapter Eleven

Vicki

After a day of being confined to the second floor, Vicki hobbled over to her studio. An eerie feeling greeted her as she entered. A dampness and the smell of moss enveloped her as if she was somewhere else.

She sighed. There must be a way she could paint. There was a chair in the bedroom and a small stool she could prop her foot on. *That could work.*

She picked up her phone and called Jenny downstairs.

"I hope you aren't in the middle of something."

"No, I'm just finishing up with a customer. Is there something you need?"

"Yeah, I'd like to move some items into the studio."

"I'll send Brooke right up. Anything else?"

"No, thanks."

Brooke arrived shortly, and Vicki showed her where to put the chair and stool.

"I thought you were supposed to rest," Brooke replied, looking around at the backsides of various canvases. "Why do you have these facing the wall? Don't you want to look at them?" she asked.

"I'm trying not to copy the same image over and over. When I have something I'm happy with, I'll show you."

After Brooke left, Vicki set up a fresh canvas and stared at the blank surface, wondering what it hid underneath. Maybe if she added a line here and a bold stroke of brown there—a little blue mixed with green slid from her brush.

She got busy adding shape and color to the board. A pendulum swung in her head, ticking away as she added more definition to her painting. Each stroke was a moment in the girl's life she was creating.

Satisfied, Vicki stood back and brought the tip of the brush to her mouth. Even though she had previously turned her paintings to face the wall, she was replicating the same girl over and over again. It was like she was a tree, and all these paintings were leaves unfurling out of her mind. That seemed odd, but who was she to question her muse? At least she wasn't painting sailboats and shells.

VICKI EASED her way the final few steps downstairs, clutching the railing for support to keep any pressure off her injured leg. She sighed as she reached the floor and shuffled to the kitchen. At the same time, a tremendous growl erupted from her belly, making Brooke turn from where she was making coffee.

"Can I see what you've been painting up there all this time?" she asked.

"Sure. Let me eat something first, though. I'm starving." Vicki opened the refrigerator, took out a plate of cold pasta, and put it in the microwave for three minutes.

Brooke handed her a cup of fresh coffee and leaned on the counter with her arms. "It must be cool to be able to paint things."

"Sometimes it's fun. Other times, it's just work." Vicki sipped her coffee. "You're a bit of an artist, too, you know."

"I guess so. I'm good at decorating like Jenny, but that comes easy. I'm just moving things around. It's not like I have to create them."

The microwave pinged, and Brooke motioned for Vicki to stay put as she fetched her pasta for her.

"Thanks," Vicki said. She took her first bite, and her stomach seemed to cry out with joy. "Well, I don't know if you'll like my paintings or not, but you're welcome to take a look at what I've done so far."

Vicki finished up her lunch, then motioned for Brooke to follow her upstairs—slowly, of course. When they eventually reached the studio, Brooke's eyes widened.

"I didn't know you painted native girls." She looked back at Vicki. "That girl looks young. Like she's just graduated from high school."

"Does she look like a Native American girl to you?" Vicki asked, scrunching up her face and studying one of her paintings.

"Yes, but she has some Caucasian in her because her nose isn't as wide and is pointy. She looks more mixed race. Her skin color is more like a tan than a true native color, but that may be because of your choice of paint. My dad was white, and I have some of his features. I've been told by my grandfather that my face is narrower than my ancestors. But I guess you can make your paintings look any way you like."

"I just saw her as the girl in my imagination. I wasn't intentionally making her a descendant from any particular ethnic group." However, Vicki now recognized what Brooke was referring to. She was right. The girl in her painting looked like a Native American teenager.

"I hope you don't dress her in buckskins and headdresses. That would be so uncool."

"What about fur? Would you find that offensive?" Vicki didn't want to come across as insensitive.

"I guess not."

"Wow, those are incredible!" Jenny commented from the doorway. "So, these are the paintings you've been doing while hibernating up here?"

"Aren't they cool?" Brooke added, turning to Jenny with a big grin on her face.

Jenny put her arms around Vicki's shoulder and gave it a squeeze.

"Thanks. I'm glad you like them." She sighed with a mixture of exhaustion and appreciation.

"Like them? I love them!" Jenny went over and squinted, examining the image more closely. "I always knew you were talented. You need to take them downstairs so I can hang them in my shop."

"Do you think any of your customers would buy these?"

"I bet people will snatch them up. What are you going to price them at?" Jenny asked, turning to face Vicki.

"I don't really know. I don't want to price them too high, but I don't want to just give them away, either."

"How long does it take to paint one?"

"I haven't kept track. I just zone out until I get blurry-eyed." Vicki bit her lip.

"Well, it's about time you start thinking about what these are worth. In the meantime, I'll look for a place to hang them."

Vicki was thrilled at the idea of seeing something of hers besides boat pictures on a wall.

Chapter Twelve

David

"How's Vicki doing?" David asked, wiping his feet on the doormat before stepping all the way inside the shop area. The rain had picked up outside, and he didn't want to track dirt across the floor. He slipped off his wet coat and put it on the hook. His mind was on Vicki. He'd been worried about her since the accident, and he couldn't shake the feeling that something else was going on.

Jenny got up from her desk and came around to greet him, giving him a quick hug. "She's in the kitchen," she said, then called loudly to the next room. "Vicki? David's here to see you."

Vicki strolled out with a cup in her hand. The blue leggings she wore stopped above her knee so he could see the bandage covering the wound on her lower leg. It had been several days since her accident, and apparently, her pain was gone, judging by how she walked.

"Hi, David, how's the house coming?" she said, flipping strands of her blond hair over her shoulder.

Yep, she was back to normal. He cleared his throat. "I'm sure Shaun has told you that we've been busy working on a couple of other places and are short-handed right now."

Jenny nodded, adding, "Shaun's still looking to hire more qualified workers, but that takes time."

"We'll start work as soon as we can."

"What am I supposed to do until then?" Vicki asked, slumping her shoulders. "I just wish this never happened in the first place."

He knew how much her house meant to her and how much she wanted to get back to normal. But he also knew her stubbornness could work against her, too.

"It's okay, Vicki." Jenny put her arm around Vicki's waist and gave her a squeeze. "Everyone knows what a burden this is for you."

David wanted to avoid Vicki's criticism, so he strolled over and looked up at the new pictures hanging on the wall. "Are these your paintings?" He immediately picked up on how the girl's eyes seemed to follow him as he moved.

Brooke piped up, "She's doing portraits of a native girl."

"Yes, I can see that. You've done several of the same person. Nice." He thought that was a bit odd but didn't mention it. Vicki was very talented, but the subject choice wasn't what he had been expecting to see. Sea life and boats had been her specialty.

"When can I go into my house again?" Vicki asked.

David stopped himself from sighing. He knew that question had been coming. He turned to answer. "Well, I'd prefer you wait. You saw what happened last time you went inside. Besides, the power and water are currently shut off. We've scheduled a plumber to come out and replace the broken pipes that were leaking in the bathroom."

"Swell," Vicki grumbled.

"I'm sorry. I know that isn't what you wanted to hear." David looked at the paintings again, avoiding eye contact with Vicki. "So, tell me about your model. Is she a local gal?"

"I'm not using a model. I'm painting from my imagination."

"Well, you seem to have this girl down pat. Will you be painting portraits of other girls, too?"

Vicki just shrugged her shoulders. "I don't seem to be inspired to paint anyone else right now."

An awkward silence followed, and he got the feeling their conversation was over. Unfortunately, things didn't go as well as he would have liked. He wanted to spend time alone with Vicki, to ask her out. However, it was obvious she wouldn't be receptive to the idea.

"I better go now. See you gals later."

He left feeling sorry for Vicki. She didn't look very happy. Something other than her house was bothering her. He just couldn't put his finger on what that might be.

David put his coat back on and went out onto the porch.

"David."

He turned to find Jenny right behind him. She had a peculiar look on her face as if worried about how he would react to what she was about to say.

"You may think this is nonsense, but my mother's ghost still lives in my house," she started. "And the other day, when I went upstairs while Vicki was asleep, I crept into my mother's room. I sat on the bed to say hello and that I hadn't forgotten her since I moved out. She told me—well, she doesn't actually speak directly. Anyway, she told me there was another spirit in the house and that it was strong. I thought she was talking about Vicki, but maybe she wasn't. Are artists' muses considered spirits too?"

"I don't know if they are or not. Mine don't seem to be."

He'd encouraged Vicki to follow her muse, but painting the same image over and over wasn't what he'd had in mind. He suspected there was more to her compulsion than she was letting on.

THAT NIGHT, he wanted to talk to Vicki but wasn't sure what to say. He picked up his phone, his fingers hovering over the keys. He wanted to hear her voice.

He put the phone down, his heart heavy. He knew that Vicki was going through something, something that was affecting her deeply.

Finally, he called.

"I'm glad to see you are walking around again," David said, his voice filled with genuine concern. He could picture her in his mind, the determined set of her jaw, the spark in her eyes.

"Yes, I guess it wasn't very smart of me to go inside my house alone," Vicki replied, her voice tinged with embarrassment.

He wasn't going to rub salt in her apology with an "I-told-you-so" comment again. Instead, he chose to steer the conversation in a different direction. "You looked tired, though. Not been sleeping well?"

"No, I have—it's just—there is a lot going on."

David's eyebrows shot up. "Ah, trauma can do that. That tree really took its toll on you."

"Yeah. I guess so."

There was a pause, and David could sense that Vicki was holding something back. He wanted to press her, to ask her what was really going on, but he knew that she needed to come to him in her own time.

"Well, remember, if you need anything, just give me a call," he said, his voice gentle.

"Thanks, David."

The conversation ended, but his concern for Vicki lingered. He sat in his living room, the phone still in his hand, his mind racing. He thought back to the paintings he had seen in her shop, the haunting images of the native girl, the way her eyes seemed to follow him. He couldn't shake the feeling that there was something more to those paintings, something deeper. However, he'd keep his thoughts about her artwork to himself.

He'd learned that Vicki was a private person, that she kept her emotions close to her chest. She could be bothered more than she was letting on about having to stay with Jenny while waiting for the repairs on her house.

He wanted to help her, to be there for her, to support her as she worked through whatever was going on in her mind. But he also knew that he needed to be careful, to give her space.

He got up and went to the window, looking out at the

night. The rain had stopped, and the stars were beginning to shine. He thought about Vicki, about her strength, her determination, her spirit. She thought she could manage all the problems in her life. But we all need help now and then.

He wanted to be there for her, to support her, to help her. Because that's what friends do, and that's what he decided the safest place for his relationship with Vicki to remain—as friends.

Chapter Thirteen

Vicki

Vicki was in the shop, standing on the ladder and adjusting one of her paintings.

"I think it's straight now." Jenny stood back. "Yes, that's perfect."

The bell above the front door rang. They both glanced over to see who it was.

"Hi, Ben. I haven't seen you in a while. Is this a social call, or are you here on business?" Jenny left Vicki and went over to greet the stocky Native man standing near the door.

He tipped his hat and said, "Well, I thought I'd drop by because I was in the neighborhood, but now I'm not sure."

Vicki climbed down the ladder and stood nearby. She had met Ben Stone before, but they had never really spoken. He was the Lummi private investigator Shaun and Jenny had hired several years ago to work on Shaun's case.

The story Ben had come up with about Orcas and spirits always struck her as bizarre, but it had worked because Shaun was now a free man, and he and Jenny were happily married.

"What do you mean? Jenny asked.

"I took a look in your window before I came in and saw that painting. It surprised me."

"Oh, how so?"

"Well, the portrait looks like a girl I once knew."

"Really? She looks a bit young," Jenny replied.

"Not in that way." He grinned. "The daughter of someone I know."

He strolled over to the other three paintings Vicki just hung on the wall next to the cash register. He hummed and asked, "Who did these?"

"Vicki Milikan." Jenny turned to Vicki and smiled. "She's staying here until her house is ready to move back into. A tree fell on it."

"The one a couple of doors down, I presume?" He nodded to Vicki. "That's unfortunate."

"Yeah, I'm afraid so," Vicki replied.

Brooke approached Ben with her eyes wide. "Does the girl in the painting look like someone who disappeared from the reservation? Is that why you're asking about her?"

He turned and nodded to Brooke. "Maybe."

"Did you want to buy a painting?" Vicki asked.

"Actually, I'd like to know more about the girl,"

Ben was staring at her, and she was uncomfortable. "Oh," Vicki replied, taking a step back.

"Did you paint these from a photograph?"

"No, I painted them from my imagination." Vicki

Strokes of Desperation

tossed her head, throwing her eyes up as though this girl had just beamed down into her mind.

"Interesting. They're very lifelike."

"I seem to be consumed with painting her lately," Vicki replied, somewhat embarrassed.

He turned to her. "Do you have any more?"

Curious about his interest, she replied, "Yes. Would you like to come upstairs and see some of the others I've done?"

She led him up the stairs, then down a hall to an open door. "I have a lot of her. For some strange reason, I keep drawing and painting this same girl over and over." Nervous, Vicki drew her hand across her head, flicking her hair over her shoulder.

Everywhere around the room were drawings and paintings leaning against the walls and lying on the floor. On an easel was one not yet complete. The poses varied, starting with just hair hanging down the woman's bare back, then several profiles, and gradually, the woman's face turned until she was looking directly out at the viewer.

"Have you ever met her before?" Ben asked. "Do you know who she is?"

Vicki thought about his question. Could this girl be a compilation of all the Native girls she had seen in the past? It was possible. She had visited the reservation a few times but had no reason to go there these days.

"No, like I told you earlier, she just exists in my imagination," she said.

"Think hard, Vicki. Is there anything, anything at all, that might connect you to this girl? A memory, a dream, a feeling?"

"No, she just revealed herself while I was painting. I

wasn't looking at a photograph or a magazine. Nothing I can remember."

"That's interesting. Because the girl you're painting resembles a girl by the name of Catori Rein. She's been missing for the last ten years."

"You've got to be kidding." Vicki's face scrunched into a confused look. "I don't get it. That's bizarre. You think I'm painting someone who's missing?"

"Yes." Ben squatted down, eyeing one painting of Catori, and pointed to the birthmark on the woman's side. Turning his head to face Vicki, he asked, "This came from your imagination, too?"

Vicki nodded.

"What about your dreams? Do you dream about her at night?"

Vicki remembered the visions she had while painting.

"Daydreams, maybe. I sort of just let my mind wander while I paint."

Ben stood, pulled out a card, and handed it to her. "Call me if you start getting visions of what happened to Catori. I'm curious about her whereabouts. No one was able to trace her after she disappeared."

Vicki smiled uneasily. "Sure."

As he left the studio, Ben pulled out his phone and punched in a number.

Vicki was left standing in the studio, her mind reeling from what Ben had told her. The room, filled with the haunting images of a girl she had never met, suddenly felt oppressive and surreal. She looked around at the paintings, her heart pounding, her thoughts a whirl of confusion and disbelief.

Could it be true? Could she really be painting the image

of a girl she had never met, never seen, never even heard of?

She thought about the compulsion that had driven her to paint this girl, over and over, in different poses, different settings, and different moods.

She recalled Ben's words about the girl's name, about the birthmark, about the mystery of her disappearance.

It all seemed impossible, unbelievable. And yet, there was something in Ben's eyes, something in his voice, something in the way he had looked at the paintings, that told her he believed it even if she didn't. That he thought there was something more to this, something deeper, something that went beyond mere coincidence.

She sat down, her legs weak, her mind still racing. She looked at the paintings again, her eyes drawn to the girl's face, to her eyes, to her expression. She felt a connection, a bond, a link that went beyond mere imagination. But she doubted that Ben was right about this being the same girl that disappeared.

Chapter Fourteen

David

It was an overcast Saturday, and David was in his shop with his tables.

"Hi, Ben." David cradled the phone, setting down the rag he had been using to polish a table, and went to the office in his shop.

"I understand you used to be a cop in the Midwest."

He pulled a bottle of water out from the tiny fridge he kept in his office. "Well, that didn't quite work out," he replied, twisting the lid off. "I have this tendency to get myself in trouble because I don't always follow the rules." He took a quick swig.

"I understand you are intuitive."

"Yes, but it has a mind of its own. I've been trying to ignore it. It gets me in trouble. I don't like knowing things sometimes. Why?" He took another drink.

"I want to find out what happened to a young Native girl."

David set down the bottle. "Oh?"

"She went missing ten years ago. The police in Bellingham didn't put much effort into looking for her. Natives aren't a priority. I tried locating her as a favor to the girl's father but didn't have the time or resources back then."

"So, why the sudden interest in finding her now?"

"The gal who owns the art gallery where the tree fell is now painting pictures of this missing girl."

He knew there was something odd about her paintings. "Vicki? You can't be serious?"

"She has a room full of the girl's image, and I don't think it's a fluke. One painting even had the exact birthmark. I bet there's some strong supernatural stuff going on there."

"Okay, now you're losing me. You think a ghost of this missing or dead girl is making Vicki paint these pictures?"

"Yeah, I do, and I want to know if Vicki can provide us with information as to what happened to this girl. Catori Rein."

"What do you want me to do about it?"

"I'd like you to work on the case with me."

David rubbed the back of his neck. "Jeeze, I don't know. I've got a regular job, and we've been busy lately filling table orders, so I can't do much."

"How about I work around your schedule? I want a fresh pair of eyes and your intuition if that's okay. You might be able to generate some leads."

David looked out of his office window toward the water. His hunches had been haunting him a lot lately. Perhaps his bad feelings about Vicki might somehow be connected to this girl Ben was telling him about. Maybe he shouldn't ignore them. Unfortunately, sometimes they'd rise up and then disappear, leaving him baffled about their meaning.

"Okay, sure. Just let me know what you want me to do."

"I'll come by with the old files so you can look them over. Then we can discuss where to go from there."

They hung up, and David sank onto his desk chair. He had been cursed with premonitions since he was a kid. They weren't about anything significant in the beginning. He knew where Mrs. Baker's cat was hiding when everyone thought it was lost. Also, he knew that Tommy's bike would be stolen from outside of the drugstore. Sometimes, he told people, but they would tease him, so he learned to keep his mouth shut.

Other times, though, they were important and shouldn't be ignored because the consequences were devastating. He'd never forget what happened when he didn't respond immediately to the premonition about his sister Rachel.

It was while he was at football practice in high school. Rachel was his biggest fan, never missing a game and often watching him at practice. That morning, she had told him, "I'm coming to see you today."

But for some reason, he knew she wouldn't be there. After school, he suited up and went out on the field. His coach was having him go through different plays when he got a flash and a gut-wrenching feeling that something bad was going to happen to Rachel. He dropped the football he was carrying and went to the coach. "I need to leave," he said.

"David, you can't leave. Whatever it is, it will have to wait until later."

Strokes of Desperation

"I have to go now." The feeling was eating him up inside.

"Kid, if you leave now, don't come back. I'll cut you from the team."

David stood there, then started to walk back to the field. But the feeling only grew stronger. He couldn't ignore it. He ran to catch a ball. Every minute he delayed made him more nervous, and the anxiety made him break out in a sweat.

Finally, he took off his helmet, left the field, and ran to the gate, then jogged out to the street. He had a horrible image in his mind. After running three blocks, a truck drove by with its window down, country music blaring. It accelerated through a light that had just turned red ahead, then slammed on its brakes with a long screech. There was a thump. Rachel's body went sailing through the air.

He immediately ran to where she lay. Her leg was twisted and broken; blood was pooling on the asphalt where her head hit the ground. He knew she wasn't going to make it.

"I love you, Ray," he told her.

Then he screamed. It was the same sound that woke him in the middle of the night every time he watched someone die that he wished he could've saved.

After Rachel's accident, all the what ifs fell upon him. Why had he waited so long? He could have prevented this if he had responded sooner to his hunch. He had lost his mother to cancer two years earlier and now his sister. He couldn't save his mother, but he could've saved Rachel. The next few months were hard. He was swirling in grief, feeling alone, and slipping into depression. Unable to concentrate, his father took him to the construction sites where he worked so they both could deal with the loss. Working with their hands was good therapy: pounding nails, sawing boards, lifting lumber, making something—new homes for families.

It took a year of struggling in darkness, but his premonitions finally returned. Now, he listened and acted upon important ones, saving fellow construction workers from falling or getting hit by something heavy. While in the army, he knew where the enemy was hiding. It was a responsibility he often didn't want, constantly feeling powerless to do anything and then witnessing the results when the outcome wasn't favorable. Haunted with guilt, he had nightmares about those that died. He was no Superman, and he didn't pretend to be. Still, he struggled with what to do when he got these feelings.

Now, when he had hunches about minor things, he let them go, living with the results. Sometimes he questioned the logic behind the feeling he got. Maybe life would be better off if he didn't try to interfere in other people's lives. Still, he felt the need to help if he could. Especially right now, with Vicki, but she wasn't letting him.

Chapter Fifteen

Ben

An hour later, Ben slipped off his coat and hung it on the back of the chair, then removed his brown Stetson and placed it on the corner, revealing dark, shoulder-length hair threaded with silver. He rummaged through a worn, tan leather backpack, then tossed a folder onto David's dining table.

David liked Ben. The man struck him as a mixture of a smart investigator and an Indian shaman—searching for clues both above and below the surface. As for being much help on this case, David didn't know if he had that much to contribute. It wasn't like he had a foot in the supernatural world with his limited abilities. He couldn't unravel the past or point to a guilty party; no. Finding who was responsible for Catori's disappearance would require old-fashioned feet on the ground work.

"You want a beer?" David asked, opening the refrigerator.

He tossed David a look. "Sure, what you got?"

"Some local beer from a Bellingham brewery."

"Great. No glass. The bottle's fine."

David popped the lid on two bottles of IPA and brought them over, taking a seat.

"Take a look at these." Ben pointed to the open file with a pen he held in his hand.

David leaned over to the photo clipped to the report. Apparently, the picture was one from Catori's high school yearbook. She was dressed in black and had a lot of makeup on as if trying to look tough and older than she was. Inside the file was another larger photo of her standing next to a beat-to-shit car outside a cinder block house. He also found a photo of a drawing; in it, Catori was nude, sitting on a chair. One leg was crossed over her other knee, her elbows resting on the arms of the chair, and her hands sat in her lap, covering her private area. Strands of her dark hair fell over most of her chest, though one breast peeked through. Her eyes were outlined in dark pencil, and she was looking to the side. Her face held a faint smile like she had a secret or was being naughty and knew it. The drawing wasn't as good as Vicki's artwork, but you could definitely recognize they were both of the same gal.

"I don't get it. Why is this girl's image showing up in Vicki's paintings now?" David turned to face Ben.

Ben threw back his shoulders. "I believe her spirit is restless and found a way to manifest itself through Vicki's paintings somehow."

David cocked his head to one side and rubbed his chin. "I can't see how her paintings are going to solve this case."

"They may not. But they're a piece to the puzzle. That's why we need to pull out all the other clues and see how Vicki's paintings fit in with the whole picture."

"So, you believe Vicki may lead us to the killer without realizing it?"

Ben took a sip of his beer and wiped his mouth with the back of his hand. "Interesting that you say, killer. Most people think she just ran away." Ben smiled sadly. "But I now believed her abductor may have killed her."

David nodded, but a twist in his stomach made him ask, "Do you think the killer knows Vicki is painting these pictures?"

"I don't think so. At least not yet if they are only hanging in Jenny's shop in Cook's Cove. However, it's possible once she gets some exposure elsewhere, her artwork will draw attention to the crime, and the killer will be curious as to why Catori's image is suddenly appearing."

David furrowed his brows. "Will this put Vicki in danger?"

"Maybe, but I'd be more worried about Catori's spirit worming its way into her mind. We don't know how it will impact Vicki's behavior and what the spirit is up to."

That was what bothered David the most. He could protect her from people and objects but not from a spirit.

"What can you tell me about Catori?"

"She was only seventeen when she disappeared," Ben said.

"That's pretty young to try to make it on her own."

"I just regret not spending more time looking for the girl back then. I knew her father and was searching for her as a favor to him. But I was busy working on another case that paid, so the missing girl didn't take priority. I'd watched her grow up, and she was a pretty good kid." Ben took a gulp from his bottle, then continued. "At the time, I thought she just ran away and would either come back or someone would spot her, and her father could quit worrying about her. But when that didn't happen, I figured someone had snatched her and forced her into prostitution. You can see how attractive she was."

Picking up the photo of Catori standing next to the car again, David noticed a resemblance to Vicki's shape; their curves and height were remarkably similar.

"My detective friend at the department in Bellingham told me they get so many reports of missing Native kids they don't bother to log them into the system. I asked that they add Catori's name to the list of missing persons. However, I don't believe anyone made a real effort to find her, though. I went out and talked to some people on my own, but all the leads were cold by then."

"Is anyone paying you now to look for her?" David asked, wondering why Ben had formed this sudden interest in resuming the search.

"No. I had a dream that her spirit was in the area, that it was restless and unhappy. Which to me means it wants us to solve this case so it can be at peace."

David had never dealt with spirits before, but he didn't doubt their existence.

Ben pulled out a crude schematic of all the people Catori had been in contact with before she disappeared. David smiled at the simplicity of it: a stick figure representing Catori was in the middle. One line led to another figure with the name Joey Black underneath.

Ben pointed with his pen and circled the name. "This

kid was her boyfriend at the time. I'd like to talk to him again."

Another line went to a box labeled Sea Haven Art College. "This was the art school where she took a job working in the cafeteria. I found out she lied about her age to get hired."

Ben tapped the point of his pen next to the second box. "This other line goes to a youth shelter in Bellingham. This is where the homeless kids go to sleep and get fed. She was last seen there. That is where the case went cold. No one spotted her leaving with a stranger. We have no idea where she went or who she went with."

Ben placed a red question mark next to the name William Rein. "Even though he wanted me to look for his daughter, Catori's father wasn't the easiest man to work with on this case." Ben set down the pen and sighed. "He demanded answers and would muck things up by charging in and threatening people—such as the head of the school where Catori worked. Seems that William was able to pry out of them that his daughter was doing some modeling in the art class, as well as working in the cafeteria. That sent William off in a rage. After that, the school was tight-lipped and told everyone asking questions to talk to their attorney. I believe a teacher got fired over the incident."

"You don't think he could have been involved?" David asked.

"William had his demons to deal with. I believe he's an alcoholic. The reservation police have been called to his place many times regarding domestic abuse, but his wife always drops the charges, retracting her statements about William hitting her. I'd seen William angry before and knew he was a strict father, but I doubt he would kill his own daughter. Still, I've worked as a private investigator long enough to know not to assume anything."

David shook his head. "None of this tells me why Vicki would be chosen as the one to be painting Catori."

"That's what I want to know. You know her, right?" Ben turned his body to face David.

"Sort of."

"Could you keep an eye on her and report back to me any unusual behavior she displays?"

"Sure."

"Well, I'll leave you to go through everything. Let me know if anything pops out at you that you think I've missed."

After Ben left, David found himself torn between his feelings toward Vicki and his genuine concern about her as a person. He didn't know how much he should get involved. Lately, he'd been getting the feeling that something was going on with Vicki that she wasn't telling anyone about. He knew she had secrets, but this was different.

He had picked up on another strange vibe, like a shadow sneaking around out of sight behind her eyes. Could that be the ghost Ben was talking about?

Chapter Sixteen

Vicki

Jenny knocked on the door to the studio, then poked her head in. "There's a man downstairs who's interested in your paintings. Do you want to talk to him?"

Vicki had just finished cleaning her brushes. She wiped her hands on her smock and took it off. Glancing at herself in the mirror, she undid her ponytail and fluffed up her hair.

Vicki was pleasantly surprised by who was standing there when she went out to the shop. A handsome fifty-year-old man wearing slacks and a white button-down shirt looked over at her with a smile.

"Mr. Tomasie!" she cried, running into his open arms.

After a crushing hug, he held her back. "How are you, my dear?" He slowly scanned up and down her body.

She beamed. "Fine," she replied, not knowing what else to say.

"So, you are the artist behind the magnificent painting in the window?" His eyes sparkled at the news.

She nodded, still in shock at seeing her old art instructor admiring *her* paintings.

He lingered, taking his time to inspect them all with an expression she couldn't quite read.

"I always knew you were gifted, but these?" He pointed to the paintings on the wall. "They are beyond anyone's expectation of true talent."

She blushed. "Mr. Tomasie, you're too kind."

"Please, don't call me that. I'm not your instructor anymore. Call me Anthony."

"Thank you, Anthony." She couldn't help but think that he was good-looking for his age. He had a little gray at the temples of his dark, curly hair and some lines at the corner of his brown eyes.

"I've always wondered what happened to you. I thought you had real promise. And I kept expecting to see your work hanging in some of the galleries back east or at least mentioned in one of the art publications."

"Well, my career is a lot more modest than what you imagined." She looked over at the counter, where Jenny pretended not to be listening. "What about you? I understand you left your position at the art college?"

"Yes, that was years ago. I moved on to better things." He kept staring at her curiously.

"Like what?"

"Are you free right now?" he asked in a soft voice.

Her face lit up at his question. "Yes, I don't have

anything I can't put off. Why?" she replied, biting her lower lip.

"I have an idea. Why don't I take you for drinks and an early dinner so we can catch up on what we've both been doing all these years?"

It was nice seeing him again, but dinner? "Go on," a voice in her head nudged her. "I—sure. Let me go change first. I'll be right back."

She ran upstairs and into the bedroom. Yanking open drawers and tossing clothes onto the bed. She had no idea what to wear. This was just a friendly dinner to catch up on old times with her art teacher. It wasn't a date. She pulled on a pair of slacks and picked up a high-neck sweater. After pulling out her necklace and grasping it in her hand, that voice in her head yelled, "No, pick something sexy instead."

She pulled off the sweater and slipped out of her slacks. Then raised the tip of the wooden pendant and placed it to her lips. What should she wear?

Opening a drawer, she found a sexy lace bra and silk panties, then slammed the drawer shut. She flicked through clothes on hangers in her closet and finally settled on a low-cut silky cream blouse that showed off her cleavage, a pair of black pants, and red high heels. She grabbed a red sweater, and her purse, then ran down to meet him.

When she returned, Anthony held out his arm for her to take. They walked down the stairs outside together and over to a white Maserati with its top down. He opened the passenger door for her. "Hop in, and I'll take you someplace special."

Chapter Seventeen

David

The sun was hanging above the horizon as David's truck rumbled down the road. It had been a long day, filled with back-breaking labor. All he wanted was to head home, take a hot shower, collapse on the couch, and zone out watching a game on TV. But as he was about to turn onto the road out of town, a sleek white sports car with its top down roared past him, cutting him off so sharply that he had to slam on his brakes.

His hand shot to his horn, anger flaring in his chest, but before he pressed it, he froze. The blonde hair flying in the wind he recognized instantly. Vicki was in the passenger seat, her face lit up with joy, and the sight of the unknown man at the wheel sent a flash of anger through David's mind. Warning bells were going off, and he had a gut feeling that this guy was someone Vicki should not be with.

His heart was pounding as David followed the sports car at a discreet distance, his mind a whirlwind of concern and confusion. He watched as the sports car pulled into a restaurant's parking lot, Vicki and the mystery man getting out, laughing and chatting as they headed inside.

David's truck rolled to a stop on the side of the road, and he sat there, his hands gripping the steering wheel, his eyes fixed on the restaurant's entrance. His mind was racing, flooded with questions and disturbing images. Images of this guy with other women. It's definitely not what he wanted to see at the moment. He didn't need to know about this guy's past conquests.

He ran his hand down his face. How did Vicki know this guy? Were they on some kind of date? Was this a romantic relationship she had failed to mention?

He pictured them inside, sitting across from each other at a cozy table for two, candlelight flickering in their eyes, Vicki twirling her hair and leaning in close as the man whispered sweet nothings in her ear. The image was so vivid, so real, that David's hands clenched into fists, his knuckles turning white. A volcano of emotions erupted inside him - confusion, jealousy, anger. He had no claim over Vicki. They weren't in a relationship. But the thought of her with this man made his blood boil.

Something inside him was screaming at him, telling him to go inside and jerk her away from this stranger. That this guy was trouble.

One foot was out the door before David paused, a moment of clarity breaking through the storm of emotion. What was he doing? Causing a scene like some crazy, jealous boyfriend would only push Vicki away.

Taking a few deep breaths, he tried to think rationally.

Vicki was her own person, free to go out with whoever she pleased. As much as he wanted to, he had no right to interfere. He leaned back into his seat, the leather creaking beneath him, and turned the key in the ignition.

As he pulled away from the restaurant, his mind churned, replaying the scene over and over. Why did he have such a negative reaction from seeing Vicki with someone?

David drove back to Cook's Cove, his thoughts a tangled mess. This was a perfect example of why he needed to ignore these crazy urges sometimes. Vicki going out with someone else wasn't the end of the world. He had no claims on her. They were just 'friends,' he reminded himself. That's what he wanted. That's what she'd been communicating to him in subtle ways, too. So, what was the big deal? What horrible thing did he think he was going to rescue her from? He was pretty sure she knew how to take care of herself around men.

He pulled into his driveway, the gravel crunching beneath his tires, but he didn't get out of the truck. Instead, he sat there, staring out at the darkening sky, lost in thought. He tried convincing himself he'd be better off if he kept his distance from her. Not let his feelings get involved. But now, everything seems to be changing. The lines were blurred, and he didn't know how to redraw them.

He finally stepped out of the truck, the cool air washing over him, but it did nothing to clear his mind. He made his way into the house. He knew he should eat, shower—do something to take his mind off Vicki, but he couldn't. He couldn't let go of the nagging feeling that something wasn't right about that guy Vicki was with.

Chapter Eighteen

Vicki

They drove the winding road along the coast. Vicki's hair flapped in the wind, and she smiled as the trees flew past her. After a while, they reached a restaurant on the cliff known for its oysters and crab. Mr. Tomasic pulled into the parking lot and opened her door for her—something younger men rarely did anymore. She giggled at his chivalry.

He took her hand as they walked inside.

"I'd like a secluded table with a view," he told the hostess.

"Of course, Mr. Tomasic."

Vicki could hardly contain her pleasure. This was a very expensive restaurant, and from what she had just observed, Anthony Tomasic frequently dined there.

Vicki started to take a seat across from him, but he motioned for her to sit next to him in the booth, pointing to the view out the window, so she slid over.

"So, tell me all about yourself." Anthony beamed, putting his arm along the back of the booth and angling his body toward her. "You were one of my favorite students. I think I even tried to kiss you once."

She blushed at the memory of the time she stayed after class to finish up a piece and him nuzzling her ear while she added a touch of paint to her work. His hot breath had given her chills. When she turned, his lips found hers, and for a moment, she was in heaven. But then a bell rang, the spell broke, and he left her to clean up.

Rolling her eyes, she shyly confessed, "I had a crush on you back then, but what girl didn't?"

He laughed, then winked, and whispered, "I found you attractive, too, and now what can I say? You're even more gorgeous."

She blushed at the compliment.

"This calls for wine." He raised his hand, signaling the waitress over. When she arrived, he told her the wine he wanted. He also ordered oysters on the half-shell and lobster for them to eat.

Vicki couldn't believe she was sitting in this expensive restaurant, drinking wine and eating lobster with Anthony Tomasie. The other girls in his class would have been so jealous.

"So, how was your trip to New York with, ah—what was that boy's name?"

"Jerrid." She looked down. "I decided that the New York art world was a bit bizarre, so I came back and opened my own small gallery." It was partially true and sounded more impressive than it was.

"So, where's your gallery?" He focused his attention on her, taking in her features.

She dropped her shoulders. "I had to close it recently because of the damage sustained during a windstorm."

He squeezed her arm. "Oh, that's too bad. Is that why you were showing your work in that little decorating store?"

Vicki suddenly felt ashamed of having her art in Jenny's shop. "I'm afraid so."

He sat back, watching her. "You know, I have a lot of friends in the art world now. Why don't I arrange for you to do a show of your paintings at a gallery in Seattle?"

Her heart skipped a beat as she tried to suppress her excitement. "You could do that?"

"Of course, no problem, my dear. Like I said, I have friends in the art world. As a matter of fact, I have launched the careers of several young artists." He took a sip of his wine, then sat back, smiling at her. "I work as an art broker and consultant now. I find pieces for Fortune 500 companies to display in their lobbies. My clients and stable of artists span the world, so you'd be in good hands. I could launch your career if you let me."

Vicki suddenly felt intimidated. "The only paintings I have right now are of the girl you saw earlier. But I could come up with something else if you prefer." She bit her lip. *Was he serious?*

"No, those are perfect! The girl will be your signature image. Do you have enough to do your own show?"

She gulped. "Yes." She had a room full of sketches and paintings. "What percentage do you charge for doing that?"

He reached under the table and squeezed her knee. "I

think we can work something out that is favorable to both of us."

Not sure what he meant by that, a knot tightened in her stomach, but she smiled. "Yes. I'm sure we can."

After dinner, Anthony whispered to her, "Let's go to Bellingham and watch the stars."

She hesitated for a moment. The reality of the cost of having Anthony help her career was sending off alarm bells. She began to question if this was a good idea. She was about to suggest he take her back to Jenny's when a voice whispered in her ears, "This is what you've always wanted. You may never have this opportunity again. Go."

She swallowed, and something shifted within her. Now she found herself suddenly drawn to him, and not just because of his good looks and charm. It was for what he could do for her, which was an aphrodisiac she couldn't deny. The words, "I'd love that," came out of her mouth as if spoken by someone else.

━━━

THE WIND TUGGED at her hair as they flew down the road, whisking up memories. She pictured herself as the young, naïve eighteen-year-old trotting up the steps of the three-story tan brick building with its arched windows and a sign that read *Sea Haven Art College for Visual and Performing Arts*. This was the private art college she had worked so hard to snag a scholarship to attend, with an enrollment of just six hundred students. She was thrilled to have the opportunity to go.

Some students came from money, whose parents indulged their darlings' fantasies of futures working as

Strokes of Desperation

dancers, musicians, actors, or artists, while other parents spent their lives cultivating their children's interests in culture. Very few students were from a background like Vicki's, where they had no supportive parent in the shadows rooting for them.

After interviewing, Vicki was thrilled to snag a job at the art supply store that would give her a twenty percent discount on supplies. Working there, she'd never seen so many paint colors or such a wide assortment of brushes. They even sold canvases that you could mount yourself. She was in heaven.

Vicki had been full of butterflies as fall classes started at Sea Haven. The halls were packed with kids determined to learn their craft in hopes of achieving their dreams, no matter how unrealistic they may be. Music drifted out into the halls from the classes where musicians were practicing. Vicki would lean against the door, listening to the skat of jazz and imagining each note as a color—blue, purple, magenta.

Farther down the hall, the sound of classical music, along with the slap of ballet slippers on the floor, would greet her. A peek inside revealed students in leotards and leg warmers going through their steps, legs held at levels that could only be achieved from years of stretching their muscles like the years Vicki had spent learning to control her hand so she could draw what she saw.

Stepping past the drama class, she heard Shakespeare recited like poetry by the advanced students while others stumbled over the words as they got caught in their mouths like a foreign language.

On the first day of her drawing class, she found a pile of tools randomly placed on a cloth in the middle of the room. When Anthony Tomasie entered in a black T-shirt that hugged his muscular torso, several girls swooned. He had thick, dark hair, possibly of Italian descent. Vicki remembered one of the girls commenting that Tomasie looked like a Roman god she'd like to sculpt.

Tomasie moved about the room, eyeing the faces of all the pretty young girls. "I'd like you to sketch these. I know you may not be familiar with these items, which is why I chose them. By not being familiar, you will have to study their shapes and where the light falls on them."

Some students adjusted their easels, securing the paper they would be drawing on, and then began tentatively pushing their pencils across the sheets. Others pondered where to start first.

"You'll be sketching these items for the next week before we move on to something else. However, you won't be drawing from a live model until your junior year, when we'll focus on the human figure."

Vicki was used to duplicating light and shadow from all the years of drawing things she had found on the beach, so this was an easy assignment for her. After several classes, it wasn't long before Anthony complimented Vicki on her talent. He would lean over and whisper in her ear, "Incredible," giving her chills.

At the time, there were rumors among the art students that Anthony Tomasie was seeing some of the girls on the side. But who could turn down a handsome, dark-haired, thirty-five-year-old Italian with swagger, even if he was their art instructor? The school was a pretty liberal private college, subsidized by wealthy donors that supported the arts, and Anthony was good at schmoozing, so people looked the other way, ignoring his side activities.

Strokes of Desperation

However, Anthony was part of Vicki's happy memories of her days at school. He'd encouraged her to pursue her career back then. Being with Anthony now was fun and exciting, like running into a childhood friend and rehashing old memories.

They followed the road into town, driving by her alma mater. As he passed the school, Anthony raised his hand and waved, honking his horn. "To all my lovely students!" he yelled, laughing.

When they reached the Seaside Marine Hotel, Anthony picked up a bottle of wine and glasses from the bar to take upstairs. Vicki peeked around; his hotel room was nice. The bathroom even had a jacuzzi tub big enough for two. Anthony slid the curtains across and opened the slider. Outside, they sat in chairs, looking up at the sky, drinking wine, and watching the golden orb disappear, exhaling its last breath in a display of color before drowning in the dark water.

If she were to paint the sunset, she wouldn't be able to do it justice. Nature was like that. Trying to capture its beauty was nearly impossible—even with a camera. That was what was wonderful about painting. You could embellish and add a bit of your own magic.

"I travel a lot these days." Anthony took a sip of his wine. "So, when I'm in the area, I like to enjoy myself. And what is better than spending my time with a woman like you, my dear?"

He stood up and came behind her, rubbing her shoulders. He kissed her neck, nuzzling her ear. "I'm lucky I ran into you today," he told her. "And to find out you were the artist of those wonderful paintings. Your skills have come a long way."

A strange otherworldly shadow flickered just beyond her vision like she was being watched, but she dismissed it.

He stood in front of her and took her hand. "Come on inside. Let's make those art school fantasies about me come true."

She looked over at Anthony as he unbuttoned his shirt. He had broad shoulders, a lean body with tight abs, and long legs—very sexy for someone his age. But did she really want this? To play this game? Hadn't she moved beyond this sort of thing? A voice reminded her that it was the only way to consummate their agreement. If she refused, he'd disappear, and her chance would be gone forever.

While the jacuzzi filled with water, she let him undress her. He removed her top and kissed the mounds of her breasts. He unzipped her pants and slid down her panties, dragging his lips across her stomach and then lower.

When he threw her onto the bed, she found herself detaching, going to that place in her mind—watching the performance. She clutched the part of her that would never surrender to any man. She didn't love Anthony, and he didn't love her, but she would need to impress him to keep him focused on helping her. As long as she was in control, she would remain safe.

Afterward, they both slid into the warm, whirling water of the jacuzzi. She leaned back. Wasn't this what she had told herself she always wanted? To be spoiled by a wealthy man and have a successful career as an artist? That dream was now within her grasp.

Anthony reached over, touching her necklace. "Where did you get this?"

"I found it in a box in the basement of the house where

I'm staying." She pushed the water aside with her hands, making little swirls.

A far-off look entered his eyes. "Interesting."

She looked down at the wooden necklace. "I kind of like it."

"Yes, yes." His smile widened, pulling her over to him. "I like it—and you, too."

Chapter Nineteen

Vicki

Anthony dropped Vicki off in front of Jenny's shop, then took off down the street, waving goodbye with one arm in the air.

Inside, Jenny was waiting on a customer but looked up and nodded hello. As Vicki calmly walked over to the stairs, her mind was whirling with thoughts concerning her future. Was this real? Was she finally going to do an art show of her own at a prestigious gallery?

The outfit she wore yesterday was hung back in the closet. She slipped out of her lace undergarments and tossed them in the dirty clothes basket in the corner, then looked at Anthony's mark on her hip where he bit her this morning. She wasn't pleased with his aggressiveness, but she was safe as long as she maintained control.

She had a lot to think about. Anthony had a list of

things he wanted her to do. He had asked her to come with him to Chicago so he could manage her career.

"Living in that tourist town is holding you back," he'd said. "You have a world of opportunities out there. You just need to get out and show your work to the right people."

She knew what he was telling her was true. He had reawakened her dream. If she was going to be a successful artist, she had some serious painting to do. She could hardly contain her excitement. Anthony was going to make all the arrangements for her opening night at the gallery in Seattle.

After changing, Vicki made a cheese sandwich and drank a pop to ward off the hunger plaguing her since leaving the hotel. From her stool in the kitchen, she heard Brooke and Jenny talking in the other room, so she went out to investigate. She found the shop empty of customers and Brooke leaning back against the counter.

"Did you see the news last night? They did a story about the missing native girls," Brooke said.

"Yes. It's just so awful. All those girls and they have no idea what happened to them," Jenny said, placing a jar of sand and shells onto a table. "Maybe if more people cared, they'd still be around."

Brooke tossed her hair to the side. "I'm only glad that never happened to me. At least Susan was nice enough to offer me a job when I was in high school."

Jenny shook her head. "I saw where you once lived in town when I went looking for you after the fire. I was ashamed that I paid you so little. Staying in that rundown apartment with that boy. I realized then how much I appreciate your contribution to my business, and I wanted to start paying you what you're worth."

"Thanks, Jenny. That apartment was better than some places, though."

Curious, Vicki asked, "What are you guys talking about? What girls?" she walked further into the shop.

"According to the news report last night, in 2016, there were over five thousand cases of missing Native American women reported nationwide to the National Crime Information Center. But only a hundred and sixteen of them were recorded in the U.S. Department of Justice's missing persons database. Can you believe that?" Jenny told her.

"I can. The cops don't care about us," Brooke replied with a frown. "Look at how many Lummi girls have disappeared over the years."

"What do you think happened to them?" Vicki asked.

Brook's voice filled with disgust. "They either end up with pimps or dead. Men treat them like dogs."

"That's awful," Vicki replied quietly.

"No one sees their value. They just disappear like they never existed."

Just then, the front doorbell jingled. Jenny went back to her computer. Brooke smiled and went over to greet the customer. Vicki slipped back upstairs.

Hearing about the missing Native girls stirred up memories for Vicki. Once she was inside her studio, she stared at her portraits. Was what Ben told her true? Had she been painting the missing girl, Catori? How in the world did she know what Catori looked like? She'd never seen the girl before. This was too weird—it had to be just some strange coincidence.

She paced back and forth. Why had an image of a

Native girl come to her instead of a white girl? She wasn't of Native descent; she was Caucasian.

Then Vicki thought back to something her grandmother had said once, "That wild savage mother of yours."

At the time, Vicki thought it had just been a derogative comment, but now she wasn't so sure. She concentrated. Her mother had been adopted by Mr. and Mrs. Farley. She remembered her mother having darker skin, and her hair color was—what? Vicki tried to remember if she ever knew what her mother's natural color was; she always bleached it blonde. Her father had a thick head of dark-blond hair, that much she remembered. Her mother's heritage was a mystery. It was entirely possible that her mother was part Native American. However, Vicki had no way of knowing now because both the Farleys had died years ago.

Vicki sat on her stool, dumbfounded. What if she were part Native American? That put the stories she'd imagined about Catori in an entirely different realm. What if they were related? Now, she was curious to learn more about this spirit that was invading her life.

Tilting the mirror, turning her head left, then right, she studied her profile in the reflection. She flipped her hair over to one side, draping it down her front, and brought the wood from her necklace to her mouth, pressing her lips to it, playfully tipping it up and down. What pose did she want the girl in now?

An idea flashed in her mind. The necklace dropped from her mouth. Vicki grabbed her purse, ran downstairs, and dashed out the back door.

At the drug store, she went up and down the aisle, looking at the different color hair dyes instead of the bleach blond she usually colored her hair. Heck, she'd been bleaching her hair since junior high and didn't have a clue what her natural color was anymore. However, she guessed it was a mixture of both parents—a mousy brown. She held up each box next to her head in a mirror until she found the perfect shade of black/brown to match the girl in her paintings. The lipstick selection was overwhelming, but she narrowed down her choice to raspberry and plum, blending the colors with her finger on her wrist. Perfect. She'd need darker eyeliner and mascara too. There were as many eye shadows as paint colors. Intrigued by the iridescent shades, she picked a sparkly green and pink. And, of course, a bit of blush. Happy with her choices, she took her basket to the checkout counter and pulled out her credit card.

"I'm sorry, Vicki, but your credit card has been declined." The cashier handed the card back.

Oh, crap. She'd reached her limit buying art supplies and hadn't sent in her minimum payment. Her mortgage and car payments had been deducted from her checking account, and she hadn't been able to make a deposit, so she knew she couldn't use her debit card either.

Taking out all the cash she had, which turned out to be fifty dollars, she laid the money on the counter, then dug down to the bottom of her purse until she found some change. Counting it out, she had twenty-five cents left over after paying her bill. She blew out her breath.

Walking through town, Vicki passed several shops with customers milling around. In the window of the gift shop were several pairs of handmade earrings she'd once listed for sale in her gallery. Another shop sold cards with beach scenes like the ones she used to paint. She quickened her pace back to Jenny's home, passing her house along the way without looking up.

———

AFTER DRYING her freshly colored hair, Vicki used a flat iron to smooth it so her hair would hang down flat over her breasts. With the dark, smoky kohl, she lined her eyes and darkened her eyebrows, then added mascara. With her fingers, she smudged a glittery green across and under her eyelids. A plum color was applied to her lips and just below her cheekbones. She ran a line of plum down her nose and dotted the apple of her chin.

In the studio, Vicki planted herself in front of the mirror, seeing the reflection of not only her but one of the paintings behind her. Wow, the resemblance was amazing.

She set out a large canvas and then tilted the mirror. Opening her robe, she gazed at her nude body. Her reflection looked nothing like her; her once-blond hair was now dark brown. She dimmed the lights to cast a shadow on her skin. Her eyes were now sultry and mysterious. Then she smiled. *This is going to be fun.* She could make believe that she was this mysterious girl and create her own backstory about this girl's life.

Vicki took a gulp of wine and then set the glass next to the bottle on the shelf. Closing her eyes, she conjured up an image of this strange young woman. Now she was falling through space between here and now and somewhere else, sailing like a nymph through the woods, carefree, happy, and laughing.

As the girl ran from her, Vicki grinned at this sprite who was pulling her into the painting. They played peek-a-boo, hiding from one another, giggling at their game. Who was going to catch who first? Peeking out from behind trees, the two merged, and Vicki became the girl running in the woods. Free from her life to create another world for herself to play in. A place without worries, far from reality.

She found herself resting on a fallen log with one knee up, strands of hair covering parts of her breast as she looked up at the sky, holding the branch of a light green fern above her like an innocent spirit.

Vicki opened her eyes and returned to her surroundings. She took another gulp of wine, then another, letting the sweet alcohol fill her with a pleasant buzz. Picking up a drawing pencil, she made a preliminary sketch, posing her body, looking back and forth at her reflection and the canvas until she was satisfied. Then she began smoothing color into her drawing, breathing life into it—hers and this mysterious girl's—and splattering paint on her own naked body as she continued into the night.

Once satisfied with the results, she left the painting to dry. A wicked smile crossed her face. Anthony would love it. She'd give it to him as a special gift.

Tossing the empty bottle of wine in the garbage, she went to work on other paintings, combining two of them, delving into a world of shapes, shadows, and highlights, bringing the white flat surface into another realm, painting with a passion that her other paintings didn't have.

After Vicki finished, she went into the bathroom, where she saw the rainbow-colored dots on her chest. Looking down, she realized paint was everywhere. She shoved her hair in a shower cap, laughing a drunken laugh. In the shower, she turned on the faucet and began scrubbing the pigment from her skin, watching as the colors ran down her legs and mixed with the water, then disappeared down the drain.

"*Be careful of the cost of your dream.*" The shower water splashed around her. "*Be careful of mixing your memories. You are not her, and she is not you.*"

Vicki shut the water off and stepped out. She wrapped herself in a towel. In the mirror, mascara and florescent green shadow ran down her cheeks. She reached for a washcloth and blotted the darkness away.

"*You are not her, and she is not you.*"

Vicki turned. Where was that voice coming from? Ignoring it, she went to her bedroom. She didn't care if it was Susan's ghost. What she was doing was none of Susan's business. She was going to keep painting this girl. These paintings were now an extension of herself.

Chapter Twenty

Vicki

Dragging herself up and into the bathroom that morning to get an aspirin for the hangover, she startled herself when she caught her reflection in the mirror. Bringing her hand to her mouth, she laughed at her image. She didn't want to show Jenny her new look just yet; she'd save the surprise until later.

After dressing, Vicki wrapped her hair in a scarf, making sure no dark hairs poked out, then went quietly downstairs and found something to eat to take up to the den, where she could relax without any interruptions. After finishing her food, Vicki got comfortable on the couch on the second floor and fell asleep.

She ran through the forest, confused, looking for a place to hide. Laughter boomed in the air, then changed to the sound of a crow cawing.

Strokes of Desperation

When she awoke, the house was quiet. Vicki went to the stairs and listened, then crept down to the main floor. Yes, Jenny and Brooke were gone for the night. She pulled out her phone and called Anthony.

"Hello, beautiful."

"Would you like to come over tonight?" She knew the place wasn't up to his standards, but she thought she would ask anyway.

"Oh, I'm sorry, I'm entertaining a guest right now." Vicki heard a giggle in the background. "Remember, we set up a date for tomorrow? We can talk then about your upcoming show," he added.

"Okay."

She set the phone down. If she planned to keep him interested, she would need to up her game. She didn't want him to change his mind about helping her launch her career as an artist.

⸻

ANTHONY CAME by and whisked her off to the same hotel in Bellingham.

"I love what you've done to yourself! Very sultry. With your hair and makeup, you look so much like the girl in your painting. You have me hot with desire for you." He beamed. "But I'll have to restrain myself until later."

As they ate their dinner on the patio of the hotel restaurant, Vicki looked out across the water, wondering what it would have been like to grow up on the Indian reservation nearby. She had only visited it a few times as a teenager. She remembered the houses were not much different from the one she had lived in. The people appeared poor. Rusted-out cars littered the yards. It felt like a world of broken dreams—life suppressed, with no reason to stay. Though the reservation was only a few miles away from a city built on the lumber industry, none of the Native Americans enjoyed the white man's riches.

The smell and the buildings of the old mill were gone now. And just like during the prosperous years, the Native people living there had nowhere else to go. Moving was out of the question, with the high cost of homes elsewhere and lack of job opportunities. Quality education was lacking, and most kids never completed high school. Vicki had been lucky to have her art to carry her. However, its reliability was always in question. Thank God for Anthony right now. She better not screw this up. He was her only ticket to success.

Vicki took a sip of her wine. Thoughts of life on the reservation must have been triggered by her own curiosity about her heritage. She should be enjoying herself instead, not dwelling on stuff that may or may not concern her. After all, she was here to forget the past. She downed another glass of wine.

After dinner, Anthony took her to his room, where he lit up a joint and handed it to her to take a hit. She was already spinning from the wine and hesitated, shaking her head no.

"Come on, Vicki, don't act so innocent. What artist doesn't enjoy a little weed once in a while? Let's indulge ourselves. It makes having sex so much more pleasurable, and I'm looking forward to a night of lust."

She hadn't had any marijuana since her college years. She took a long inhale and handed it back to him, then smiled and blew out. After a few more times, she was floating. She giggled and inhaled again.

"Come strip for me," he said, leaning back against the wall.

She put her hand to her mouth and laughed.

"Strip, come on," Anthony begged. He undressed and crawled on top of the bed, propping up a pillow to watch. "I'm waiting," he murmured, bringing a joint to his lips.

She shook her shoulders and shimmied as she removed her top, then slid down her pants and tossed them to the side. Next, she slowly stepped out of her panties.

"Now, make me insane for you," he commanded.

"What?" She was feeling dizzy and didn't want to fulfill his request. But something was propelling her to give in and do it, anyway.

"Show me you're worth making a star."

She tried all sorts of things, indulging his whims until he cried, "Yes! That's my beautiful girl."

He suddenly grabbed at her like an animal and began ravaging her as if she was his plaything. She was high and went along with whatever he wanted, though he seemed savage and rough. When he mounted her, he was lost in his own world of pleasure and demanded, "Purr for me, cat."

Vicki honored his request and purred.

⸺

VICKI THREW BACK the covers and started to get up, but Anthony pulled her back to bed. "Stay put." He grabbed a robe and answered the door; their breakfast had arrived.

He prepared a plate for Vicki and brought it to her,

setting it on the bed. She propped up some pillows and sat up to eat her eggs and toast.

"You excite me. So fresh and willing," Anthony told her. "It's a pleasure to be with you."

Vicki smiled. "I'm glad you came into the shop so we could reconnect. You've inspired me to express myself more."

He pinched her leg. "I love the way you express yourself."

Anthony's cell rang, and he glanced at the number. "Sorry, my dear, I have to take this." He stepped out onto the balcony in his robe and closed the door. Then, he walked to the far end and leaned on the railing, looking out. He spoke for a couple of minutes, then came back in.

He went into the bathroom and then returned. "Would you like a mimosa?" His back was to her while he poured them both a glass from a pitcher, stirring one with a spoon. Vicki glanced at the time. It was eight a.m. Still early, but she wasn't in a hurry to get back to Cook's Cove.

He handed her the drink. "I have someone I'm meeting with. It'll only take half an hour. Then I'll be right back." He got dressed, then tied the laces on his expensive shoes.

She stood up, stretched, and reached for her clothes that were scattered across the floor where she'd left them last night.

"No, no." Anthony stopped her, gently pushing her back onto the bed. "I want you to stay just as you are. I don't want you to get dressed just yet."

She thought about his request. She was learning that, along with being demanding, Anthony had a very active libido.

"Finish your drink," he said.

She sipped her glass and then set it on the table next to her.

"I'll be back shortly." He kissed her goodbye, then slipped out the door.

Vicki wondered what to do while she was waiting. In the bathroom, she took a robe from the hook, picked up her drink, and went outside. It was bright, and she raised her hand to block the sun as she stood at the railing. The large marina below was dotted with boats. This was a life she could get used to.

Someone honked from down below, and she realized they could see her bare body as the wind blew open her robe. She smiled and waved, though her smile stretched into a yawn.

With all of her late painting sessions, she was finding it difficult to be alert in the morning. She drained her glass, went back inside, and sat on the bed. Overcome with tiredness, she laid her head on the pillow. She could get in a quick nap while Anthony was gone.

She stirred. Opening her eyes, she found Anthony naked next to her, stroking her.

"I've been waiting for you." He smiled.

"Sorry." Glancing over at the time, she couldn't believe it was two p.m. already. She must have been exhausted to have slept that long.

Anthony continued playing with her body, trying to get a response from her. She let him, though she wasn't in the mood, and her body was numb. However, she made sure he was satisfied before he left the bed that afternoon.

Anthony drove her back to Jenny's. Before she got out of the car, she stopped with her hand on the dash and a sly grin on her face. "I have something for you." Then she ran inside while Anthony waited by the car. She returned with his painting wrapped in a protective covering.

"I made a special painting for you. It's a combination of me and the girl."

"*Bellissimo.*" He kissed her. "I will cherish it as I do you." He carried it out and put it in the backseat of his convertible with the end sticking out. He strung a bungee cord across it so it wouldn't fall out. "I'll be careful and drive slow."

Vicki beamed with delight at his appreciation of her work.

He then came over to her, taking her hand. "Sorry, Vicki, but I need to leave town for a while. I've got meetings with some corporate clients, and I'm trying to secure some art for their new buildings. Maybe I can sell them the picture you just did for me." He winked.

Her face dropped at the news. That painting was private, not to be displayed in a public building.

"I'll call you if I can get away, but with so many late-night dinners, I'll probably just drop into bed when I get to the hotel. I'll text you when I'm back, and we can get together then."

She shrugged her shoulders in disappointment.

He ran his finger down her nose. "Hey, beautiful, don't look so sad. This will give you more time to focus on your art. You're going to sell a lot of paintings—trust me. And seriously consider what I said about coming with me to Chicago. I'll set up a show for you. You'll be a hit, I guarantee."

Anthony kissed her passionately, then reached down and squeezed her tush. He pulled back and laughed.

Strokes of Desperation

Whistling, he leaped into the driver's seat of his car, waving goodbye as he maneuvered down the road.

She dropped her shoulders and then slowly walked back into the house. Anthony was right. Without him as a distraction, she could get more paintings done. She stopped in the kitchen and poured herself a glass of water from the tap. She had only just now realized how thirsty she was as her tongue seemed to stick to the roof of her mouth.

Jenny came into the kitchen, placing her arms on the counter. "You colored your hair."

"Yes, I thought I'd try something different for a change. Do you like it?"

"I liked you as a blonde, but I'm sure I'll get used to it."

Brooke followed Jenny into the room and put her hands on her hips, giving Vicki a curious look. "You look different. And what's up with the hair?"

"If you want to know, it helps me with the portraits I've been painting."

"I liked the way you looked before better." Brooke inspected Vicki from different angles.

Jenny glanced over at Brooke and shrugged. "She's trying to get into her character."

Brooke rolled her eyes. "Whatever," she said, then turned to go back to the shop area.

"So, you and Anthony seem to be an item now." Jenny took a glass and poured herself some water.

"Yeah, he arranged for me to do a show in Seattle."

"Congratulations."

"Thanks," Vicki said with a confused smile at her best friend. Jenny didn't sound overly excited about her good news. "But it means I'll be working my butt off getting ready."

Jenny set her glass down and sat on a stool across from her. "Vicki, can I ask you a question?"

"Sure."

"Are you going out with this Anthony guy just because he can help with your career?"

Vicki faked a look of surprise. "No," she replied. "Why would you think that?"

"I know you like going out with wealthy, older men, but—it's just that—well."

"What? You can tell me." Vicki set down her glass and glared at Jenny.

"When I started dating Robert, he was quite charming, and I fell for it. You saw how that turned out. He almost destroyed me and Shaun. I would hate to see you get yourself over your head with Anthony. He comes across as a player to me. I don't think he's good for you."

Vicki crossed her arms. "You're wrong, Jenny. He adores me."

She nodded slowly. "It's your life. I just thought David—"

"Jenny, I told you before, David isn't my type."

"Okay, okay." Jenny threw her hands up. "Don't say I didn't warn you."

Chapter Twenty-One

Vicki

Vicki stared at the text beneath Anthony's name: **I found the perfect place for U to stay in Chicago. U R going to love it.**

Chicago. She grinned. *The big city. Home to several famous galleries.*

She pulled out her laptop and typed *Anthony Tomasie* into the search engine. A handsome photo of him came up, along with pictures of him next to various paintings. There was a short bio mentioning his accomplishments as an art broker.

This was a once-in-a-lifetime opportunity. He was her ticket to success. Vicki shut down her computer and did a happy dance, then skipped downstairs, taking the steps two at a time.

"I'm thinking about selling my house," she announced as she reached the bottom.

"What?" Jenny spun around from her desk in the corner of her shop. "You can't be serious. I thought you loved it in Cook's Cove."

Vicki waved her hand dismissively; she wasn't surprised by Jenny's look of shock and disappointment.

"What about your business? You've been fretting over it ever since the tree fell on it. I thought that was why you've been working so hard on your paintings."

"I don't know if I want to run my gallery anymore. A new world is opening up, and I can't do both. Besides, selling my art around the country has been a dream of mine since I was a little girl."

"Are you sure this is your idea, not that guy Anthony's?" Jenny's brows were up, letting Vicki know she was displeased.

"Well, he told me he'd help get me into the best galleries in all the big cities."

"And you believe him?"

"Of course. I looked Anthony up on the internet. He's a successful art broker and sells art worldwide. So why wouldn't I?" She was defending her decision, but she had to admit the idea of leaving Cook's Cove and her friends behind was unsettling.

"I'd give this a lot of thought if I were you. You've worked so hard to get your gallery up and running. I'd hate to see you just throw it away on a promise that seems a bit—"

"What?"

"Honey, I don't want to dash your dream, you know that, don't you? But there is something about Anthony that

I don't trust. Why don't you see how your show goes in Seattle before you decide?"

"Okay," Vicki grumbled. Couldn't Jenny see she had no other choice? She was so close to making it. If she didn't follow her dream now, she might never have another opportunity again.

Vicki returned to her studio. After positioning a blank canvas, she sat back and stared at it. Should she try to control her painting or let the muse do it? She rubbed her necklace between her fingers for luck, then got up and positioned the full-length mirror so she could see her reflection as she painted. After a few squeezes of paint on her palette, she was ready to begin. But nothing came to her.

She closed her eyes and took a couple of deep breaths, envisioning the face of this woman that Ben called Catori. Slowly, an image materialized.

Like the evergreens that grew nearby, trees came into focus behind Catori's head. She was walking into a forest. Catori was looking over her shoulder; her body was angled, and she was holding out her hand as though she was expecting someone to grasp it.

Vicki smiled and went to work outlining the image. This would be the composition of her painting. For guidance on the proper proportions, she stood and angled her own body, reaching out her hand to the mirror like it was another world. Once her mind's eye had recorded it, she got busy documenting the shape on the canvas.

While dabbling in the paint, Vicki let her mind wander through the woods. Soon, she had the sensation that she was actually walking among the trees. The damp smell of the rotting forest filled her nostrils. Above in the branches were the sounds of chirping birds and squirrels. She placed her hand on the trunk of a tree, feeling the bumps and ridges. She was there. Then she wasn't.

Now the observer, she gazed at this mysterious girl reaching out to her. Picking up a new brush, Vicki filled in the light glowing on her canvas with pigment, giving Catori a realistic cast.

Once the painting was complete, Vicki stood back and admired it. The trees appeared thick with bark—not flat but rutted with a texture like real ones. Catori's face held a mischievous grin as though she was beckoning a lover to follow her into the woods.

Vicki closed her eyes again, trying to conjure up an image of where the girl was leading her. A rapid sequence of scenes flew through her mind. Catori was holding hands with a boy who had long, dark hair flowing halfway down his back. They were running together along a path, sneaking to a secret place.

Once they arrived, the boy set the tan blanket he was carrying on the ground, carefully spreading it out over the leaves, then removing his shirt and pants. Catori lay down, and he curled up next to her. Vicki touched her own mouth as the boy began kissing Catori's lips. Now she was Catori, experiencing the moment, looking through the girl's eyes at the boy hovering above her. His long hair tickled her bare skin as he lowered his hips, entering her.

As Catori's lover rhythmically brought them to a climax, Vicki's body flooded with sensations. Oh my God. She caught her breath and then giggled. Had she imagined this?

Opening her eyes, Vicki shook off the dream while putting away her paints for the night.

Strokes of Desperation

She crawled into bed, thinking about Catori and her boyfriend. Their love was innocent and sweet, full of goodness. She remembered the feeling of totally giving herself to someone, wondering if she'd ever feel that way again.

During the night, a yell brought Vicki out of her sleep. It was coming from the hallway. She grabbed her robe and peeked out the doorway. A sliver of light pushed from under the door of her studio. She swore she heard voices arguing.

But as she opened the door to see who was there, she found the room empty. The arguing had ceased, and in its place, she heard the sound of someone crying. Catori's face came into her mind, red and wet with tears. What had caused the girl to be so sad?

Vicki sat cross-legged on the floor and studied the paintings of Catori she had done. Puzzled, she leaned against the wall and looked over to the window. Moonlight was spreading across the room. A sudden gust of wind fluttered the curtains. A painting fell off its stand onto the floor. An image of the boy's face entered her mind's eye, full of rage, yelling, shaking Catori by the shoulders.

Why? But the reason didn't come to her, only Catori's heartache.

Vicki got up and set out a board to paint on. She squeezed colors onto her palette and made several bold strokes, creating an outline of Catori's face. She held the wooden middle of one brush in her mouth while she painted with another, then switched back and forth, adding details as they came to her.

Red, swollen eyes looked back at her, and she stopped painting. Immediately, Vicki's own disappointment and heartbreak surfaced, remembering when her boyfriend Jerrid had abandoned her in New York City. The betrayal, the anger she'd felt.

Vicki got up and put her brushes in the can to soak. She swirled them around and watched as the paint mixed with the liquid, causing the release of a thread of colors. As she continued to stir, the strands meshed into a bloom of murky brown while images of Jerrid rose to the surface. She hadn't thought about him in a long time, but Catori's sadness was all too familiar.

At Sea Haven, she'd been convinced she had found the boy of her dreams. They were from different backgrounds, but he made her believe it didn't matter. Jerrid Berk was from an upper-class family and had gone to private schools, but he was rebellious and liked to think of himself as a bad boy. She found him extremely sexy, unlike any guy she'd ever met before. He wore his hair long on top but shaved the sides of his head. His body was a piece of artwork, with tattoos on his arms, legs, and chest. She was crazy about him.

Jerrid was always painting. Once, he used her nude body as his canvas, decorating her with finger paints. She was convinced they were soulmates. They'd lay in bed while Jerrid would spin tales of seeing his paintings in the hottest galleries in New York and Chicago. So, when he told her he was leaving for New York City after graduation to pursue his dream, she jumped at the chance to join him.

She packed her art supplies and a few T-shirts and jeans in Jerrid's Honda, and they drove across the country, listening to hard rock and rap music on the radio. They slept in cheap motels most of the time, other nights out under the stars in sleeping bags. Being with Jerrid was exciting, fun, and magical. She never wanted it to end.

Vicki shut down her thoughts, got up, and dumped out the water in the sink in the bathroom. There, she rinsed the brushes under the faucet, then laid them out on paper towels to dry. She caught a glimpse of herself in the mirror. She looked exhausted.

Another memory flashed before her. She and Jerrid arrived in New York City, and the excitement she'd felt overtook her mind. She remembered rolling down the window and shouting, "We've made it!" as if they had already achieved their dream.

"Well, we're just getting started," Jerrid had assured her.

She recalled how they got lost traveling through the busy streets of the Bronx, Vicki using the GPS on Jerrid's phone to navigate them to their destination. Jerrid had told Vicki he had an old girlfriend living in the city who knew about an artist commune where they could rent living space and paint. He'd called ahead to the warehouse, so they were expected.

After driving in circles, looking for a place to park Jerrid's Honda, they finally arrived at the front door of the artists' warehouse. It was covered with graffiti and posters that advertised different art events. Setting down their boxes full of paints and brushes, Jerrid rang the bell. Eventually, someone let them in.

Inside the warehouse was an odd jumble of studios where people had put up makeshift partitions to close off where they worked and slept. From the looks of things, Vicki was pretty certain this arrangement was probably against city code.

Walking around, looking for someone to tell them

which room was theirs, Vicki noticed, surrounded by scaffolding and theater lights, a gigantic piece of art that someone had been working on. She swelled with excitement at the thought of being there in New York City and becoming a legitimate artist.

A guy named Sam showed up dressed in paint-splattered clothes, with his hair in a ponytail, introduced himself, and gave them a tour of the building.

"The bathrooms and showers are over there." He pointed to a couple of gray doors. "There are lockers inside for your clothes. We don't have separate bathrooms or showers. We are the same here. I hope you're not modest because everyone uses the same facilities. It's like going to the gym, only not as nice. Also, you'll be taking a cold shower most of the time 'cause the hot runs out pretty quickly." He laughed.

"There's a sink next to the bathroom for rinsing out water-based paints and cleaning up. Be sure to put your chemicals in the right containers so we can properly dispose of them.

"The kitchen area is over here." Sam pointed, walking in that direction. Along the counter were several hot plates and microwaves. The large sink was full of dirty dishes. Two refrigerators sat side by side. "Once a week, we go through the fridge and throw out anything that has green on it. Write your name on your stuff so people know it's yours. Of course, that doesn't guarantee someone won't take it."

Next, Sam showed them the pantry, which was just rows of metal shelves with canned goods and boxes. Names were listed below the shelves. Vicki and Jerrid would need to make a label to put on a shelf for their stuff.

Strokes of Desperation

When Sam showed them the cubby hole where they would be sleeping, Jerrid slapped his head and groaned. A dirty mattress sat on the floor without sheets or a blanket. In the corner sat a few empty cardboard boxes to be used for storage.

"Here's your key to the front door. You'll need to get a paddle lock for your room. Rent is $800 a month," Sam said. "If you don't pay on time, you'll be kicked out."

Vicki gulped. Even splitting the rent with Jerrid meant the two thousand dollars she'd saved wouldn't last very long.

Vicki and Jerrid counted out their cash and handed it to Sam.

Later, they took the subway and searched for the recommended art supply store to buy canvases. On the way back, they stopped at a deli to grab food before returning. Everywhere Vicki looked was crowded with people of all different ethnic groups. Having lived in her local area her whole life, she'd never seen such diversity.

That night, after having sex, Jerrid lay quietly next to Vicki in his sleeping bag.

"What's wrong?" Vicki asked. She could tell he wasn't happy with the arrangements.

"Are you okay with this?" he asked.

"I think it's wonderful. It's exciting to be around other working artists."

Two days later, Vicki returned from exploring the neighborhood to find a note on top of her sleeping bag:

"*Vicki, I think this place sucks. Glad you're happy with it. My old girlfriend Jennifer told me I could stay with her. Sorry, but she said she didn't have enough room for you too. Good luck pursuing your dream. It was great knowing you. Jerrid.*"

. . .

VICKI TOOK a breath and left Jenny's bathroom, the memory fading from her mind. Returning to her studio, she glanced at the half-finished painting of Catori on the easel. They both had suffered because a man left them to fend for themselves.

Fend for ourselves. Vicki looked at the row of paintings. What did Catori do after her lover left? It couldn't be as bad as what she endured in New York City—could it?

Vicki got a flash of Catori sitting on the curb, her head down, crying. The room began to spin, and Vicki reached behind her to break her fall, knocking over a picture as her knees buckled. She lay there, surrounded by a gang of paintings. Overpowered by emotions, she curled into a fetal position and sobbed. Thoughts of New York City pushed at her like a river breaking through a damn.

In the beginning, she had been hopeful, even optimistic, about making it on her own as an artist in New York. She figured if she just put her head down and got to work painting, things would work out.

Wandering the vast, empty warehouse, Vicki found a little corner to call her own. As she pulled out her supplies with trembling hands, she stared anxiously at the blank canvas on the easel before her. She took a deep breath to steady her nerves. Concentrating was impossible, with the pounding rap music blaring relentlessly in the background, fraying her already scattered thoughts. What on earth was she going to paint? Still life? Landscapes? She didn't know how to even begin to break into the cutthroat New York art scene.

As she half-heartedly dabbed at the canvas, she

Strokes of Desperation

overheard a group of artists talking and laughing nearby, listening to them discuss scrambling to get shows at hole-in-the-wall galleries across the city.

One girl caught sight of Vicki's quaint little seaside scene taking shape and let out a laugh that cut straight to her core.

"You must be out of your mind if you think anyone wants cute beach paintings in this city," she sneered, her eyes glinting cruelly. "No one can relate to that crap. You need raw portraits of real people and their struggles or colorful abstracts if you actually want to make it here."

She blinked back humiliated tears as the girls chuckled amongst themselves. Doubt crept into her mind, strangling her fledgling confidence. Maybe she didn't have what it takes after all.

Over the next few soul-crushing weeks, she desperately lugged her artwork around on buses and subways, going from shop to shop, her blistered feet screaming in agony. All she encountered were slammed doors, and dismissive head shakes. Her hard-earned savings dwindled as she replenished her rapidly disappearing art supplies.

Desperate, she spent the last few precious dollars renting a booth at an outdoor fair, hoping against hope to finally make a sale. But the crowds drifted past all day, barely glancing at her work. By the time she packed up that evening, she was drained and on the verge of tears.

Then the absolute worst happened—she discovered her cash box stolen. Shock and rage boiled inside as she realized some thief had taken all she had left when she was at her lowest. Finally, the floodgates opened, and she collapsed in wracking sobs, hugging her knees tightly to her chest. At that moment, her last remaining shred of hope had vanished. There was no possible way she could make next month's exorbitant rent. Her dream was over before it had barely begun. Utter defeat and despair consumed her.

Hungry, she waited until almost midnight before she went to the pantry. Her shelf was empty. Looking around to see if anyone was watching, she took a can of beans and a package of noodles from someone else's shelf, tucking them under her shirt. Scurrying over to the kitchen, she washed out a dirty pot in the sink. She put water in it to boil, then opened the can of beans. Dumping the beans on top of the noodles when they were done cooking, she grabbed a clean fork and ate out of the pan while sniffing back tears.

That night, she lay looking up at the tall, open warehouse ceiling, listening to the sounds around her. A couple was making love, someone else was snoring, and others were laughing, whispering, and playing music. It smelled of burned pizza, marijuana, and coffee. She knew deep inside that she couldn't live like this by herself. The excitement of being there had worn off.

Then she remembered the card one of her instructors at college had given her when she informed them she was going to New York. She recalled being told to contact this guy if she fell on hard times. But she wasn't going to call the stranger just yet. She'd figure something out.

Walking the streets, she found an abandoned entryway to a boarded-up shop to sit. She set out several of her paintings next to her. She lowered the price each day until she listed them for less than the boards they were painted on.

That evening, she cried herself to sleep. The dream world she had envisioned crumbled into a reality she didn't want to experience. Alone. She was always alone, trying to figure out how to survive.

Early in the morning, she was outside, going through the dumpsters along with the homeless, looking for something edible. However, she couldn't bring herself to eat after she saw the cockroaches scurrying across the side of the metal container.

She was going to be homeless soon, too, if she didn't come up with a plan. *A plan.* As if setting a goal would make a damn bit of difference right now. She felt tired and lightheaded; her energy was draining away.

Finding her spot in the entryway of an abandoned building, she sat down, setting her last three paintings next to her. Two days had passed since she'd had any food to eat. With her arms wrapped around her knees and her head down, she quietly prayed for a miracle.

After a while, someone cleared their throat, and she looked up to find a man standing in front of her. He was a short, balding, beady-eyed middle-aged man in a poorly fitting suit. He smelled of cigarettes and Aqua Velva aftershave. She doubted he wanted a painting.

He smiled. "Can I buy you lunch?"

She had chewed the ends of her brushes into a splintery pulp while trying to fend off her hunger. Her stomach ached, so she nodded and stood, packing her paintings and putting them in her art satchel.

He took her to a fast-food place and ordered two hamburgers, a Coke, and fries while she waited at a table. When he set down her food, she ate it eagerly. After finishing her Coke, the man leaned over and asked, "How about some dessert?"

He winked, and his smirk meant he wasn't talking about ice cream.

She lowered her eyes and replied, "I'm not that kind of girl."

"You're here with me now, so I think you *are* that kind of girl."

"No." She shook her head. She wasn't going to do that.

"One hundred dollars says you are."

Vicki had once heard that hunger and desperation could make people do things they would've never considered before. She'd arrogantly believed she would never be controlled by circumstance. But that was before she came to New York City. Before Jerrid had left her. Before she had lost all her money. Now, she needed to eat to survive. Letting out a sigh, she nodded.

"Okay."

━━━

AFTER RETURNING TO THE WAREHOUSE, Vicki stood in the shower in the bathroom as the lukewarm water splashed her body and hid her tears. She felt dirty and numb. Oblivious to her surroundings, she was unaware when a man stepped into the shower behind her. Before she realized what was happening, he'd pinned her against the wall. She tried to scream, but he covered her mouth with one hand and shoved himself into her with the other, pounding her against the wall. She closed her eyes. She was dead—alive but dead inside.

When he was done, she crumpled onto the floor. He left her in a puddle as the water pounced off her body. She had been in New York for less than two months, lost all her money, and had sex forced upon her by two strangers on the same day.

VICKI JOLTED up from the nightmarish memory. She looked around the room at all the eyes in her paintings, watching her, whispering in her ears. *"You are a loser. You don't deserve love."*

Fleeing the room, she hurried down the stairs, through the dark, empty shop, then opened the door, went outside into the night, running to her house. Jerking the door handle when she arrived, she pounded on the door. "Let me in, damn it!" It wouldn't budge. David had secured the house again to keep her out.

Looking around, she spotted a rock. She picked it up and hurled it at the window, cracking the glass. Then she picked up another, and this time it made a hole. But the window was too high for her to reach. Tears ran down her cheeks. There was nothing inside for her. This wasn't her safe place anymore. There was nothing here to make her feel better.

She heard a door slam.

David. She wasn't sure but wasn't going to take the chance. Vicki took off, sprinting around to the back of the house, then went along the alleyway to Jenny's and let herself in.

Not ready to go back upstairs, she pulled out a bottle of wine from the refrigerator and poured a glass. Sitting on a stool with her head in her hands, she tried to shut off the chatter in her mind. She needed to get a grip. Her constant painting was making her crazy.

She gulped down the glass of wine. She needed a

release—someone to hold her. To pretend someone cared about her, to make these feelings go away. Anthony? No, he was out of town. Maybe she should call someone else. Who? Not David: she had just ditched him at her house. Perhaps she could call Jenny and tell her what was happening. No, that would complicate things.

She let out a sigh. There was no one to turn to. She dropped her head into her hands. She was alone. Like always. Alone to figure things out.

Grabbing the wine bottle by its neck, she dragged herself back upstairs. Avoiding her studio, she went to the den. There, she drank herself into believing she was just experiencing a minor setback.

Vicki closed her eyes and lay down on the couch. Dreams of running through the forest looped over and over; she couldn't escape.

When she awoke, she was glad to be no longer dreaming. Her mouth was dry, and her head ached. Making her way back to the bedroom, she jerked open the curtains and looked out the window at the water beyond. A sliver of light was breaking through the night. The sun was beginning to rise.

I need to get away. Someplace secure. My life is going nowhere here.

Chapter Twenty-Two

Vicki

After another day of cat naps and a long night of painting, Vicki left the house. She pulled up the hood on her raincoat to protect herself from the spring rain—not that she minded the drizzle much. It somehow felt refreshing. She headed toward town without a destination. She just needed a break.

Misty gray skies cast a different look on the town of Cook's Cove. With fewer strangers milling around, the locals could come out and get their shopping and visiting done.

Once, when she was ten years old, she snuck into town and hid under the stairs of one of the restaurants. She sat listening to neighbors and local workers chat about their lives, dreaming she could go home with them. To a real home, not the house where her father lived. A place like what was on TV, where parents loved each other and cared about their kids. Like Jenny and Shaun's home.

Vicki didn't know what brought up that memory and shook it off. Flashes of uncomfortable feelings she thought she'd buried deep were now haunting her. She'd have to try harder to deny them. Painting had always been her escape, but now she wasn't sure if living in her visions was helping or contributing to her anxiety.

Outside Joe's Coffee Shop, she decided to go in and get a coffee. When it was her turn to order, she realized she didn't have any money and couldn't use her credit card.

"What can I get for you, Vicki?" the barista asked.

Vicki stood for a moment. Should she leave? "I'm embarrassed to say I've left my wallet at home."

"Oh, just pay next time you come in."

"Thanks, Holly. I'll have a double latte then." Vicki scanned the display case. "Can I have one of those too?" She pointed to a poppyseed muffin.

"Sure. Anything else?"

"No." Vicki took her drink and muffin to a table. She set her muffin on a napkin and pinched a piece off, popping it in her mouth and savoring the flavor. She hadn't had a muffin in a while—it was one of the pleasures she'd had to forgo since the money had stopped coming in.

Upbeat music played in the background while she sipped her latte. She loved this town and hated it at the same time. Her house and her business had sustained her for years. It had been her rock, grounding her but also holding her here. Was she ready to move on, to leave this for her dream of success? Her best choice was to put her house up for sale, as Anthony had suggested. Break her ties here. He'd promised her if she went to Chicago with him, he would support her until her work started selling. She just needed to trust him and leave Cook's Cove behind. Is that what she wanted—to leave?

She watched the rain fall outside. Right now, she didn't want anyone to know how broke she was. Not even her best friend, Jenny. The insurance deductible, mortgage, car payment, health insurance, and credit card had all drained her accounts. She *could* ask Anthony for an advance on the sale of her paintings—the exhibition was only a few weeks away—but then what would he expect in return? She was already having sex with him whenever he wanted it.

A chair pulled out next to her, and David took a seat in it. Immediately, she wanted to disappear through the floor. Why him, and why now?

"I almost didn't recognize you with your new hair color. How are you doing? I haven't seen you for a while." David set down his cup of coffee and leaned back in his chair. He still had his coat on, and it was dotted with raindrops. His hair was slightly damp, and he smelled of wet wood.

Vicki huffed. "I'm doing shitty. Are you happy?" She slumped down in the chair, dropping her head.

He set his forearms on the table and gave her a concerned look. "Why would I be happy about that?"

"Because you always seem to show up when I—" She frowned.

"Need a hug?" he whispered.

She wanted to tell him to get lost, but something about David made her want to crawl into his arms, to feel his warmth and compassion. Her lip trembled, and her eyes began to fill. *Damn him.*

David reached over and touched her face as her tears

rolled down her chin. "Come with me." He stood and reached out his hand to her.

Vicki shook her head. She needed to do this on her own. She couldn't have him thinking he could rescue her whenever something didn't go right in her life.

"Come. Let's talk."

Why was it so hard for her to go with David when it was easy to go with other men who never gave a shit about her? Was it because he could see into her?

Vicki reluctantly got up. She'd lost her appetite, so she tossed the muffin and the remainder of her drink in the garbage, then took his hand. He led her out to his truck. Inside, she watched the rain as it fell on the windshield, distorting the world beyond their little cubbyhole, giving her a little reprieve from reality.

"We can talk in here without other people listening," David told her.

She looked at her hands in her lap. What was she going to tell him?

"What can I do to help you?" he asked matter-of-factly, adjusting his body to face her.

Her frustration was mounting inside. "I don't know."

"Tell me."

She looked over at him. "You could magically make the mess I'm in go away. Get my house fixed so I can move back in. Paint pictures I can sell. Stop my—" She wanted to say cursed obsession but didn't.

"Is there something you aren't telling me that you need?"

Oh, crap. Now, he was stripping away her façade again. She had a hard time lying to him. "I'm dead broke. I couldn't even pay for my damn coffee. I had to promise to pay for it later," she blurted out, covering her face in shame.

"Ahh, Vicki. I'll give you some money. Just tell me how much you need." He reached for his wallet from his hip pocket.

Vicki put her hand on his arm to stop him. "I don't want your money. I should be able to pay for things myself. It wasn't supposed to be like this. That damn tree ruined my life." She sniffed.

David handed her a tissue, and she blew her nose.

"Vicki, if you need money, I'll loan it to you. You don't have to suffer like this. I'm here to help you, remember. Heck, you could ask Jenny and Shaun for help, too. That's what friends do. Help one another."

She had to turn away from his intense blue eyes. "I—can't." She couldn't take David's money. He was a nice guy, but she didn't want him tangled up in her mess or Jenny and Shaun either.

He was silent for a moment, then said, "You're pushing yourself pretty hard, girl. Do you think that's a good idea?"

She looked back down at her hands again. "I don't have a choice."

David moved the hair from her eyes and looked at her like he really did care. "Have you thought about getting a job somewhere?"

"And giving up my painting? I'm too close to making it as an artist. I can't give up now." She was in this too deep. She wanted to tell him the girl she was painting wouldn't let her quit.

David pulled Vicki over to him and put his arms around her. She sunk into him, laying her head on his chest. The feel of him immediately calmed her—his hugs were the only thing that made her feel safe, even if the sensation was only temporary.

He pushed her hair to the side, and it caught on to the chain that held her necklace. Vicki lifted her head and adjusted the pendant.

"Where did you get your necklace?" David asked, sliding his hand under the piece.

"Oh, this piece of wood? I found it in a box of junk in Jenny's basement."

"It's very unusual. Would you mind taking it off so I can get a better look at it? I'm always fascinated by wooden objects."

"It won't come off. I think the lock on the chain's broken. I've gotten used to wearing it all the time, so it doesn't bother me to leave it on."

David held it near to his eyes, turning it over. "Wow, at first, I thought the artist added some sort of metal to create the little veins. But now that I look at it closer, I can see a patina, and if I didn't know better, I'd swear it was moving." He set it back on her shirt.

Vicki looked down at the wooden coin. "That's weird. I can't see that. Are you sure?"

"Maybe it's just the light playing tricks," David said, then hesitated before saying, "Ben wanted me to ask you if you've had any strange thoughts while painting lately."

She pulled away from his chest and stared at him. "Like what?"

"He wondered if you had any dreams about the girl you were painting, something that might explain her disappearance."

She hadn't had a day free of the Native girl's face in weeks, either in waking or while sleeping. "No."

"You would tell me if you were, wouldn't you?" David probed.

Vicki met his eyes. "I don't know if we're even talking about the same person. The girl in my paintings may look like that other girl, but she isn't her. What was that girl's name again?"

"Catori. Catori Rein. Ben believes Catori's spirit could be trying to communicate with you."

She threw her head back and rolled her eyes. "That's crazy!" But was it? She wasn't sure; she wasn't sure of anything anymore. But she wasn't going to tell David about her daydreams or the nightmares; she couldn't risk destroying the muse. She needed to keep painting. This girl's image was her ticket to success. This was her dream, and she wasn't about to let go of it now.

He pulled her back to his chest. She looked up at him. His blue eyes dilated, and she felt the connection. She stared at his chiseled jaw, the dark stubble on his face, and his soft pink lips. God, she wanted to kiss him—but if she did, the threads holding her life together would unravel, and then what would she do?

Chapter Twenty-Three

David

After leaving Vicki, David stopped by the grocery store and bought several bags of food, then dropped them off at the back door of Jenny's house. He wasn't going to let Vicki starve. If she wouldn't take his money, he'd figure out another way to help her. He left a message for Jenny without explaining Vicki's situation so Jenny would know he'd left bags on the back porch that needed to be put away.

Once he got back to his house, he paced the floor. Something was going on with Vicki. He had driven to her house in the middle of the night, thinking she was trying to get in. But once he got there, she was gone, so he drove back home, confused. Maybe his constant worrying about her was making him a bit crazy, too. She was acting strange

—and scared. He didn't care for her new hair color and makeup.

David got out his phone and called Ben. "I saw Vicki, and she's starting to look like Catori. She's colored her hair and is all made up to look different now. When I asked, she claimed she hadn't received any strange messages from Catori, but I'm not buying it."

"I wonder how much control this spirit has over her. I'd like to find out what Vicki knows," Ben replied.

"So would I. Have you found out anything new yet?"

"I'm working on it. Let me know if Vicki starts sharing anything."

"That may be a bit hard to do. I rarely see her out in town anywhere. I only run into her when I get the feeling she needs me."

Ben chuckled. "Needs you? How about taking her out on a date?"

"I—" David wanted to ask her, but he was sure she'd turn him down.

"Anyway," Ben continued, "I'd like you to come to Vicki's art show with me. I want to check out the guests and see if the show arouses any interest from Catori's abductor."

"Sure. I was planning on going anyway."

"Great. I'll call you later. And David. Find out a way to keep an eye on Vicki."

David sighed as Ben hung up, lowered his phone from his ear, and then dialed Jenny. She answered almost immediately.

"I'm glad you called. I'm worried about Vicki. She's been going out with a guy I don't like."

"Who?"

"Anthony Tomasie. I guess he was her old art teacher in college."

David's heart sank. Damn it. Was he being played? "How long has that been going on?"

"Not long. He saw her art in the shop window and dragged her off with him. But I don't like him at all, David. He seems to be a bit of Romeo if you ask me. I feel like he is just playing with her."

This must have been the man he saw her go into the restaurant with. After how he'd felt watching the guy drive past, David had suspicions of his own but wanted to hear it from Jenny. "What makes you think that?"

"The guy is promising to set up art shows for her back east. He's trying to convince her to sell her house and go off with him to Chicago."

"You're kidding me."

A bell rang in the background. "Sorry, David, a customer just arrived. I'll have to talk to you later."

What was going on? He ran his fingers through his hair as a sudden anger flared. He wasn't going to go through this shit again. Let a woman jerk his feelings around. Hadn't he learned from Kelly that women could easily manipulate men to get what they wanted?

He sat down and took a couple of breaths. Maybe he was overreacting. These were two different women. Vicki's situation was different; she needed to sell her art. Maybe this Anthony guy was sincere about helping her. So why was he so upset? He had no claim on Vicki.

He could find out what was holding up the construction of her house. Maybe Shaun could get a crew out there right away. Reorganize some of his other projects so she wouldn't have to wait. If Vicki's house was repaired, it would take a load off her plate. Hell, he'd pay for it out of his own pocket if necessary.

God, he wished Vicki would look to him for help instead of this Anthony creep.

Chapter Twenty-Four

David

"Thanks for joining me," Ben said.

David buckled his seatbelt. "I don't know if I'll be much help. It's not like I have any control over my hunches. As I said earlier, they come and go on their own."

"Well, I thought we'd visit some of the places where Catori was last seen and talk to a few people. I'd like your input just the same."

Once they arrived in Bellingham, they parked and walked down the street toward the youth center. A cold breeze whipped around the corner of the old brick buildings near the waterfront, sending a chill with it. David saw five teenagers huddled together. A whiff of marijuana floated by, and David tapped his nose with his finger.

Ben gave him a quick glance. "I just hope that's all

they're doing, but I suspect crack will be making its rounds once the dealers spot the new kids."

"Have the police tried sending someone undercover?"

"These are Native kids. The city doesn't care what happens to them until they start stealing—then they want to haul them all off to jail."

David stopped and glanced at the sandwich shop across the street. "I'll be right back." He ran across to the shop and went inside, returning a few minutes later with half a dozen assorted sandwiches and pops.

Ben just shook his head.

"I know this isn't much, but it's something I can do for them." David walked to the group huddled together. A girl looked up at him. Her eyes flitted to the left and right. He motioned for her to take the bag from him. "It's just food. I don't want anything from you." Finally, she took the bag he held out, and he knew she was one of the lucky ones and would be okay. The kids eagerly dug out the food and started ripping into the paper, shoving the sandwiches into their mouths. One kid whispered, "Thanks, man." Another just nodded. David looked at the group and felt a darkness swirling around the kids. It made him sad. Some would be dead within five years. Looking away, not wanting to remember their faces or who would live and who would die, he cursed inwardly. There was nothing he could do to change their future. Just like Ben, his hands were tied.

He returned to the old Native, who watched with a similar morbid look hidden behind his eyes.

"Let's head over to the youth center," Ben said. "The receptionist has worked there a long time. Maybe you can pick up something from her."

"I haven't used my gift on old events. My intuition works on the future, not the past."

"Anything is worth a try, David."

David pursed his lips and nodded, extending his arm to allow Ben to lead the way inside the old brick building. They entered through double glass doors, stiff on their hinges and in need of a little oil. Beyond the portico, the hardwood floors were scratched. Ripped, overstuffed chairs and couches were grouped in a corner. There were tables and fold-up chairs in the middle of the room for games. The place looked adequate but not the least bit cheerful. They were greeted by a gray-haired woman in a sweatshirt and jeans.

"Hello, Sally," Ben said as he walked over to the receptionist's desk.

"Hi, Ben. I haven't seen you in a while. Looking for someone in particular?"

"How do you know this isn't a social visit?" Ben smiled.

"I know better. Between you and the cops, you have no other reason to come here. And I sure as hell didn't call and invite you over for a cup of tea."

Ben laughed. "Sally Coppell, this is David Garson, a friend of mine. I asked him to come along to help me solve an old case."

Sally came out from behind the desk and looked David over. She couldn't be more than five foot two and was built like a bear, David thought, with her big arms and stocky body. She stuck out her hand to shake his, gripping it firmly.

"So, what can I do for you boys?" She placed her hands on her hips.

"I want you to think back to ten years ago." Ben pulled out his phone. "Remember this girl?"

Sally placed the reading glasses hanging from a chain around her neck onto her nose and took the phone from Ben. She squeezed her thumb and forefinger, then spread them to make the photo larger. "Yes, I remember this one. Rein's daughter. She was running from him—and life in general."

"I know you've been asked these questions before. However, it would be helpful if you could repeat your answers for David."

"Sure, what do you want to know?" She went back behind the counter and sat down.

Ben indicated to David to go ahead, so he asked the first question. "When did you first notice Catori coming here?"

"I think it was the night of a bad downpour. The kids aren't inclined to sleep outside in weather like that. We had cots set up and hot soup for them. I remember her looking a bit lost, afraid to be out on her own. You feel bad for these kids."

"Was there a boy she was particularly friendly with when she came in?"

"No, she came by herself. I thought she looked sad. Most kids develop this tough façade, like they know more than adults and that staying here is some sort of joke. But deep down inside, they're all scared.

"Now, Catori, I noticed right away. She looked fresh and vulnerable, not streetwise yet. I asked her the next day if she would like to stick around and help me, and she did. I like to weed out the ones I think we might be able to help."

"How long did she work here?"

"Oh, not long. Two weeks, maybe. She swept the floor,

and because she'd worked at the art school in the cafeteria, we put her to work in the kitchen. She'd hang around when Ms. Meyers was here. I think Christine thought she could rescue Catori. Christine took an interest in some of the girls, talking to them about going to school and making something of themselves—which, in my opinion, was a waste of time 'cause these Native kids come from families who don't have the means to go to school. Christine was heartbroken when Catori disappeared." Sally let out a heavy sigh. "It's hard when you get attached to one of the kids and then realize you couldn't save them after all."

David was internalizing the hopelessness that loomed over these kids. It was easy to believe that you could rescue them if you just tried. But how do you fix the problems that brought them here in the first place—the broken homes, the poverty, and the lack of education?

"Do you have any idea what happened to Catori?"

"No, I had a couple of days off, and when I came back, she was gone." Sally set her hands on the desk. "I prayed for her. I prayed that nothing bad would happen to her. Don't know why she disappeared, but I never saw her after that."

"Did you notice anything odd before you left? Anyone watching her? Any strangers talking to her?"

"No. She didn't strike me as being the type to go off with a stranger."

"What about her father? Did he come by?"

"Don't know. Like I said, I wasn't here at the time. I know Mr. Rein came in afterward in a huff. I felt sorry for Catori, growing up with a father like that." She scowled.

"How so?" David asked.

"He was a loud, demanding man. He wanted to search

the place, thinking we were hiding her from him. No wonder the girl ran away."

David scratched the back of his head. "Some people don't realize the impact they have on their kids. Extreme strictness never works. If often just makes matters worse."

"Ain't that the truth," Sally replied.

David let out a breath through his nose. He hadn't had much of a feel for the girl until now. Catori sounded like a lost teenager with the odds stacked against her. "Thanks, Sally," he said and nodded to Ben to let him know they were done.

"Sorry I couldn't be of more help," Sally said as they left.

At the car, David thought about Catori, trying to clear his mind of all else. He waited for something to tell him what might have happened, but nothing came, so he turned to Ben. "Do you think she left with someone she knew? One of her friends, maybe?"

"I spoke with kids around here at the time, but they were no help. They seem to think men like me are the enemy. Being a Lummi myself didn't earn me any points, I'm afraid."

Their next stop was a hardware store to talk to the woman who had covered for Sally while she was away. A checker directed them to an office where they would find Helen Brigs. Ben knocked on the door and then opened it.

"Hi, Ben." A tiny Native woman in her late thirties stood up and pointed to two chairs across from her desk. The cabinet behind her was lined with bobblehead sports figures like she had a team that always agreed with her.

David pulled out his chair and sat down. A scar ran through her left eyebrow, skipping her eye, then picking up again on her cheek, traveling to her chin. Ben had mentioned on the way over that Helen had gotten her scar while escaping from her kidnappers when she was a homeless teen.

Ben introduced David. "I brought David with me because he is intuitive, and I'm hoping he can help me find out what happened to Catori Rein."

"Oh, a shaman?" Helen's eyes opened wide.

"No, I'm afraid not. Just someone that gets strong premonitions," David said.

Ben set his arms on the table. "So, Helen, tell me about the day Catori disappeared."

She bit her lower lip and looked up at the ceiling. "Well, I wasn't familiar with her. I only filled in at the center when they needed me. I was going to school at the time. I remember I was studying for a test, so I had my nose in my books."

"Did you notice anything unusual that day? Anyone acting strange?" David asked.

"No, can't say that I did."

"Did you see Catori leave with anyone?"

"No."

"What about Christine Meyers?" Ben asked.

"Oh, sure. I thought you were talking about someone else—a guy, maybe."

"A guy?" Ben leaned forward, shooting David a quick look.

"Yeah, some guy stopped by that I think she knew. But they only talked briefly, and then he left."

"Do you remember what he looked like?" David asked.

"Let me think—" She drummed her fingernails on the table, closed her eyes for a moment, then opened them again. "He had dark hair and was tall and lean. That's all. I don't remember what his face looked like anymore. I just got a glimpse of him."

"So, Ms. Meyers was there that day?"

"Just briefly."

"Did you see Catori leave with her?"

"I think they went to lunch. Yeah, that's what Christine said. They went to lunch, and then she dropped Catori back off at the center. Christine told me she had some errands to run after lunch, but I never saw Catori come inside. Maybe she came in the back door while I was studying, and I missed it. But she wasn't there later to help with dinner."

A knock sounded, and then a man stuck his head in the door. "I need you to order some doors for a customer."

"Okay, I'll get right on it," Helen replied.

"We'll not use up any more of your time," Ben said, getting up from his chair. "Thanks for your help, Helen."

"Hope you find out where she went. I know a lot of those girls don't make it. I was lucky."

Back in the parking lot, David asked, "Why didn't they have surveillance cameras watching who was coming and going?" The lack of suspects frustrated him.

"I guess they didn't have the money or chose not to spend it on surveillance," Ben replied.

David shook his head. Everything reinforced the idea that what happened to these kids wasn't a priority. "What happened to Helen?" he asked suddenly.

"A couple of boys tried to sell her for drugs. They threatened her with a knife. While she was trying to get away, she got sliced in the process. Fortunately for her, the police showed up and arrested the guys offering her for sale.

The buyer vanished, though, and was never caught. Everything was arranged through an anonymous source. After the news did a story on Helen, several people came together and paid her medical bills and for her to go to school to become an accountant."

"I had no idea this was as bad as it is. I understand now why you want to find out what happened to Catori. It's much bigger than just one girl." He met Ben's eyes. "I have a feeling that Catori's story involves several people. I don't know who they are and if they're still at it, but I'd like to see them behind bars."

Ben put his hand on David's shoulder. "I appreciate your help."

Chapter Twenty-Five

Vicki

After nights of painting, the day had finally arrived for Vicki to pack up her work for her big show in Seattle. After pondering over her choices for too long, she decided on the pieces that best portrayed a mysterious, alluring, sensual, yet innocent young woman. Satisfied, she prepared them for hanging and crated them for shipping. Anthony was sending a van and movers soon to deliver them to the gallery.

When the men arrived, Vicki watched as they carried her work out the back door. It was as though part of her was leaving. She waved as the van disappeared down the alleyway, then she ran back to her studio. All the orphans remained. Vicki could see the sadness in their eyes.

They're just paintings, she told herself, though she knew

she was lying. She was selling off part of her family. The remaining pictures were grieving.

This was crazy. She would create additional work after the show, so it wasn't like her time with Catori was over. This was the beginning of her career. Still, it didn't come without a price. Besides the stress of painting, there was Anthony to deal with.

Several hours later, Anthony arrived to whisk her away. He picked Vicki up and whirled her off the ground. "You ready to show the world what a great artist you are?"

"I guess so." The jitters were driving her crazy. One minute, she wanted to call it off. The next she wanted to shout from the rooftops, "I made it!"

"Guess so? I know so." He grabbed her hand. "Let's get this show on the road, beautiful."

While he drove, Vicki looked out the window, listening to the music on the radio and daydreaming about doing art shows across the country—people admiring her work and telling her how fabulous she was. This was the beginning of something great, she told herself, and before she realized it, they were pulling up in front of their hotel. Anthony grabbed their suitcases and carried them to the lobby, where they checked in.

It was a classy hotel, and she marveled at the surroundings. They had both a front room and a separate bedroom. Fresh flowers sat in a vase on the coffee table. Vicki smiled. She could get used to staying in nice places like this.

After unpacking, Vicki stood in front of the mirror, trying to decide which outfit to wear from the ones Anthony had bought her. She settled on a short, green velvet dress with a scoop neck; it went perfectly with her wooden necklace. As she slipped into the bathroom to freshen up, Anthony entered behind her and slid his arm around her waist. Then he rubbed her shoulders and kissed the side of her neck.

"Maybe I could do something to release your tension," he whispered.

"No, I'd rather not right now." She didn't want to have to deal with him. She wanted to bask in her feelings, not satisfy his wishes.

"Suit yourself." He unwrapped himself from her and approached the door. "Just remember you owe me big time later."

She rolled her eyes at her reflection, combed her hair, applied some lipstick, then went out to join him.

―――

VICKI WALKED around the Hillman Gallery, taking in the fact that these were her paintings hanging on the walls. She still couldn't believe it. All the hours spent with this girl's image were about to pay off. Her heart swelled with pride, and she laughed, spinning around like a little girl with her arms out. If only her father could see her now. She'd made it, despite what he'd always said.

Once people started to arrive, however, Vicki's confidence began to wane, and she was a bundle of nerves. She chewed the quick of her left thumb. It might as well be *her* stripped naked and hanging on the walls, waiting for everyone to hurtle criticisms at her. Would they like her art?

She made her way through the crowd to the back wall, where a table held information about her. A flyer claimed Anthony discovered her and that she was set to go on tour.

However, the idea that he would be managing her career made her uncomfortable. Self-doubt in her abilities haunted her as much as the ghost she was painting. Could people tell she was a fraud and not worthy of their praise? That these images didn't come from her, but from an unexplainable source instead?

She swallowed her fears and smiled the best she could like nothing bothered her. People moved about with glasses of champagne, nibbling on cheese Anthony had provided for the occasion. Vicki observed people's responses as they shuffled by, viewing her art. Her intention was for each painting to reflect back what the viewer wanted to see—a vulnerable girl or a siren daring someone to touch her. They had magic to them, a technique she'd perfected. Catori was an illusion, but here she was—real in the viewers' mind.

One woman walked back and forth in front of a painting, trying to find a spot where the painting's eyes didn't follow her. A man reached out, moving his hand in the air as though he could brush the hair that covered the girl's breasts.

"I swore that I could see her chest move. That she was breathing," one man commented to his friend.

"Her skin glistens like she has pores."

"So seductive. I wonder who the model is." A man chuckled, rubbing his chin.

The man standing next to him elbowed the guy and agreed, "Yes, I wouldn't mind getting to know her myself," then stood back, eyeing the portrait.

Vicki grinned. Viewers were captured by the spell of her art.

"Vicki!"

Vicki spun to see Jenny and Shaun approaching, hand in hand.

"Wow, look at all the people admiring your work," Jenny said as she gazed around. "You must be ecstatic. I remember when you were a little girl sitting on the dock, drawing birds and sailboats."

Vicki beamed. "Yes, I can't quite believe I painted these."

"Good luck." Jenny kissed Vicki's cheek, and then Shaun led her away to look at some of the other pieces Vicki had done.

Out of the corner of her eye, Vicki spotted David in the crowd. He looked handsome in his navy blue shirt and leather jacket. She debated if she should go over and say hi or just wait for him to come to her.

Someone cleared their throat, grabbing Vicki's attention, so she politely turned to answer questions about her art.

"Tell me about this girl," asked a man in his forties wearing a yellow bowtie and a striped vest. He leaned in to hear her answer.

"She is the girl in my dreams."

"Someone told me you're clairvoyant, that this girl is dead, and you've been channeling her." His brows went up and down, and a grin filled his face.

Vicki looked up at the ceiling and let out a breath, not knowing quite how to respond. "She does resemble a girl that disappeared years ago. But I hate to disappoint you; I'm not a medium and don't communicate with the dead. The woman I paint is just a figment of my imagination."

"Amazing. You're very talented," he said.

After the guest moved on, Vicki noticed David had

disappeared into the sea of bodies. Secretly, it was his praise she wanted most. But now, he seemed to be lost in the crowd of strangers.

As her eyes skimmed the sea of people, still looking for David, they instead landed on Anthony, who was chatting with a tall, attractive brunette. The woman appeared to be in her forties, but judging by the shape of her arms and the way her dress clung to her, she had a great body. Vicki watched as the woman placed her hand on Anthony's chest, straightened his tie, then kissed him. Anthony let his hand slide down the woman's thigh as though it was a natural thing to do.

A rush of heat rose into Vicki's face, and she made her way through the crowd to them. The woman had disappeared by the time she arrived, but Anthony must have guessed that she had seen her because he volunteered, "Oh, that was Christine Meyers. We were in a relationship once. She shows up occasionally to see what new artists I'm promoting."

Vicki wasn't surprised that Anthony had been with such an attractive woman. Still, it bothered her that she was here, stealing his attention on *her* night. Anthony seemed to sense this and wrapped his arm around her waist, pulling her close to him. He smelled of a tart mixture of champagne and cologne.

"This is the beginning of your career, my beautiful. You've proven you can capture a crowd. Now we can take the show to other cities. I'll finish lining up that one in Chicago for you."

"Yeah, sounds great," she murmured, searching the crowd for David again. She was a bundle of mixed emotions and could really use one of his hugs right now.

Strokes of Desperation

After all the anticipation and build-up, the event turned out to be a letdown. Sure, people liked her work, but she was a fraud masquerading as an artist. Disappointment loomed around her. The show hadn't changed anything. She was still the same person with the same emptiness inside. Had she been expecting something magical to happen to fill that space?

Perhaps her expectations had been too high. She'd always believed recognition would somehow heal the wounds of her past. Now she knew that wasn't true.

Chapter Twenty-Six

David

David and Ben arrived together but decided to split up. This was so Ben could survey the crowd while David relied on his intuition to discover if anyone here might know something about Catori's disappearance.

David's senses were on high alert as he strolled around, looking at Vicki's paintings. He was getting strange vibes from them. Observing her artwork, he couldn't help but think something was disturbing about them. They appeared hypnotic and eerie, almost supernatural in how they glowed from the canvas.

As he walked past one, he got the impression that it was covering something up. An emotion, or perhaps several emotions, were hidden under layers of paint. The eyes were intriguing but a distraction from the soul.

Strokes of Desperation

He found another painful to look at. The image was of a beautiful young girl, but she seemed afraid, as though she was embarrassed for people to see her naked and vulnerable in this setting. One was seductive. He was bothered by all the men gathered around it, having fantasies about the image. The girl was a teenager, for God's sake. She may have even been molested or raped before she was killed.

Killed? David thought about the reality of that. Was it something he had just assumed or a genuine hunch?

He spotted Vicki clinging to her benefactor. She was nervous, he suspected. Anthony Tomasie struck David as an arrogant showman—polished on the outside and a slimebag on the inside. He noticed how Anthony's eyes wandered. He had a way of looking at women, sizing them up based on their vulnerability and sex appeal. What did Vicki see in this jerk, anyway?

From a distance, he spied Jenny and Shaun and headed in their direction to say hello. Before they could reach him, someone grabbed his arm.

"How's it going?" Ben asked.

David just raised and lowered his shoulders. "Have you found anyone suspicious wandering around?"

Ben squeezed David's shoulder. "I'm still looking, but I'm relying on you to let me know if you receive any strange vibes from anyone."

"Sure, I'll meet up with you later." David looked around; Jenny and Shaun appeared to have moved on. As he strolled to the edge of the exhibition to look over the crowd, a strong sensation pulled him farther down to a hall where a door was left slightly ajar. He put his ear to it first, hearing moaning, then peeked in the crack. Anthony was in the room with a tall brunette, and they were going at it from the looks of things.

David threw open the door, and both guilty parties looked over. The woman quickly lowered her skirt, and Anthony zipped up his pants.

"Who the hell are you?" Anthony demanded.

"A friend of Vicki's." David flew across the room, landing a punch to Anthony's jaw. He was furious. He wanted to beat the guy to a pulp. How dare this slimebag screw a woman at Vicki's show!

The woman shrieked and darted away. He was about to hit the guy again when someone stopped his punch mid-air by grabbing his arm. David spun around to find Ben standing there.

"Come on, David, leave the lovebirds alone."

"I'm calling security," Anthony said, rubbing his jaw.

David's hand still held a fist. He wanted to show that creep a thing or two, but Ben shoved him out the door. "Calm down. No need to cause a scene. This is Vicki's special night, remember?"

"But—" He couldn't believe Vicki was with this sleazy guy.

"Let Vicki have the night to believe she's made it. She'll have plenty of time later to deal with the truth."

He still wanted to beat the shit out of the guy, but Ben was right; it probably wasn't a good idea and wouldn't win him any points with Vicki. He gritted his teeth and asked Ben, "Have you learned anything new tonight?"

"Other than Anthony Tomasie being quite the lover boy?" Ben rested his arm on David's shoulder, escorting him from the scene. "If it makes you feel any better, I'll check to see if the guy has a record."

"I hate to see Vicki involved with him. She deserves someone better than that scum bag."

Ben just shook his head. "Like you, maybe?"

"What? I'm just concerned, that's all." He lied. This really shook him up inside. He wanted to protect her from men like Anthony.

"Right now, the woman Anthony was banging in that room has piqued my interest. I'm pretty sure she's Christine Meyers, the same gal that's on the board of the organization that runs the youth shelter in Bellingham." Glancing back at Anthony, Ben said, "I wondered if Tomasie has a thing going on with her or if she's just another one of his conquests."

David turned his attention to Vicki, who was mingling on the other side of the room. He felt sorry for her. She probably had no idea what a dirtbag Tomasie really was. He wanted to warn her, but she should have her night. He would approach her about him another day.

"What do you know about the necklace around Vicki's neck?" Ben asked. They both looked over as she nervously held it, rubbing it between her fingers.

"She told me she found it in a box of junk in Jenny's basement. I took a look at it. It's an odd piece, that's for sure."

"Something left over from Susan's time there?"

"I guess."

"I'd like to check it out, find out who made it."

By now, Anthony had reclaimed his spot next to Vicki. He was kissing her cheek like nothing had gone on. David's anger reared its head again. "I don't want to get too close to that bastard."

"Okay, just stay behind me and keep your head down. There are enough people here that you can blend in."

David hung back as Ben approached Vicki. "Can I get a photo of you next to one of your art pieces?"

"Sure, any particular one?" Vicki looked at the walls where her paintings hung.

"Yes, that one." It was a large image of Catori's face.

Vicki made her way through the crowd, posing in front of a portrait of Catori, looking out at the viewer. David could see what Ben was doing; this was an excellent composition, and he would get a good shot of the necklace. After taking a few more pictures of Vicki, Ben turned and got several shots of people standing around with his phone. Satisfied, he pointed to the exit. David followed, and they went outside.

"Now we need to do some research to track down information about Vicki's bauble."

Ben pulled out his cell phone and leaned against the passenger side of his car. He motioned for David to get out his phone, too. David watched as Ben looked up jewelry stores in Seattle—ones that made specialty items. They each called the numbers, hitting several dead ends until finally, David got a lead.

"You might try Forgotten Gems in Fremont," the woman on the phone said. "The guy who owns the place works with natural elements. I don't know if that's what you're looking for. Still, he might know someone."

Ben looked up Forgotten Gems.

"I think we've found what we're looking for. The store is owned by Joey Black, Catori's old high school boyfriend. I've been wanting to talk to him."

Chapter Twenty-Seven

David

The shop was a small cubby hole next to a store that sold old record albums. The door creaked when they walked in.

"Hey." A Native man lifted his eyes from working on a piece of jewelry at a counter. He looked to be in his late twenties. His long, black hair was tied in a ponytail, and he gave them a pleasant smile.

David glanced around the shop at the necklaces displayed on the walls. They all had pendants made from different colored stones, each wrapped in a silver cage, looking like sea glass caught in a wire spring.

Ben stepped over to the counter. "I'm looking for the person that made this necklace." He held out his phone with the picture of Vicki in front of Catori's portrait.

The guy set down his pliers and leaned in for a better look. "Whoa." His eyes widened, and he put down the piece of jewelry he was still holding in his other hand. His jaw twitched ever so slightly, and he shifted his body on his stool. "That's weird."

"I'm Ben Stone, and this is my friend David Garson."

"Joey Black." The guy held out his hand to shake.

"Tell me about the necklace," David said.

Joey ignored him, eyes still on Ben's phone. "Who's that girl?"

"Which one? The girl wearing the necklace or the girl in the painting?" David asked.

Joey's eyes flicked back and forth. "They look almost the same, but one in the painting looks like a girl I once knew."

"Catori Rein?" Ben said.

Joey nodded.

"We spoke years ago," Ben told him.

"Yes, I thought you looked familiar. Weren't you the private investigator Catori's father hired?"

"I was helping him look for her back then. So, do you think this girl in the painting is Catori?"

"I don't know, could be."

"Well, that's what we'd like to find out."

"Where's she been hiding?" Joey asked.

"We were hoping you might know the answer to that," David said.

Joey's face contorted. "Heck no, I haven't seen her in ten years. She just disappeared one day, and I never saw her again."

Ben pointed to the photograph. "Did you make this necklace?"

"I—" Joey moved closer, squinting at the image with a frown. "I gave it to Catori when she was my girlfriend. I'm confused. What is this other girl doing wearing it? Where did she get it?"

"So, Catori never contacted you after she disappeared?" Ben pressed.

"No, I'm afraid not. I thought she just ran away. She hated her dad and living on the reservation. She couldn't live with me, though. I was still living at home and had no money. Plus, her dad hated me. He was always punishing her for seeing me."

"But that didn't prevent you from sneaking out with her."

Joey grinned, his eyes staring off as he revisited a memory. "No. We had the hots for each other, and there was a spot in the woods where we'd get it on. It was our secret place."

"You never mentioned the spot in the woods before," Ben replied.

"Heck no, I didn't want her father finding out. He would've killed me if he'd known I was screwing her," Joey said.

"Maybe you can show me where that was." Ben pulled up a map on his phone, blowing up an area so they could see the roads.

Joey pointed to a small line off the main road, miles from town. "It was up in the woods above the state park, away from everyone. You had to take a dirt road that went back into the hills. It was a few miles from where guys liked to practice shooting. We occasionally could hear gunshots in the distance. Kind of spooked us, but it made it more exciting, too. There was only one house up that road, but we avoided it."

"Did you ever go back after she left?" Ben asked.

"No."

David studied Joey; there was that twitch in his jaw again. He was hiding something.

"What's up with that girl with my necklace? She kind of looks like Catori." Joey added.

"Yes, she does. But she's not. She's an artist," David replied.

Joey smiled. "She looks hot, though."

David didn't like the vibes he was getting from Joey.

"Tell me again why you broke up with Catori?" Ben asked.

Joey blew out his breath. "She took a job working at that art school in Bellingham, and I wasn't happy about it."

"As an artist model," David clarified.

"Yeah. At first, she worked in the cafeteria, but then one of the art instructors asked her to be a model in his class. Turns out he wanted her to model without any clothes on. Heck, she lied about her age to get a job working in the cafeteria. She was supposed to be twenty-one. But the school didn't check to see if that was true."

Joey shifted his weight from foot to foot as he spoke. "I was pissed when I found out. She had a smoking hot body, and, well, she was mine. I didn't want word to get around about her modeling and having other guys hitting on her. I thought she loved me. But her modeling gig just pushed me over the edge. Heck, her father would have beat the shit out of her if he found out she was naked in front of people."

"What happened after you broke up?" David asked.

"She ran away and was living on the street in Bellingham with a bunch of homeless kids."

"Did you look for her?"

"Yes. Last time I saw her, she was sitting on a corner, begging for money."

"Did you talk to her?"

"No, I was upset. I thought by then she'd be hooked on drugs and tell me to get lost." Joey glanced to the side. "I had enough of my own shit to deal with then. I couldn't help her."

"Why did you think she'd be on drugs?"

"I just figured that was what most kids did on the street to cope."

"But no one told you she specifically was using meth?"

"Not really."

Why would he jump to that conclusion? David wondered. What else did he think Catori was doing? "You were angry when you saw her?" David asked.

"Do you blame me? I thought she'd never do shit like that. She told me she loved me. But when I criticized her for sitting naked in front of those people in the art class, she told me it was her body, and it wasn't like she was stripping for a bunch of ogling men. She said there was nothing kinky about it—that it was all very professional and tastefully done. I still didn't want her to do it. I told her it was over between us if she didn't quit. She could have gotten a job working at a burger place, but she didn't. I just couldn't deal with her anymore."

Ben motioned to David, then spoke to Joey. "Well, thank you for your time. Here's my card. If you remember anything else, give me a call."

David glanced at the funky hole-in-the-wall Mexican restaurant across the street. "You want to get something to eat?" He motioned to the place.

They found a table, sat down, and ordered a couple of

beers and burritos. Ben sat in silence, chewing slowly on his food. Meanwhile, David's own thoughts were bugging him, and he hardly touched his.

"Do you think Vicki is in danger?" he suddenly asked. Maybe he was being overly suspicious, but he didn't like the idea she was with Anthony. His alarm bells were going off big time every time he thought of them together. He wanted to protect Vicki and pull her away from the scumbag but felt that would just blow up in his face. He also wasn't fond of Joey and got the feeling the kid knew more than he was telling them.

"Other than from Catori's ghost haunting her?" Ben asked.

"Yeah. I wonder if all this attention is going to stir up interest from the person that killed Catori, and they may go after Vicki."

"It's possible," Ben said. "Dial in your radar and keep an eye on her."

"Oh, put it all on me to protect her." He glared at Ben.

Ben leaned forward. "Hey buddy, I can only do so much. You are the one with the ability to sense things."

David sat back. He was worried. He had a job in construction, and Shaun needed him on site. It wasn't like he was still working as a cop. He had no badge or power to arrest anyone, and he couldn't use a gun if needed. *Shit.* What was he supposed to do to keep Vicki safe?

Chapter Twenty-Eight

Vicki

Once in their hotel room, Vicki kicked off her shoes. She was hiding her disappointment behind the smile she'd been wearing all night.

"Great job, beautiful. Most of your work sold. Aren't you proud?" Anthony snuggled up behind her. "I want you to list your house now. I'll have a real estate company handle everything. I'll set you up in an apartment with a studio in Chicago, so you don't have to worry about expenses. You can just paint."

"I don't know." Her stomach fluttered.

"What are you afraid of? Success, money, living your dream?"

"I have more paintings I'll need to finish first." Why was Anthony pushing her to move so soon? Her house wasn't ready yet. Everything was happening so fast. Was she just afraid? This is what she wanted, right?

But now that she'd tasted it, this wasn't what she'd imagined success to be like. These paintings didn't come from her; they came from—somewhere else. She shouldn't be taking credit for them. What if her visions of this girl disappeared? What if she'd have to paint something else, and people found out she wasn't any good?

"I don't want to go," she blurted.

Anthony laughed. "You're going. You're just nervous, so don't argue. I have a business trip I need to make, but when I get back, I'm taking you to Chicago." He handed her a glass. "Have a drink. Let's celebrate."

After tasting it, she made a face. "What's in this?" She'd never had anything like it before; it was sweet but had a kick. She usually just drank wine and beer. Mixed drinks were not her thing.

"Oh, just a fancy cocktail. Here, let me help you relax." Anthony unzipped her dress, and she stepped out of it. He kissed her shoulder.

Standing in her underwear, Vicki held the glass to her lips, finishing the contents. Anthony slid his hands down her stomach. She was tired and reached down to stop him before he went any further. "Anthony, can we do this later?"

"You owe me, beautiful," he whispered into her ear.

"I'm sorry, I'm just not in the mood." A wave of dizziness came over her.

He scooped her up and laid her on the bed.

She willed herself to sit up. The room spun around her. She pressed her hand to her forehead. Why was she so dizzy? She slid her legs over the side and tried to stand up, but her legs were like rubber, and she fell back. Her brain wasn't working clearly. Her eyelids were heavy, so she closed them.

In the distance, she heard a knock on the door, then the muffled sound of male voices.

The bed shifted. Anthony leaned over and asked, "Vicki, are you awake?"

Things went in and out of focus. "I—" she mumbled. Shadows moved around her. Then the bed jiggled again, and she fell into a deep sleep.

HER EYES FLUTTERED OPEN. She tried to focus but found herself still dizzy, only half awake. She was in a hotel room. Realizing she was naked underneath the blanket, she pulled it up to cover herself, then pushed herself up, clutching it with one arm.

"Are you hungry? Would you like me to call room service for breakfast?" Anthony asked. He had dressed and shaved already.

"I'm still groggy. I could use some coffee. What was in that drink last night? It must have knocked me out because I can't remember anything after having it."

"Why don't you take a shower before our food arrives?" He leaned over. "Unless you'd like to wait until I—"

She scowled at him. "I'm not up to making love right now." He was such a pest.

Vicki threw back the covers, stumbled into the bathroom, took some aspirin, and then brushed her teeth. She felt out of sorts, like she had just run a marathon. Thank goodness the show was over, and they'd be heading back to Cook's Cove later today.

Chapter Twenty-Nine

David

The day after Vicki's big night, Ben drove David to Sea Haven Art College, where Catori had worked, hoping it would trigger something inside him they could use in the investigation.

They trotted up the steps to the door of the building. Students scurried past as he and Ben walked down the hall to the frosted glass doors of the director's office.

While Ben spoke with a receptionist in a bright green sweater, David looked at the plaques on the wall. This was a prestigious art school with many awards for its outstanding contributions to the art world.

"Right this way," said the woman, leading them to a heavy wooden door. "Mr. Bradshaw is expecting you."

Inside, a man with a tuft of gray, curly hair stood up

and held out his hand for them to shake. After the introductions, David sat in a chair next to Ben.

"I understand you want to talk about that Native girl that went missing ten years ago. You know, you'd be better off contacting our attorney about it," Bradshaw said, clasping his hands and setting them on the desk in front of him.

"We're not here to discuss the issues of hiring an underage girl," Ben replied, and David noticed the man flinch at Ben's statement. "I just want to better understand what she did while she worked at this school."

"That was a long time ago, and we told the police everything we knew then."

"I was hoping you could shed some light on what you know about the girl."

"As I said before, she originally worked in the cafeteria. One of our former art instructors asked her to be a model in his class. He liked her features, I guess. Unfortunately, he didn't go through the normal channels, as I assumed. Just so that you know, we have a policy of only hiring professionals as models."

"How long did she work here?"

"You're asking about the modeling position, I take it? She only sat for a few classes, then quit."

"Do you know why she quit?"

"I'm not sure. Our records indicate that she gave no reason. She just turned in her notice and didn't show up after that. Maybe she wasn't comfortable with sitting motionless for an hour. I've been told it can be difficult to hold a pose for extended periods of time. Perhaps she just decided modeling wasn't what she expected."

Ben nodded. "So, she didn't report that anyone was harassing her?"

"No, she didn't. If someone had been bothering her, I would have been informed. We don't tolerate that kind of behavior."

A lot goes on in colleges that those in charge like to pretend doesn't, David thought.

"What can you tell us about Christine Meyers? Ben asked.

"Ms. Meyers?" Bradshaw sat back and folded his arms across his chest. "She is involved with several fundraising events in Bellingham. You should be aware of that already."

Ben nodded. "And for the college?"

"Christine chairs the Sea Haven Art Gala every year." Bradshaw sat up a little straighter. "She brings in a fair amount of money and features the works of some of our best students. It gives them the opportunity to perform and show off their work in front of an audience. The event draws people from around the country, not just Seattle."

"What can you tell us about Anthony Tomasic?" David interjected, and the director stiffened.

"I'd rather not voice my opinion of the man. He is one of our donors."

"You don't care for him, I take it?"

Bradshaw averted his eyes, then stood up. "Good luck with your investigation."

David followed Ben out into the hall.

"What do you make of our conversation?" Ben asked.

"I think he doesn't want to cast suspicion on anyone that's a donor."

"Did you get any vibes that might tell us anything?"

"Nothing you didn't pick up on." David slowed down as they passed a couple of students in conversation coming down the corridor. One had a backpack slung over a shoulder, and the other was carrying a large portfolio case for artwork. A bell rang, and he and Ben stepped aside to dodge a rush of bodies coming at them. David spun around, watching them file into classrooms down the hall.

"Vicki went to school here, didn't she?" This was something she had never talked to him about.

"I'm pretty sure she graduated before Catori disappeared," Ben replied.

"It still seems strange that she's painting pictures of someone who vanished ten years ago unless there's some connection we don't know about." David pushed open the main door, and they stepped down the stairs and headed in the direction of the car.

"I suspect there is. And I think our best source is Vicki," Ben said.

"Vicki." David shook his head and sighed.

"Is there any way you can get her to open up?" Ben opened the car door.

"I wish." David opened his side and slid in.

Chapter Thirty

Vicki

"Where the hell is she?" an angry man's voice resonated through the shop.

Vicki heard the sound of a chair slamming to the floor. Curious about the commotion, she stayed in the kitchen out of sight but peeked around the corner, holding on to her coffee mug. She watched as Jenny walked over and stood in front of Brooke, whose mouth was hanging open and eyes were wide.

"Please, lower your voice," Jenny said.

A large Native man stood near the entrance with dark, shoulder-length hair, dressed in jeans and a tan shirt that looked too tight across his barrel chest.

"I want to know where the woman who painted that picture you have in the window is," he demanded, walking over to the paintings on the wall. He lifted his arm, pointing to them. "And these too."

"And why do you want to talk to her?" Jenny's voice cracked.

"That's my daughter, and I want to know what their connection is." He moved around the shop like an angry bear looking for something to destroy.

"She doesn't know your daughter," Jenny said.

"How do you know?" his voice boomed.

"Because she told me that the girl's image came from her imagination."

"Dreams?" he bellowed. "These are from *dreams*? Evil spirits are more likely. The ones who know what happened to my daughter."

"I'm sure this is just a coincidence. I don't know where people get their ideas. I'm not an artist." Jenny moved over to her checkout counter, looking around until she found her phone.

Vicki swallowed hard. This was Catori's father? He seemed so much like her own father—a stupid, loud-mouthed fool.

"I want to talk to her," he demanded.

Jenny looked up, phone in hand. "She's not here, so you better leave now, or I'll have to call someone to remove you."

He grunted. "Tell her Catori's father is looking for her. I need to talk to her. I want to know where she got these images." He glanced around the room, then left, slamming the door behind him.

Trembling, Vicki came into the shop area.

Jenny ran over and pulled her into a hug. "Are you okay?"

"Yes. Wow, that guy was upset." Vicki's coffee almost sloshed out of her mug with how badly she was shaking.

"He's gone now. I'm going to call Ben and let him know that Catori's father showed up. Maybe he can talk some sense into the man. I don't want him coming back, expecting to find you here. And you be careful when you go out. He may try to intimidate you."

Vicki nodded and trudged back upstairs. Maybe she *was* painting a real person—the girl David and Ben had been concerned about. She was hesitant about doing any more paintings of Catori, but she needed to finish the one she'd already started.

By now, Vicki knew all of Catori's emotions and could recreate her expressions with ease. A fine line in the corner of her mouth could turn a smile into a pout. Eyes that were once soft, even playful, now held a severe new look, intense with emotion.

The joy of painting the girl had vanished. The images were now disturbing. Vicki caught herself just before adding silver teardrops to Catori's face. She was extracting pain and sorrow from her own life, mixing it with dabs of shaded color.

"You're just like your mother!" It was her father's voice, so similar to Catori's father's, haunting her from a memory she'd tried to keep locked away. She remembered her father snatching her arm and dragging her back inside, slamming the door and locking it.

"Go make dinner. I'm hungry." Her father fetched a beer from the refrigerator, plopped down on the couch, and turned on the TV until it was time for him to leave for work.

Vicki jolted back, recoiling from a slap. Staring at the

canvas, she realized she had painted a glowing red mark on Catori's face and a purple bruise on her arm.

Now Vicki's own nightmares were seeping out of the tubes of blue and green, the muddy browns pushed into the bark of the family trees, their limbs broken by the harsh winters. Memories of her and Catori's father and the men who wanted to control them swirled like pools of pigment on her painter's palette. There was no painting over the damage the men in their lives had caused.

Vicki had run into the arms of a man at the age of sixteen, hoping to be rescued, only to find out the man wanted to use her for sex, and when he was done, he'd dumped her.

Somehow, Vicki knew Catori had also run from her father into the arms of a man to be rescued, only to be used —and then what? Abused?

The door was swinging both ways, in and out of each other's past. Memories were spilling like paint all around. There was no way Vicki could ignore any of it, all the guilt, anger, and pain inside her, the things she never wanted to face. She was in hell, and it was her fault. She was a child again and didn't know what to do or how to stop the bad stuff from happening.

It was her younger sister, Veronica, that Vicki hadn't been able to protect from her father. Veronica was younger and easier for her father to catch when on one of his rampages.

"Is something going on at home?" the school nurse had asked.

Vicki's eyes widened as the nurse pulled back the sleeve of her sister's shirt, revealing the dark, bluish-purple mark.

This was the third time the nurse had inquired about the signs left by her father's anger.

Not knowing what would happen to either one of them if she revealed the truth, Vicki lied. "She was climbing over the fence in the backyard and fell on a pile of wood."

The nurse glanced over at the principal. "I think we should call protective services."

"Maybe the girl did fall," the principal responded. "Why don't we wait a while?"

That day, on their walk home, Vicki told her sister, "I want you to come into town with me."

"There's nothing for me to do while you sit and draw. Besides, Daddy doesn't like it when I'm gone. He wants me to take care of him."

"Take care of him?"

"Yeah. You know, make him feel better."

"You stay away from him. Do you hear me?"

Veronica just shrugged her shoulders. Drawing was Vicki's escape. Veronica didn't have one.

The day Vicki came home from sketching at the beach and found Veronica pointing a gun at their father was a day she would never forget. Her father kept his gun lying around "for protection." But he liked to wave it around and pretend to shoot things when he got drunk. When Vicki arrived, bullets were scattered around the box on the kitchen table. The gun was loaded this time, and it was no game. Her father cursed her sister, yelling the same names he called both of them—"Pieces of shit."

Veronica didn't shoot him when he lunged for it but instead turned the barrel to her own head and pulled the trigger. That day, something broke inside Vicki. She swore she would never forgive her father. Though he cried and

Strokes of Desperation

screamed, begging to be forgiven for his sin of not loving his daughters, Vicki knew then she was on her own. No one was coming to rescue her. They had all abandoned her.

Tears ran down her face and mixed with her paints as she pushed her sorrow into teardrops on the image of Catori.

Drained, Vicki set her brush down. Painting was now becoming a nightmare. Catori's face wasn't staring back at her; it was her own. It was a face of raw emotion. Gutting her. Them.

Vicki stared at her arm, then picked up her X-ACTO knife. She made a fist with her wrist out, ready to draw the blade across, half expecting to see paint shooting out once she sliced the surface. Then she froze and dropped the knife.

Pacing back and forth in her studio, she was full of nervous energy; her insides were exploding with the urge to run. Why were these images appearing? Was it because she was afraid of him—still, after all these years? Was Catori fearful of her father, too? Was this a combination of both their fears manifesting themselves together? Carrying her own past was heavy enough without Catori's seeping in, as well.

Her mind had been too active for a nap these days. The rare times she could doze, her mind would fill with snippets of dreams, either about running in the woods or the girl she was painting. Often, she'd wake up only to find the images dissolving into a wash of watercolor running down a page.

The mirrors she had placed around the studio were playing tricks on her mind, confusing her. Had Catori taken on movement now, or was that only her reflection? Reality and her dreams were merging, and Vicki was exhausted from trying to distinguish one from the other. Sometimes, they came as holograms projected in front of her, appearing like a movie.

She needed to get out of this house.

She pulled off her sweats, throwing them on the floor, then pulled on a pair of jeans and slipped on a sweater and some boots.

"I'll be back later," she called to Jenny as she walked through the shop and out the front door. She chose not to look at her house as she passed it.

Walking along the beach with the cool breeze on her face, she tried to shut out the images that had been ruining her life. Nowhere was safe from the ghost of this girl! Catori was like a shadow that no amount of light could make disappear. Vicki took off, rushing out to the retreating water. Maybe if she ended her life, she would find peace.

At the water's edge, she heard a voice.

"Vicki."

Before reaching the tide, she dropped to her knees, covering her eyes with her hands. It was him. He always managed to show up when she was vulnerable. *Damn it.*

David sprinted over and bent down. "I knew you'd come here. I've been waiting for you."

She looked up at the softness in his eyes and stood up. Mud covered her knees.

"What's going on?" he asked.

She blurted, "I don't know what's happening to me. The girl in my paintings is taking control of my life. She reminds me of myself, dredging up memories I don't want to revisit."

"Like what?"

"Painful stuff I've never told anyone about."

"You can tell me."

"No, no, that's never going to happen." She turned her back to him.

He took her shoulders and made her face him. "Why? I won't judge you."

"The hell you won't. If you knew some of the shit I've done, you'd run the other way." She pushed away his arms.

"I think you've misjudged me. I've seen a lot of heartache in my life, too. People I love die—bodies blown apart. Crimes committed I could have prevented. You're not the only one that's suffered from painful memories. I have nightmares, too."

Seriously? He had nightmares? He always appeared so together.

Vicki bit her lip, and he took her in his arms. He caressed her head as she began to shake.

"I can't shut off my mind. My muse won't leave me alone. She's with me everywhere I go."

"Come with me."

Once they reached David's house, he led her to a fire pit he'd built near the water and lit the wood stacked inside the circle. Sitting down, he put his arm around her.

She watched the wood as it crackled and danced like spirits. She even thought Catori's face appeared for a moment within the embers.

"I'm losing it. Hell, I don't even know what's real anymore." She sniffed.

He took her chin in his hand. She looked into his eyes for answers.

"Maybe you're just burned out. You need a break."

At this moment, she wanted him to rescue her from the craziness she was going through. To lift the burden from her shoulders. She closed her eyes. The warmth of his hand cupped her cheek, and she pressed against it.

"Can I do anything to help you?" he whispered.

"Just hold me."

He wrapped both arms around her, and she snuggled into him. He kissed her forehead. After a few minutes, she looked up at him. His eyes went from concerned to serious. He hugged her, kissing the side of her head.

"Can I stay with you tonight?" Vicki asked, wanting to feel the warmth of his comforting body against hers.

He pulled back. She couldn't tell what he was thinking. He ran his hand through his hair as though pondering what to say.

"I—"

"I shouldn't have asked." Vicki stood up, yanking back her feelings. "Can you take me home?"

"No, it's just that—"

"I know, I know. I'm sorry I asked." She looked around for his truck. Once spotting it, she ran toward it and opened the passenger side, getting in, then slamming it shut.

She watched out the window as David looked down and kicked a rock at his feet, mumbling something. Then he came over and started up the engine.

Neither of them said anything as he followed the road back to town. When he pulled up in front of Jenny's shop, Vicki reached for the door handle to get out, but he grabbed her arm.

"Vicki. I'm sorry."

A mixture of emotions ran through her—embarrassment, disappointment, a longing for comfort, not just sex—but she dismissed them.

"There's nothing to apologize for." She looked up at the door to Jenny's.

"I want to help you. I do," he said softly.

"Thanks. You keep saying that, but that's not what I want. I want to be able to help myself, damn it." She pushed his hand away and crawled out of the truck, then ran up the stairs.

Chapter Thirty-One

Vicki

Vicki once again outlined her lids and brows with a heavy black kohl pencil that accentuated her eyes, then added an iridescent green shadow, like a peacock's tail, above and below her lids. In her studio, she caught a glimpse of herself in the mirror, giving her an eerie feeling.

Pulling over the stool, she sat down, then hesitated after picking up a tube of blue paint to squeeze onto her palette. For some reason, her heart wasn't into painting right now.

Going to the window, she looked out. What would she do with her time if she didn't paint tonight? Bringing the wooden piece from her necklace to her mouth and flicking it up and down with her lips, a thought occurred to her. Why not go out? The idea of having a beer at Silvers sounded nice. She was pretty sure she could talk a free one out of Nick, the bartender.

Going to the closet, she took out a blue knee-length cashmere cardigan and a pair of boots. Then she pushed her hair back and added a scrunchie, making a ponytail.

Jenny closed up and left a while ago, so it was dark when Vicki reached the main floor. She locked the door behind her as she left.

Outside, a breeze snapped at her, but she reminded herself she'd be inside soon. It was a moonless night, and clouds created a darkness that ate up the stars. An uneasiness crept up on her as if something was watching her.

She took a couple of deep breaths, then went down the steps and headed off down the street. She refused to look at her house as she walked by. After reaching the corner, another odd sensation poked at her. A rustling sound came from the bushes. She ignored it.

I've gone into town by myself a million times before. There's nothing to be frightened of.

A cat in heat let out a loud screech, calling for a mate, then scampered off into the darkness. Vicki wrapped her arms around her chest and picked up her pace. It was quiet now, except for the small voice in her head. "He's here." She ignored it.

On the sidewalk near the alley that ran behind the restaurants, she came to an abrupt stop.

In the dimly lit alley, a tall, shadowy figure loomed before her, leaning casually against a grimy dumpster. Her instincts screamed she better move, and she attempted to avert her gaze, lowering her head and trying to slip past unnoticed.

However, the figure emerged from the darkness, stepping directly into her path. His face was hidden in the shadow of his hood. He extended a large, imposing hand, pressing it against her chest with a chilling firmness, halting her escape. Vicki's body froze. Her breath caught in her throat, a silent scream trapped within. He shoved her roughly, propelling her backward.

Her boot heel snagged on a jutting rock, throwing her off balance. She stumbled, but he hauled her upright before she fell to the ground.

He pushed her deeper into the alley, away from the glare of the streetlights, until the world beyond ceased to exist. Abruptly, he shoved her against a cold brick wall. She felt its hard edges digging into her back.

"Take my purse. There's no money in it. Just let me go." She held out her bag for him to take. When he didn't, she dropped it to the ground.

His face was hidden inside his hood, but his dark eyes contained a flicker of distant light.

Desperate, Vicki looked around, searching for any chance of escape.

Suddenly, his hand shot up, gripping her chin and yanking her gaze back to him. "Catori? Is that you?" he demanded.

Vicki swallowed the lump of terror in her throat. "No," she managed, her voice barely a whisper.

He reached out, yanking the scrunchie from her hair. His fingers cruelly weaving through her strands, letting them fall like a curtain across her face. "Don't lie to me," he hissed, leaning in close, his grip on her hair tightening, pulling at her scalp.

Vicki began to shake uncontrollably.

Releasing her hair, he then pulled down his hood and unzipped his sweatshirt, revealing his bare chest. "It's me,

Joey," he said, with a twisted smile on his face. "Did you forget about me? I've never forgotten about you."

Vicki's gaze was drawn to him despite the terror clawing at her insides. His black hair cascaded around his shoulders, and as he tilted his head, his face briefly emerged from the shadows. His skin, a dusty clay hue, seemed almost ethereal, while his dark eyes held her captive in their intense gaze.

As he turned his head, scanning for onlookers, Vicki's eyes caught a glimpse of intricate red and black Native symbols tattooed across his torso. An energy crackled in the air, charged with a raw, almost primal magnetism.

Vicki's heart pounded, her thoughts in a whirlwind of confusion and dread. She bit her lower lip, struggling to make sense of this surreal encounter. He was the man she had imagined passionately entwined with the girl in her art. It seemed impossible, yet here he stood, a figure from her fantasies made real.

"Catori?" he probed again.

With a shake of her head, Vicki tried to assert her reality. "Please quit calling me Catori and let me go," she pleaded, her hands clenching into fists.

"How do I know you're not her?" Joey challenged.

Vicki could feel the intensity of his stare, as if he was trying to unravel her very soul. "My name is Vicki," she insisted, her voice a mix of fear and defiance.

"Hah. That is what you want me to believe. But I know better," he scoffed, his tone dripping with skepticism and an unsettling confidence.

Joey's gaze dropped ominously to Vicki's chest, and with deliberate slowness, he reached out, his fingers grazing the fabric of her sweater. She felt the cold touch of his hand as he began to unfasten the top button. His fingertips brushed against her skin underneath. Her lip quivered uncontrollably.

He proceeded to undo each button, his actions deliberate and invasive. As the cardigan fell open, revealing her black lace bra, Vicki's breaths came in sharp, rapid bursts, her chest heaving with a mix of fear and vulnerability.

"Nice," he murmured, his voice a disturbing blend of approval and menace. Then, dragging his fingernail slowly from the hollow of her neck down to her cleavage, he sent a shiver through her.

His attention then shifted to the necklace she wore. He picked up the pendant with his long fingers, turning it over in his palm. The wood began to emit a soft glow under his touch. His eyes flicked up to meet hers.

"Why are you wearing this if you aren't her?" he demanded.

"I found it in a box of junk," Vicki stammered, her voice barely a whisper.

"I made this for Catori. She swore she'd never take it off," he said as he admired the glowing pendant. Bringing it to his lips, he kissed the wood, and it flared up like a tiny flame.

Someone else's words blurted out of her mouth, "Yes. I know."

His eyes snapped back to hers, intense and searching. "How would you know that if you weren't her?"

"I, I—" Her words dissolved into a frightened stammer.

"Have you been hiding from me, pretending to be someone else?" His accusation hung in the air between them.

"No, I told you, my name is Vicki, not Catori." Desperate to reclaim control, she reached up to take the necklace from him. But he was quicker, his free hand capturing hers in a firm grip. The wood of the pendant radiated a strange heat, intensifying as he held it. Releasing the pendant, he let it fall back against her chest, where it left a searing sensation on her skin.

"Why did you run away?"

She swallowed hard again. "I didn't."

His eyes studied hers. "Cat?"

Clearing her dry throat, Vicki exhaled, and in a moment of confused surrender, a word escaped her lips on a breath. "Yes." Panic surged through her immediately after, and she coughed out a frantic denial, "No. No!" Her body was rooted to the spot, paralyzed by fear and an unexplainable connection to this strange man.

Abruptly, he yanked her towards him, his whisper sending chills down her spine. "I've missed you, Cat."

Instinctively, Vicki raised her palms, trying to create a barrier between them. But as her fingers brushed against his bare chest, a strange sensation overtook her. A tingling warmth spread from her fingertips, an involuntary urge to explore the contours of his torso. His presence was intoxicating, an allure that she found herself unable to resist as if he were a magnet drawing her in against her will.

Vicki's mind spun. The intensity of the moment was overwhelming her senses, leaving her with an eerie, haunting desire.

A bead of sweat trickled down her neck, heading for the space between her breasts. A pulsating light radiated from her necklace. Something was happening she couldn't wrap her mind around.

His mouth hovered close to hers. His lips were a light plum color. She inhaled his masculine scent—musk, sage, and sweat. Confused by a sudden inner desire drawing her toward him. He was breathing in her breath, and she, his, as though they were one. He looked deep into her eyes, and the darkness called to her, claiming her.

When his lips touched hers, a mysterious sensation rushed over her. He pushed his tongue inside, kissing her vehemently. Her knees weakened. Vicki reached around his neck and hung on as she and the girl in her paintings merged.

Powerless, Vicki found herself swept into a dream. Abducted by an apparition. The alley disappeared around her; she was transported to the woods—to Catori's and Joey's secret place. She was falling into a memory that was not hers. Trapped in the clutches of two lovers, she was ensnared in a dream of passion that threatened to consume her. What was real and what was imagined didn't matter at this moment. Neither did the strange calling Vicki was running toward, not away from.

Her necklace glowed, and her body lit up. She closed her eyes. Every touch sent ripples through Vicki's body as he seduced Catori. Her breath began to quicken.

"Ahh, that's my Catori," He whispered as he continued toying with her.

As she was about to surrender completely to this mind-bending experience, the sudden coldness of a hard object pressing against the bare skin of her hip broke the spell. Her eyes flew open.

Joey drew out the handle of the blade he had tucked in a holder on his belt and laid it flat against her throat. She tensed, trying to read his eyes. *What was he planning to do next?*

Joey smiled a wicked smile while she trembled. Holding the blade out to his side, he picked up her hand and pierced the tip of her index finger. A teardrop of blood formed, and he brought it to his mouth. He tasted the blood, dragging his tongue around her finger, then placed his mouth over the tip and began sucking.

Vicki became faint. He pressed his mouth to hers, giving her another disarming kiss and sending her back into Catori's memory. But this time, swirling, caught between two worlds, she resisted. Vicki tried to tell him to stop. But no words came out. She conjured up her strength to fight him off. But she was inside the dream again. Propelled by self-preservation, she took off running in the woods. Time sped backward in flashes that made no sense—a black bird, her soul taking flight, excruciating pain, running for her life through the woods, screams, fear, a dark room, muffled voices, laughter, and heartbreak. Tears dripped down Vicki's cheeks.

A sudden voice interrupted her nightmare and brought Joey's actions to a halt.

"Get your hands off of her!"

Her eyes flew open. Joey let go and turned, wheeling the knife out.

"Drop the knife, Joey," David commanded.

Ben stood beside him.

Stunned and wide-eyed, Vicki cried, "David?"

David motioned for Vicki to move away. Confused, she stepped to the right. The smell of steak on a grill from one of the restaurants filled Vicki's nostrils. The reality of where she was suddenly hit her. She looked down and quickly buttoned up her sweater. *What was she doing here?*

David whirled around and kicked Joey in the side. The

knife fell from his hand. While Joey was bent over in pain, David brought up a fist, slamming it into Joey's face several times. Joey flew against the bricks and slid down to the ground.

"I thought she was Catori," Joey said, wiping the blood from his mouth.

Ben jumped between them and pushed David back before he kicked Joey again. "Hey. That's enough," Ben said.

"No, it isn't. He needs to learn he can't pull this shit and get away with it." David scowled.

Joey dropped his head, and his hair fell, covering his eyes. "I just wanted to know if she was Catori, that's all. And if she still loved me."

Ben patted him on the shoulder. "This gal does look a lot like Catori. But she isn't her."

Vicki dashed over to David. He put his arms around her, hugging her tightly. "I was afraid Joey would contact you after we talked to him in Seattle," he whispered. "It looks like I was right."

"He was her boyfriend. They were lovers," Vicki mumbled. She was shaking, and deep nausea was threatening her insides.

David lifted her chin and looked into her eyes. "You're not Catori, so why the hell were you letting him crawl all over you?"

"I." Vicki swallowed hard. "I was ... I wasn't sure if he was real or not."

David let go of her. "Right," he hissed. "You couldn't tell the difference?"

"I felt like I was in a dream." She could see David was upset.

"A dream?"

She nodded her head.

"If that's true, you better find some way to shut down this girl's influence over you."

Vicki looked away.

"I hate to think what that guy would have done to you if we hadn't intervened. You've got to be more careful. Someday, you might not be so lucky. I don't want you to end up missing or dead like Catori."

Chapter Thirty-Two

David

David drove Vicki back to Jenny's in silence, then headed home. He was pissed. How could she let that guy touch her? Hell, from where he stood, she wasn't even putting up a fight.

Had he been kidding himself about Vicki? Was she just a tramp like his ex-wife? Ready to drop her panties for any guy. Hell, he told her as much that night of Jenny's dinner party. He must be out of his mind, thinking she was worth his attention.

Emotions swirled inside him. He had wanted to believe that Vicki was different—a victim of circumstances. Yeah, sure, chalk it up to her damn ghost, but he witnessed what was going on. That guy was coming damn close to screwing her, and she was —

God, what had he gotten himself into? When he set out

to help Vicki, he didn't bargain on having to sit back while other guys mess with her. He was angry at these men taking advantage of her. He was angry at himself, too, for not protecting her from these scumbags.

He pulled into his driveway and killed the engine. As he sat there in the dark silence, he didn't know what to think. His intuition had told him to go to the alley because Joey would be waiting for her there. That Vicki was in danger. Danger? Humm.

As soon as he closed the front door behind him, Ben called.

"I spent some time talking to Joey."

"And?" David asked, trying to contain his voice from the bitterness he was feeling.

"I've decided not to turn the kid over to the police. He was just confused."

"Confused?" David's hand flew out to the side. "Hell, he was! He knew exactly what he was doing and who he was with. We showed him a picture of Vicki and told him about the paintings. He said he thought she was hot. The guy went looking for her."

"Now, don't go into a rage. He didn't harm Vicki. Maybe scared her a bit, but—"

"Come on. The guy was all over her." David blew out an angry breath. "He would've screwed her if we hadn't shown up when we did."

"Hey. You weren't going to let that happen. You knew we'd find him in that alley with her when you called me."

Yes, David had the vision. He just didn't understand why Vicki didn't try to escape. If her willpower was so weak and her behavior was the result of Catori's spirit, this damn ghost was going to get her killed if he didn't intervene.

"So, I take it you don't think he killed Catori?"

"I haven't crossed him off the list just yet. What's your gut telling you about him?"

"Other than him not giving a damn that Vicki wasn't Catori and that he was going to take it as far as he could?"

"Yeah."

"I think he's hiding something. He might know more than he's telling us."

"That's what I thought. If I'd turned him over to the police, we'd never get any more information out of him. I think he's just as curious as we are to know what happened to Catori."

"Right. But if I catch him anywhere near Vicki again, I'll break his God Damn neck."

"Cool down. Give the kid a break. I'm sure he regrets his actions. From the looks of it, she wasn't exactly putting up a fight."

"Yes," David cut Ben off. "That's what's got me worried. That spirit must be pretty powerful. Who knows what else it can make Vicki do." He knew he was making excuses for Vicki's promiscuous behavior, but he was trying to convince himself that she wasn't in her right mind at the time.

David laid down on the couch after they hung up. His head hurt. He was trying too hard to come up with explanations for everyone else's actions. His thoughts were telling him one thing, but his gut was telling him another. The only thing he was sure of was that he wanted to get to the bottom of this pit and slay the damn dragon before Vicki went up in flames.

Chapter Thirty-Three

Vicki

Alone in the house, Vicki went to the bathroom and wiped off her eye makeup. Even after brushing her teeth and washing her face, Joey's smell and presence were still there, his taste still in her mouth.

She was exhausted from the evening's events. Judging by the fact that it was now eleven p.m., she and Joey were together in the alley much longer than she realized. To her, time stood still. Her mind had been caught in a hallucination. Did he? Did she? What actually took place between them was hard to decipher.

Confused and ashamed, her eyes began to fill, and she shoved her fists into her lids, trying to suppress her tears, but then broke down and sobbed into her hands. Why was this happening to her? All she ever wanted was to be loved, not used. She didn't want to be someone else's surrogate or fantasy. She hated her life—the constant painting of Catori, screwing Anthony and being so damn poor. How did she end up so desperate again?

The only thing good she had going in her life was David. Sweet, caring David. Now he probably thinks she's a —tears dripped down her chin. She wasn't good enough for someone like him. If he only knew about her past, he'd run the other way instead of trying to help her.

Vicki's head ached as old secrets split open and memories unspooled before her. She was back in New York City, crawling from the showers, wet, cold, and terrified after being raped. Reaching her cubicle, she rifled through one of the cardboard boxes and dug out the card of the man who was supposed to help her.

"Mr. Bianchi, I was given your number by someone in Bellingham." At the moment, she couldn't remember who. "I was told that if I fell on hard times in New York City, to call you," Vicki explained into the borrowed phone as its owner watched to make sure she returned it after her call.

"Well, I'm glad you called, then," Mr. Bianchi replied.

At the designated time the following day, a limousine arrived in front of the warehouse. With the engine idling, the back door opened. A heavy-set, bald man smoking a cigar leaned his head out. "Vicki Milikan?"

She nodded.

"Get in."

Vicki hesitated. What was she about to do? Going off with this stranger was against every instinct she had. But she was desperate. She told herself it had to be better than living on the streets. She got in, and they pulled away from the artist's warehouse.

"I'm Mr. Bianchi. You'll be working for me now."

"I will?" Vicki's stomach fluttered, not knowing what she had gotten herself into. "Doing what?"

"Here's the deal, sweetheart. I'll make the arrangements, feed you, give you a decent place to stay, and in return, you'll take care of some of my friends for me."

Vicki stared out the window as they maneuvered through the busy city streets. She was empty inside; she had no other choice. What good would it do to bolt out of the car? Who else would she end up with? A pimp on the street? She was stuck in New York City, starving, with no money and no income.

Mr. Bianchi stopped in front of a run-down tenement building. A small, plump woman with dark, permed hair and wearing too much makeup was waiting to greet Vicki.

"Come with me." The woman motioned.

Vicki followed the woman up several flights of stairs. The place was poorly lit and smelled of disinfectant and bug spray.

They stopped in front of a door, and the woman unlocked it. "When you have a customer, I will buzz three times to let you know they're here, so let them in. I'm on the first floor in the lobby. If you feel threatened, just hit the button on the wall, and I'll come by and check on you.

The woman swung the door open. "Here's your place. Get yourself comfortable. I'll send a customer by later." Then she turned and left.

Vicki let out a breath and stepped inside.

The apartment was small, with a bed in the middle of the room. A table sat on one side bearing a wide-based lamp with a smoke-stained shade. Vicki walked over and picked up the lamp. Its base was square and made of clear plastic resin. Opening the drawer to the end table, she found lube, condoms, and sex toys.

There was no phone, just a remote for a large TV screen mounted on the wall. She was pretty sure it was for watching porn. A window looked out at the bricks of the building next door. The kitchenette had a small refrigerator, a sink, a hot plate, and a microwave. All the sharp knives had been removed from the silverware drawer.

Vicki opened the lower cupboard, squatted down, and rummaged through the pots and pans. None were heavy enough to do any damage if she wanted to use them as a weapon. She stood up, remembering that the concierge had told her that all food would be delivered. There would be no need to leave her room. Mr. Bianchi made all the money arrangements so she wouldn't have to collect from her visitors, either. Vicki released a heavy sigh. She was a prisoner.

Opening the closet revealed various costumes, high heels, and lingerie inside. The only regular clothes she had were the jeans and T-shirt she was wearing.

In the bathroom was a shower. The cabinet contained a hair dryer, shampoo, and soap samples. One drawer contained a bag of pills.

Vicki went out into the main room, scanning it for something, anything she could use when the time came for her to escape. Above the bed was a mirror. She then noticed a surveillance camera in a shadow at the corner of the ceiling. *Shit.* Someone would be watching her.

The first man sent to her room told her that he was married and that his wife wasn't interested in sex—as if that was an excuse for being there. She felt awkward and sat on the bed, looking at the wall.

"Come on, honey." The man undressed. "I have to get back to work."

What was she supposed to do? Swallowing the bile in her throat, she glanced over at his potbelly and hairy body. Nothing about him was even remotely appealing.

She handed him a condom, then lay down next to him and closed her eyes.

"Hey, I didn't pay for you to act like my wife. If you're not going to do anything, at least give me a blow job."

That got Vicki's attention. She wasn't going to put his tiny dick in her mouth. Realizing that she was expected to get these guys off, she went to work doing some of the things Jack Taft had taught her and that she and Jerrid had done together.

After more than a dozen visitors, she just went through the motions, making sure each man was satisfied. She wore high heels, played roles in various costumes, and acted like a porn star while feeling like a zombie inside, pretending she was anywhere but in that room, counting the minutes until it was over. She was tempted to take some of the drugs in the bathroom, but she knew if she did that, she'd never escape.

The next man asked her to do things she decided she wasn't going to do. She was sick of this shit and these fat, smelly, disgusting perverts. This wasn't living. She had to get out of there.

When she refused him, he grabbed her hair, yanked her toward him, then hauled off and punched her in the face. "Bitch, I'm paying for you to do whatever I ask."

Whoa. Emotions raced around inside her like a rabid beast. In her nicest voice, she said, "I'm sorry. I'll do whatever you want. Let me get something that will make you feel really good."

"Hurry up." He sat on the edge of the bed and checked his phone for messages.

Sitting on the floor next to the end table on the other side of the bed, she unplugged the lamp. She watched as he scrolled through his phone messages. When she was sure he wasn't paying attention, she quickly picked up the lamp and slammed the base to the back of his head. He turned around, and she struck him in the face, breaking his nose.

His eyes were wild. "Bitch!" He reached out his arms and tried to grab her.

Vicki whirled around with a power she didn't know she had, hitting him again on the side of the head until he fell to the floor. A gash had split his scalp, and blood began forming a puddle on the floor.

She yanked the lamp cord out of the lamp, wrapped it around his ankles, and then pulled a pillowcase over his bleeding head, knotting the end.

Rapidly going through his pants draped on a chair, she found his wallet and took all his cash, which turned out to be five hundred dollars. Quickly, she got dressed in her jeans and then fled down the stairs.

Peeking over at the reception area, she didn't see anyone but heard voices; the woman was on the phone in the back room. *Shit.* She had probably watched the whole thing on the surveillance camera. Vicki ran out onto the street, where she hailed a taxi.

At the bus station, she bought a one-way ticket to Seattle, which happened to be boarding then. She had no luggage, no coat, only the clothes on her back and her purse. She kept glancing over her shoulder, expecting to

Strokes of Desperation

find someone looking for her as she ran up the stairs of the bus and took a seat.

As the bus pulled away, several men rushed into the bus loading area, looking at the passengers on the other buses. She slid down in her seat. The woman next to her stared at the developing bruise on Vicki's cheek where the man had punched her in the face earlier.

"My husband hit me, and I'm leaving him," Vicki lied.

The woman turned away and whispered, "Good for you."

As the bus traveled across the country, Vicki thought about how foolish she had been to go to New York with Jerrid. She'd never trust a man with her feelings again. Jerrid had let her down. New York had let her down. She had arrived with hopes and dreams but was leaving with disgust and shame. Maybe her father was right. She was a piece of shit whose art would never amount to anything. *She wasn't worthy of love.*

NOW, in Jenny's room, Vicki squeezed her eyes shut, trying to block out her past. No one was ever going to know what she'd done to survive in New York.

SUNLIGHT BROKE THROUGH HER SLUMBER, causing her to open her eyes. She pushed herself up and headed into the bathroom. The hot shower filled the room with steam and fogged up the mirror. Rubbing a circle with the sleeve of her robe, she thought about David. He was the only stable thing in her life, showing up every time she was in trouble. She appreciated his kindness, but she needed to somehow prove to him that she could make it on her own. Was that belief even true anymore? Caught in this web with Catori, she was beginning to have doubts.

She left the room and went downstairs. Hungry, she searched the freezer for something to eat. She pulled out a chicken and rice dinner. She wasn't picky; she just wanted the hunger to go away so she could go back upstairs and resume painting. The meal was put in the microwave, and the timer was set.

Brooke strolled into the kitchen where Vicki sat, mouth set in a grim line. "Did you hear the news?" she asked.

Vicki looked up. "What news?"

"The cops found the body of one of the missing Lummi Native girls in the woods near the state park. Her name was Holly Bear. She was sixteen. I guess someone shot her and dumped her body in the woods."

"That's awful. When did that happen?"

"They said that she'd been dead for five years. A dog found her bones. It gives me the creeps to think some sicko might still be out there, looking for girls to hurt."

The thought of that poor girl made Vicki nauseous. She got up and dumped out her meal from its plastic container, then grabbed some crackers to take up with her.

When she placed her hand on the studio door, she dropped it again and returned to the bedroom. Looking out at the water, she wondered about the missing girls. When she had been held captive, no one even noticed she'd been missing. No, she wasn't going to think about that.

Aching to go home, she took a bite of the cracker and swallowed the dry crumbs, feeling them as nothing but a lump in her stomach.

This wasn't her house. She was as much a prisoner here as she had been in the past. She dropped her head; what choice did she have? Forcing herself, she went back to her cell—her studio.

As she began to paint, it became impossible to stop her emotions from flowing through the brush. Violet, maroon, cobalt, black, and red. Rage, anger, hate. Yellow, orange, pink. Bitterness, shame, and guilt. Pigment smeared over the faces of the past.

She opened a drawer and ran her hand across her special art spatula. It was shaped like a triangle with a handle. One side was smooth and sharp; the other was jagged like a bread knife. It had many purposes for painting, but now it would be something to keep her safe—a weapon. It was time to put it in her purse. She never wanted to be without something to protect herself again.

Chapter Thirty-Four

Vicki

The sky was black and blue, smeared with broken wisps of clouds that had once been whole. Vicki went into the darkness and wandered the woods next to the shore, looking for the place in her dreams, the place Catori had shown her.

Branches scraped their fingers across her shoulders, some grabbing her hair as she walked. In front, broken pieces from old trees lay horizontal on the path, sprinkled with fungi. A split pine spread its legs in the air like a man on his back. To the left was a stump broken into a thousand slivers. Beneath her feet were decaying leaves changing into mulch. Above, squeaks and rattles from the unseen echoed and mingled with the swaying branches. A flutter of crows blocked the light from the sky. Shadows of tree spirits stepped out from behind their hiding places. Sounds

Strokes of Desperation

layered in the rushing wind—fluted phrases and whistling rhythms of the birds above—cries of gulls.

Dusk began to dim into the night, and the birds' chorus faded into the sound of hoots from owls. Frogs called for their mates in the small streams made from the runoff of an earlier storm. Vicki found a path and ran toward the shore, out from the canopy of trees and into the open, looking around for familiar signs of where she was.

A new energy was mounting in the air. The storm-laden clouds were growing steadily, led gray and maroon shapes thickening, eclipsing the last patch of blue as they merged overhead. A crack of thunder in the distance sent a chill curling around her.

A gust of wind pushed against her chest while air rushed past her ears. Her face was pelted with drops kicked up by the wind. Heavy rain began to pound her light coat, blurring her vision. Already drenched, she made her way through the turbulent, unseen powers howling and whooshing past, tearing at her clothes.

"Vicki!" she heard a voice shout in the wind.

Turning, peering through the gusty mists, she couldn't see who was calling. No one was there. Should she shout back? "Here! I'm over here."

Out of the gale emerged a shape wearing bright yellow, reaching out for her hand. Not knowing if it was real or not, she extended hers and was snatched and pulled toward a rain-splattered coat. Frozen with fear, she watched as the other hand pulled back the hood for her to see a face. Even with water in her eyes, she recognized him. "David."

Wetness dripped down his face. He scowled and led her out of the open and under the cover of trees. Her feet sank in the mud as they followed a path to his truck. He opened the door for her, then climbed in himself. Water ran down her clothes and onto the seat. He flipped the heat on along with the windshield wipers, then drove off.

He hurried her inside his house as the rain pounded the ground. Then, he hung up his coat and grabbed some towels, tossing one to her, and went to stoke a fire that he had started earlier in the fireplace.

Vicki was confused. How had she gotten to this place? She had no memory of leaving Jenny's house, walking to the beach, or wandering the forest. Had David stepped into her dream?

Chapter Thirty-Five

David

David stood as Vicki stared at him like a zombie. A shadow was vacillating between two women, one living and one dead. Her eyes were distant as if she wasn't in the present but off in another world. He knew she was cold; her lips were blue. He let out a breath of frustration. Where had Vicki gone?

He tossed a towel to her, but she never used it. Her only reaction was a faraway glare. Wanting to strip off her damp clothes but afraid of how she might react, he patted her dry instead. He took her hand; there were flecks of paint on her fingernails. Maybe she would recognize where she was if she sat by the fireplace.

He guided her over to a chair so she could adjust to her surroundings, setting down a towel on the cushion and pointing for her to sit. She plopped down and just stared off into space. As her hair began to dry, he noticed blue and yellow paint stuck to the strands next to her cheek. He touched her face, and she turned. She was so childlike. It broke his heart to see her like this.

David hadn't felt this powerless since his sister died. Knowing that if he didn't do something soon, that if Vicki didn't die at the hand of another, she would take her own life. Cursing under his breath; he hated knowing this. What good was his gift if he couldn't save her? Ben believed that Vicki could show them what happened to Catori. But seeing Vicki like this, he didn't give a damn about Catori. He wanted Vicki safe.

"How did you know where to find me?" She said out of the blue, surprising him.

He ran his fingers through his hair. "Vicki, I'm worried about you."

"Was I sleepwalking?" She looked at him. Alert now. Whatever had possessed her before had now passed.

He blurted out, "I don't know what the hell you were doing out there, but damn it, you've got to stop this!"

"Stop what?" Her eyebrows went up, and she focused on him.

"Stop driving yourself crazy, painting. You're obsessed, and it's changing you into —"

"What?" She shook her head like she was throwing off the spirit.

"Her. You've changed your hair color, makeup, and clothes. Every time I see you, you look more like Catori. You've lost weight, too."

He watched as her hand went immediately to her necklace. "Anthony says that people like me looking like the girl I'm painting. It adds mystery to my show."

She was so naïve as to what was going on. This frightened him even more. Anthony had his fingers wrapped around her mind, just like Catori's ghost. He should have confronted that guy. Told him to leave Vicki alone when he first got a whiff of his stink the day Anthony took Vicki to that restaurant.

"Mystery?" he replied sarcastically. "Don't you ever wonder why all these people want pictures of this girl?" He flung out his hands in frustration.

"Because there's something special about her. They even did an article about me in the Seattle Today Magazine. For the first time in my life, I'm famous." She sat up straight in the chair and flicked her hair back.

"At what cost?" Why couldn't she see what Anthony was doing? That he was manipulating her.

Her brows narrowed again. "What are you getting at?"

He leaned in closer to her face. "Who are these people buying your paintings?"

"I don't know. I don't care, either." She crossed her arms in front of her.

"I've asked around. I think that guy is bankrolling your success," David said reluctantly.

Her eyes flashed with anger. "Anthony? No, he isn't. He's helping my career. He's even set up a show for me at the Morris Gallery in Chicago."

"Wake up, Vicki. You're not the only girl he's—" He ran his hand over his mouth. Damn it. He shouldn't tell her he caught the guy screwing another woman.

"He's what?" She put her fist on her hip.

"Never mind." David shook his head. "He's using you, Vicki. He's dangerous, and you need to get away from him."

"What makes you think that?" she demanded.

"I just know. Trust me." *God, I wish she would believe me for once.* He looked away.

She picked at her nails. "You're just jealous."

"Of him? Give me a break!" He paced back and forth in front of her. "Guys like him are just out for themselves. Haven't you learned some things aren't worth selling your soul for?"

"I don't know what you're talking about."

"I think you do, Vicki."

She gritted her teeth. "Just butt out of my life, David! I don't need you rescuing me."

"I'm just trying to help," he pleaded.

"I don't want your damn help."

"This guy you've been sleeping with that you believe is so great. He's not who you think he is. I don't trust him. I have a bad feeling about him."

"I've heard enough. Take me home, David." She stood up and headed for the door.

Damn it! He wanted to shake her and wake her up to reality, but she was already out the door.

AFTER DRIVING Vicki back to Jenny's, David started thinking like a cop again. He needed to if he was going to help her. He called Ben.

"Vicki is losing her mind. She's convinced that Anthony Tomasie will help her career, but my gut is telling me otherwise. He's trying to convince her to sell her house and go on the road. This makes zero sense to me. She can do art shows without giving up her house. She doesn't need to go anywhere. She's making herself crazy painting Catori. That ghost has a hold on her, and Tomasic is encouraging it. Trust me, Vicki is headed for a breakdown. This guy is poisoning her mind."

Ben hummed. "I wonder why she doesn't realize that?"

"I think she's scared to death because she can't pay her bills, and Tomasic is telling her if she sticks with him, she will be a success."

"What would you like me to do?"

"Vicki told me the name of the gallery in Chicago where Tomasic said he's scheduled a showing, but when I looked online, I didn't find anything mentioning her."

"What's the name?"

"It's the Morris Art Gallery. I'm going to give them a call and find out why she isn't listed, and then I'll get back to you."

David looked up the site and then called the number listed for the gallery. "I'd like to ask you some questions about an artist by the name of Vicki Milikan."

"Of course, but I'm not familiar with that name," the woman on the other end told him.

"I just want to know if Ms. Milikan will be doing a show there in the near future. I've checked your schedule online, and I didn't see her name listed. When are you doing the art show on Vicki Milikan's paintings?" he asked.

"Vicki Milikan? Let me check on the computer."

David ran his hand through his hair. He had a feeling that this was a sham. Still, he needed to know for certain.

"I don't see her in our records. Are you sure she's doing a show with us? We're booked out through next year, and her name is not on our list."

"Are there any other galleries in the Chicago area with a similar name?"

"No. Oh, wait a minute. Maybe you were referring to a private showing at Mr. Paul McMorris's home? He is a patron of the arts and has a reputation for inviting new young female artists to show their work at his parties. However, we have nothing to do with him, as our standards don't permit artists that aren't yet established to be shown in our gallery."

"Thank you." David hung up. Well, that answered a few questions regarding Mr. Tomasie's ability to set up shows for Ms. Milikan.

David sent Ben a text: **I'd like to know if the police in Chicago have anything on a guy by the name of Paul McMorris. Can you use your contacts to find out? I'm sure something fishy is going on.**

While he waited for Ben, he went out to his shop. He needed to do something with his hands, so he sanded the rough spots on a table.

An hour later, Ben called. "You were right about the show in Chicago and McMorris. It seems Mr. Tomasie was stretching the truth to Vicki.

"Apparently, one of our missing Native girls was found dead at one of his parties. Seems she was working as a prostitute and snorted too much coke—not that anyone here cares. But it got me wondering again about where the pipeline for these girls is. I started thinking about them being shipped out of state. Maybe they left willingly, thinking they were going to a job offer. I'll contact my detective friend in Bellingham and let him know what we've found."

"Thanks." David leaned back in his chair and scratched

his head. There was something he wasn't seeing. Tomasie was a womanizer—so why, with his good looks, would he be interested in Native girls? And was there a connection to Catori other than having the girl model in his art class?

"Tomasie left the state after he was fired for fooling around with his students," Ben added. "I never had a chance to interview the guy. It would be a bit tricky to corner him now with questions."

"What do you think he's up to?"

"That's what I'm going to find out. Let me know if you get any more hunches. And David?"

"Yeah."

"Keep an eye on Vicki. Make sure she doesn't leave town."

DAVID KEPT GETTING UP and looking out the window at the trees during the breaks and replays of the game. Standing, watching them sway in the wind, he was enveloped by a strange feeling he couldn't put his finger on. Last night, he'd had trouble sleeping, haunted by a disturbing dream about looking for someone in the forest. What did it mean? Was he supposed to save someone?

His phone rang. David muted the game and reached for the phone on the second ring. Not recognizing the number, he went ahead and answered the call.

"Hi, David, this is Joey Black."

Swell, the guy who wanted to screw Vicki. He sucked up his distaste for the guy and replied. "Hello, Joey. What's up?" David's gut feeling was that Joey might call. Perhaps Joey had some information he was now willing to share.

"I'm sorry about that girl, Vicki. She looks so much like Catori. I don't know what came over me. I felt drawn to her, like she was the real thing. It was weird, and I just lost control. I wanted her to be Catori so bad. I never got over losing her."

David rolled his eyes. "Yeah, Vicki does look like Catori. So, why are you calling?" He knew it wasn't just to apologize.

"There's something that I never told anyone about when I went looking for Catori."

"Go on."

"After we broke up, I drove by the street where she hung out in Bellingham, but she wasn't there. I stopped and asked some of the kids if they had seen her, and they said no. I wondered if she had gone off with some guy to our secret spot, so I decided to go and see if she was there."

"Yes, go on," David told him.

"I parked down the road, but I saw her father drive by, so I ducked down so he wouldn't see me. Then I got out. I wondered why he was in the area. Then it occurred to me that maybe Catori had told someone about our spot, and he'd come looking for it. I walked up the road and saw Catori's father's car parked at a house. I heard shouting. He was yelling at a guy on the porch. Then he knocked the guy to the ground."

David held the phone with one hand and, with the other, pulled open a drawer and took out a pen and pad. "Then what happened?"

"An alarm went off—like a house alarm, which I thought was weird because the men were standing outside."

"What did the men do?"

"They started to walk around the side of the house. But

then someone took off running in the woods. They started yelling, 'Stop!' I got the feeling that it was Catori and that maybe she had been in the house. I thought if it was, and her dad was going after her, I better try to help her before he got ahold of her and beat the shit out of her."

"I thought you said you broke up and were done with her at the time." David set the pen down.

"I know, but I still loved her, and I didn't want anything bad to happen to her. I knew those woods pretty well and thought I'd cut around to the back and distract the men so Catori could get away."

"Did she get away?" David was trying to conjure up an image of the situation in his mind.

"I guess so because they stopped chasing her after a while and came back to the house. I went to our secret spot, and she wasn't there. I searched for her but never found her. I thought she must have found her way back to the road, then to the park, and hitchhiked back to town.

"I never saw her after that. But honestly, I wasn't even sure if that was Catori they were chasing. I just assumed it was because of her father."

"Can you give me the name of the man Catori's father was arguing with? Or a description of what he looked like?" David picked up the pen, ready to write.

"No. I was so freaked out I didn't get a good look at him. I don't know who he is."

Swell. He would've liked to be able to track someone down. "Thanks for calling, Joey. Why don't you call Ben and tell him what you just told me?"

"I don't want to talk to the cops."

"Ben isn't a cop. He's a private investigator, remember? He just wants to find out what happened to Catori."

"Yeah—sure. I'm really sorry about what I did to that girl."

David tried not to think about that night.

Joey continued, "You'll let me know, won't you—what you find out about Catori? I've thought about her for years and want to know."

"Okay."

After he hung up, he turned off the TV and looked up the area on Google, searching for the house Joey had mentioned. He found one in the area. It belonged to Christine Meyers. He called Ben, but it went to voicemail.

Restless, David went to his shop and began sanding tables, keeping his phone nearby just in case Ben called. Something was about to go down, but he didn't know what. His nerves were on edge. If his message could be clearer, he'd know where to go, but right now, it wasn't.

The phone rang. It was Jenny.

"I'm worried about Vicki," she blurted as soon as he answered. "I called Ben. Can you come over? I want to show you something."

He had a feeling that it wasn't going to be good. He also knew whatever had been eating him had to do with Vicki.

He unplugged his sander and picked up his coat. It was a good thing it was a Sunday, and he had time off. Shaun had been pretty tolerant of his need to leave occasionally to follow up on his urges. Jenny must have been cluing her husband in on Vicki.

JENNY RAN over to him as soon as he stepped in the door. Her face was contorted with worry.

"Vicki's been acting strange lately. I heard her go out the back door, and I went upstairs and peeked into her studio. It scared me. You've got to see what she's been doing."

They both turned as Ben walked in the door.

"Is there a problem?" he asked.

Jenny started rambling nervously, pacing the floor while running her hands down the sides of her hair. "I care about Vicki, and this whole painting thing about doing pictures of this girl over and over is wrong. I told her to just stop and think about stuff. But she wouldn't listen." Jenny suddenly stopped and faced David. "And this Anthony guy she's been dating has been encouraging her, convincing her she'll somehow become famous for doing these paintings." Jenny threw her arms up.

David knew nothing good was going to come from these ghost paintings.

Jenny continued, "I've tried to talk some sense into her, but it's like I'm talking to a wall. She hasn't been listening, and she doesn't want to believe what is obvious to everyone else—this guy's manipulating her, and she's going along with it. Now I'm afraid she's going to go off with him to Chicago." She brought her fingers to her lips and spoke through them. "She's always been so strong and in control. I don't know why this is happening to her. I'm worried something isn't right in her mind. You've got to see what she's done."

David followed Jenny up the stairs. Ben was right behind. Jenny went down the hall to Vicki's studio.

Scattered around the room were pictures of Catori. The expressions had been taken straight out of a horror movie—wide eyes of terror, yellow and blue bruises on faces, red blood splattered across a chest. One image was pale and looked like stone. Several of the paintings had been slashed, others broken, hanging together by threads.

"I knew something was wrong with her, but this is really bad," David said, squatting down and examining the paintings on the floor.

"What do you think this means?" asked Jenny.

"It means Vicki is in trouble. Do you know where she went?"

"She left with Anthony," Jenny replied.

"Anthony Tomasie? Did she take anything with her?" Ben asked, whipping around to face her.

Jenny stood for a moment. "She—she went out the back door, so I don't know."

David jumped to his feet and followed Jenny to the room where Vicki had been staying. She opened the closet. Half the hangers were empty.

"If she was leaving, I don't know why she didn't tell me," Jenny sobbed. "This is all his fault. I know it—promising her he would make her famous."

"Come on, let's go." Ben indicated to the door.

Outside, Ben turned to David and asked, "Do you know where Anthony took Vicki? Her safety depends on it."

David closed his eyes and took a breath. *Come on, don't fail me.* Tall evergreen trees popped into his mind. "To the woods." A house in the fog appeared. "To a place in the woods."

"When I looked earlier, I couldn't find a real estate record under Tomasie's name. Do you know whose house he took her to? I want to call for police backup."

People's faces flashed through David's mind. Then, the woman he had caught Anthony with appeared. "Christine

Meyers," David said. The map on the cell phone they had shown Joey came up. "I believe it's the same place Joey mentioned."

"Interesting."

"What?" David was already turning for the car.

"Did you hear about the Native girl found dead in the woods recently? Holly Bear?"

David frowned; he didn't like where this was going. "Yes. Why?"

"Sally called and told me she remembered Holly had gone to lunch with Christine before disappearing."

Chapter Thirty-Six

Vicki

An hour earlier

VICKI RUBBED her eyes and looked again at her artwork; the faces were of fear and horror. Before her was an inner darkness, but whose—hers or Catori's?

Vicki got up from her stool, picked up a painting, and flung it across the room. It hit another and crashed to the floor. She squeezed paint onto her palette, then took a brush, splattering red, yellow, and blue on the faces that had been haunting her. Going to one, she broke it across her knee. Flaying around, she tossed canvases of Catori's image on the floor.

Staring up at the ceiling, she knew she was going insane, and this was not the way she wanted to be recognized—the psycho who painted images of a ghost. Images that required rehashing her past and echoes of someone else's. A girl she had grown to love and also hate.

Grasping her necklace, she looked down at it. Catori's story must be locked inside this little piece of wood she wore around her neck. This had to stop. Vicki reached up and tried to unscrew the chain. It wouldn't come undone. She tugged at it, trying to yank it off, but it just cut into her neck. It didn't want to let go. *Damn it!*

Looking at the damaged paintings that now littered the room, she let out a heavy sigh. Maybe her violent paintings would sell. People liked crazy shit. But did she have to turn into a psycho to paint this stuff? God, she needed a break.

Her phone buzzed.

"Hi, Vicki," Anthony's voice beamed. "I'm back in town. You're going to Chicago tomorrow, beautiful. Pack your bags. I'll pick you up in an hour."

"Anthony, I'm not going to Chicago," she reluctantly told him, glancing around at the paintings she had trashed on the floor.

"I've already booked your flight. At least come with me to check it out. I'm sure you'll love it. Stay a week, and I promise I'll fly you back if you aren't happy with the arrangement."

"Maybe I'm not cut out to be a famous artist after all."

"Are you losing your confidence? Come on, now. You're a fabulous artist. People love your work. I'll pick you up in the alley." He ended the call.

"Go," the voice demanded in her head. Maybe he was right. She was losing her confidence. Vicki went to the closet and pulled out her suitcase. Selecting a few dresses to take, she folded them and set them inside. Next, she pulled open the dresser drawers and threw her lingerie in. She could start over in Chicago. Paint something different. Couldn't she?

Flopping down on the bed, she began to cry. She didn't really want to leave. But she felt driven by an uncontrollable source. Why was she doing this? Her mind blurred. Then she heard her father's voice. "You are a worthless piece of shit." She wiped her tears and gritted her teeth. She hated him, but she was determined to be what he told her she would never be: a successful artist.

Vicki pushed against the door and went out into the alley behind the house, where Anthony was waiting. He took the suitcase from her and placed it in the back seat of his car. Vicki turned, debating whether she should tell Jenny that she would be gone for a while.

"Come on," Anthony said impatiently.

If you go back inside, you'll never leave. Vicki let out a breath. This was her one shot at success, and she had better not blow it. Vicki gathered the hem of her skirt, then slid in, and closed the door. As they slowly passed the back of her house, she saw a fresh pile of lumber, along with roof trusses. She turned to Anthony, panicked, and yelled, "Stop!"

But he kept on driving. She slumped down in her seat. She had made her choice. Vicki took out her phone and texted Jenny.

Hi, I'm leaving with Anthony to go to Chicago. Text U later.

They drove out of town, traveling along the main coastal highway toward Bellingham. Once they passed the park, Anthony turned off onto a dirt road. Tall evergreen trees lined both sides as the car sped by, flinging dust behind them. Dark trunks with arm-like branches flickered past her eyes. At a Y, they veered right and continued deeper into the woods. It felt like they had left civilization far behind. She would have never guessed this unmarked path existed after exiting the main road miles back. An uneasiness began to grow inside her.

Eventually, they arrived in front of a modern-looking house. A motion detector immediately lit up the front with floodlights. Anthony got out and opened the passenger side for her. She looked around; this place had an eerie remoteness to it.

Vicki nervously followed Anthony to the entrance, where Anthony punched in his code and swung the door open. Vicki was greeted with a sensation of déjà vu, though she had never been here before. Across a large, open room stood floor-to-ceiling windows. She wandered over and looked out. A forest thick with trees sat outside, casting a threatening darkness into the room. A shiver went down her spine.

She turned her back to the window, noticing the simple tan leather furniture facing a fireplace on one wall. A large, white bear skin rug on the dark hardwood floor was between the fireplace and a marble table. On the right was a hall with several doors, and somehow, she knew one led to a bathroom and another to the master suite. Along the side, stairs went down to what she couldn't see, but an image of a large room with pictures on the wall filled her mind's eye. Behind a large canvas was hidden a secret room. A basement door led out to the backyard. How she knew this was a mystery.

Anthony put his arm around her. "Great view, isn't it? It makes you feel like you're a million miles from anywhere."

Vicki turned to face him. "I didn't know you had a house here." Why hadn't he told her about living nearby? She had assumed he lived in Chicago.

"Yes." He kissed her cheek. "I've lived here for a long time."

"So, why did you take me to the hotel in Bellingham?"

"I thought it was more romantic." He turned her, picked up her hand, and began to slowly dance, rocking back and forth, then bending her back.

She let out a nervous giggle. He spun her around and then pulled her toward him.

"A new world is opening up for you, my beautiful artist. I hope you realize that," he whispered in her ear, placing his cheek against hers.

"I want to let you know that I'm not going to paint that girl anymore," Vicki told him.

He dropped his hold on her and stood back. "Why? I'm disappointed. She's your signature piece." He put one hand on his hip, demanding an explanation.

Surprised by his sudden irritation, she replied, "I'm ready to move on and paint something else. I'm done with her." She didn't know if she should explain to him the toll painting Catori was taking on her. If she did, would he try to force her to continue painting the girl, anyway?

"Here, let me change your mind." He snatched her hand, leading her into the bedroom.

The room had a large window with a view of the woods. The bed was covered by a faux fur spread. She reached over and touched its surface. It was soft; she knew it would feel dreamy next to bare skin. She looked at the pillows on the bed. A flash of Catori's face peeking out from under the fur came into her mind. Anthony was on top of her.

She froze. The wheels in her mind started turning. Facing Anthony, she asked, "Did you happen to know the girl I've been painting by any chance?"

"How could I know her? She's just a painting." He tossed his hand in the air as if shooing away a pesky fly.

"Did you know Catori Rein?" The image of Anthony on top of Catori was still fresh in her mind. "Did you know her nickname was Cat?"

He chuckled. "Cat?"

"After I colored my hair, you asked Cat to purr for you when we were having sex."

"Did I? Maybe it was just a fantasy."

"A fantasy by the name of Cat? That seems a bit of a coincidence, don't you think?"

"Well, maybe I did meet someone who looked like the girl in your painting when I was teaching. Perhaps her name was Catori. That was a long time ago, and you must admit your paintings have a certain seductive quality. I was fantasizing."

"Do you do that often? Fantasize about other women?"

"I fantasize about you all the time. All the special things you do to me. You're the one I can't wait to take to bed." He pushed her down on the bed and slid his hand under her top.

She grabbed it and pulled it out. "No."

He placed his fist lightly against her jaw and said, "You owe me. I'm going to have you as often and whenever I want." Then he smiled and kissed her. "My beautiful artist. Surely you will grant me this wish for all I'm doing for you?"

The front door slammed.

"Crap." Anthony sat up and put his finger to his lips. "Go wait in the bathroom until I come and get you."

"Why?"

"Just do what I say. I'll explain later." He pulled her up, then pushed her into the bathroom and closed the door.

"To hell with this," she said to herself. She put her ear to the door.

"Anthony, I know you're here," a woman's voice called.

After he left, Vicki opened the door, crept out into the hallway, and peeked around the corner.

Anthony was walking toward a woman standing in his living room. "Hi, I didn't expect you back until next week, sweetheart." He kissed her.

Vicki recognized the woman from her art show in Seattle. It was Christine. Anthony had told her they had once been in a relationship. Vicki listened intently to what Anthony and Christine were discussing.

"Did you bring her here?" Christine snapped.

"Who?"

"That little imposter. The gal from the art show who's been painting all those pictures of Catori. Christ, can you be more obvious, Anthony?"

"Don't worry. Nobody will put the pieces together. The people that recognize the girl she's painting think Vicki is clairvoyant, that's all."

"She isn't *that* talented. Hasn't she figured it out yet that you're just baiting her? You've been dragging this one out too long."

"I needed for her to trust me."

"Trust you? What were you thinking?"

"It is easier if they trust me first."

"*She's too visible*. Get rid of her."

"I'm taking her to Chicago."

"When?"

"Tomorrow."

"What about her connections in town? Won't they suspect something?"

"She has no family, doesn't have a boyfriend, and only a few friends. She already told the woman she's living with that she's selling her house. I'll have an agent deal with it. So, who's going to come looking for her? You're making this more complicated than it is."

"I don't want her here unless she's locked up."

Vicki peeked around the corner and watched as the woman walked over to the window and looked out. While both of their backs were turned, Vicki tiptoed to the stairs and went down to the lower floor.

The room was dark. It took a minute for her eyes to adjust. When they did, she saw the walls were filled with paintings, just as she had envisioned. She moved closer to them. These were *her* paintings, the ones she thought she'd sold in Seattle.

Following her intuition, or perhaps Catori's spirit, she began feeling along the wall under a large canvas until she heard a click. She pushed, and the wall revolved to reveal a room. When she entered, Vicki swore she heard the faint sound of crying, but no one was there except her.

She turned on the light. It appeared to be an office. A table sat along a wall with a laptop on top. Drawn to it, Vicki went over and touched the space bar. The screen lit up with photos of at least a dozen girls. She stared at their faces; they all appeared to be Native American.

In the bottom row, she recognized her face. Why did

Anthony have a photo of her? She clicked on it, and a video popped up. *Shit.* He had filmed her having sex with him in the hotel room in Bellingham. Quickly, she hit return, and the screen returned to the other girls. She had a bad feeling about being in this house with Anthony.

She looked around the room and saw another door. Curious, she went over, opened it, and peeked inside. A bed sat in the corner. Straps hung from the rear wall, along with restraints. An image of being tossed on the bed flickered in her mind. When she tried to get up, she was forced back down. These were images from Catori's memory.

Vicki heard voices above.

"You got away with the others, but you failed to reign in this one, letting your dick get the best of you again."

"Hey, she's a real treat. Knows what to do, unlike those kids on the street."

"Did you sell her while you were in Seattle like you promised, or keep her just for yourself?"

"Yes, I had a couple of guys come by. She never suspected a thing. I slipped a roofie into her drink. I sold her once in Bellingham, too."

"She needs to perform, not just get used."

"She will."

"I hope you know what you're doing because I don't want any trouble."

Vicki backed up in shock, tripping over her feet and knocking a metal container to the ground. That was why she felt drugged those times. Why did he do that? *This doesn't make sense.* He said he was helping with her career, but as what?

"Did you hear something?" Christine asked.

"Crap. She's downstairs."

"You didn't have her locked up? You idiot! Go get her," Christine said.

Vicki heard footsteps on the wooden stairs. She went back to the bedroom, closed the door, and crouched down next to the bed. She rummaged through her purse until she found what she was looking for.

The door to the room opened, and Anthony appeared.

"Vicki, what are you doing in here?" Anthony hovered over her.

She stood up. "I." Her heart was racing. "I don't want to go to Chicago with you." Her sleeve was pulled down, and her fingers wrapped around the handle of her spatula.

"Wasn't being a famous artist your dream? Do you want to throw that opportunity away now? You're just on the verge of success."

"That's not why you want to take me to Chicago, though, is it?"

He laughed. "Smart girl." Then he came toward her, backing her up against the wall. She held her arm with the spatula down stiffly.

"What's going on? I want to know why you want me to go with you to Chicago."

Anthony reached over, stroked her face, then leaned in and placed his lips on hers, shoving his tongue into her mouth. His hand reached down, grabbing the contour of her butt, and pulling her toward him.

When he was done kissing her, he moved her hair from her shoulder, looked into her eyes, and whispered, "Once a whore, always a whore."

Vicki tensed. "What did you call me?"

"New York, beautiful. As I recall, you worked for a

friend of mine there." Anthony kissed the side of her neck, then bit it, holding her skin between his teeth.

"You knew about Mr. Bianchi all along?" Her stomach tightened.

"You're not the first girl I encouraged to go to New York to follow her dreams." Now, his teeth pulled on her earlobe. His breath was like warm venom on her skin.

"What about Catori? Did you send her to New York, too?"

Anthony put his hand around her throat, his fingers touching the base of her ears. "Catori. Beautiful, sweet Catori. One of my favorites. I kept her in this very room for myself. She drove me crazy. I could screw that little girl all night long."

Anthony pressed his lower body against her. His sudden arousal was obvious. Vicki knew if she had any chance of escaping this monster, she'd need to maintain control. She'd have to mentally block out what he was doing to her, just as she'd done every time before.

He dropped his hand from her throat. "When I found out that you were painting portraits of her, I couldn't believe my luck. After a little wine, you were eager to sell your services to me for an art show. Do you remember? Ah, you were a hot one that night. Then you changed your looks to be more like Catori. That made the deal even sweeter."

Vicki remembered the photos of the girls on the computer. "Did you kill that Native girl, Holly? The one in the news whose body they recently found?"

"Me? Oh heavens, no. I did enjoy her for a little while, though. Unfortunately, she and Christine had a falling out. A pity. I'm sure I could have fetched a good price for her if she hadn't tried to escape. Christine is an excellent shot, in case you were thinking of trying to get away."

Vicki felt the brush of fabric sliding up her leg and the warmth of his hand following it. His fingers inched up her inner thigh.

"You make a delicious replacement for Cat. I like it when you purr for me. Can I make you purr for me now?" He grinned, pleased with himself.

Vicki growled. She wanted to knee him in the balls. "What happened to Catori?"

"Hell, if I know. If her father hadn't shown up when he did, she wouldn't have gotten away. No one would have believed her story if they found her. Her kind are easy to steal because no one cares what happens to them. Poor, desperate girls like you are easy to manipulate. Just wave a carrot, and they come willingly."

Anthony tapped Vicki's inner thigh for her to spread her legs, testing her response to his commands.

"You're crazy." She moved her legs apart, and he smiled.

Anthony grinned, looking into Vicki's eyes, then unzipped his pants. "Come on, enough talk. I want to fuck."

While he fumbled with his member, she put her hand up, shoving him and moving past him. "Keep it in your pants, little man. I'm leaving."

"On no, you're not." He grabbed her arm, jerking her back toward him. Then, with the back of his wrist, he smacked her hard across the face.

She glared at him. *No one hits me!* Clutching the necklace around her neck, Vicki's anger exploded, and she felt Catori's energy merge with hers.

"Don't act so put out, sweetheart. You're my whore now, and you'll do what I say." He came toward her, trying to intimidate her.

With all the strength she and Catori could summon, Vicki shoved her hand forward, and the razor-sharp tip of the spatula tore through his shirt and pierced his stomach. Then she pulled it back out as blood blossomed on his shirt.

"What the hell?" His wide eyes glared at her in shock, then down at the gash. "You little bitch." His hand went out to her, but his pain caused him to drop it.

Before he could block her, she managed to shove the spatula again, harder this time, into his lower abdomen, slicing him deeper. "This is for Catori." And again, wiggling it back and forth with the handle, then pulling it out. "This is for all the other girls you screwed." And again. "This is for sending me to Mr. Bianchi and selling me to those dirty men."

Anthony put out a hand for her to stop. When she did, blood poured from his wounds, and Anthony bent over in pain.

"Hello? Anthony?" Christine's voice called. "Do you have that girl with you?"

Vicki's head shot around, and she tossed the weapon back in her purse and left the bedroom, going to the open secret door in the office.

"Ah, ah! Christine. In here." Vicki heard Anthony moan in pain as he staggered out of the other room.

Stepping out into the hall, Vicki caught a glimpse of Christine on the stairs, holding on to the railing with one hand, the other holding a gun. Anthony was leaning in the doorway now, holding his stomach, his shirt soaked in blood.

Christine ran over to Anthony. "What happened?"

Vicki's mind flashed into overdrive. There was a door down here somewhere. She went to the exterior wall, searching for it. It was to the left. She found the door, unlocked it, then went outside. An alarm went off, giving away her exit.

"Stop, you little bitch!" Christina yelled, running after her.

Stepping around lawn furniture, confused by her surroundings, Vicki crouched down behind a shed, pulled out her phone, and called David.

He picked up before it rang. "We're on our way."

She slid the phone back into her purse, then went around to the front of the house. It was midday, but a motion detector light went on, lighting up the driveway.

Vicki had no idea when David would arrive. She needed to escape now.

There was forest on each side of the house. She turned to the side where it was the thickest, dropped her purse on the path, and ran.

As Vicki went farther into the woods, her surroundings took on a surreal glow. She had been here in her dreams. Catori had been here. The sound of a gunshot startled her. She turned.

"Stop right now, or I swear I'll kill you," she heard Christine yell behind her.

Vicki glanced around. Which way was it to the main road? She knew the road forked and turned, but it was treelined, and nothing stood out as recognizable from inside the thicket. Should she make a guess and try to go parallel to the road or go deeper into the woods?

Another gunshot flew past, hitting a branch nearby.

Panicked, Vicki took off through the trees. Images flashed around her like a movie in fast-forward. Light silhouetted a grove of dark shapes, rotting stumps, fallen logs, ghostly nets of lichen, and fluorescent moss flew by. Was she running, or was it Catori? The sudden sting of a branch striking her across the face convinced her it was real. God, where could she hide in here? If she stopped, would they find her?

Anthony's house was remote. She hadn't seen any other houses along the way. Nothing made sense.

A shadow ran through the forest behind her, then stopped. Another crack whizzed by. Christine was getting closer.

Fear in every heartbeat pushed Vicki forward into the shelter of the forest. She leaped over a log, having no idea of where she was going. The trees all looked the same, yet quite different. She was compelled to head north.

Surveying the situation, she took a couple of breaths. Before her was an obstacle course she hadn't prepared for, yet intuitively knew the way. A deer path that wandered to the left off the main trail was narrow and appeared to be a dead end, but just beyond, it picked up again behind some tall ferns and broken boughs.

She moved forward, sprinting along the path, lifting her legs, jumping over roots and rocks while dodging protruding limbs. A clearing ahead was lit from above by streams of light poking down from the hidden sky. Was that a safe area, or would she be exposed? A squirrel sped up the trunk of a tree. She looked up at the light. In a forest full of pine trees, climbing was not an option.

Stepping into the shadows around the lit area, she found her feet now trampling ferns and mushrooms. A trickling stream hidden beneath a covering of rotting leaves and bark flowed beneath her feet, making the ground slippery. The smells went from sweet fir trees to wet, earthy soil mixed with bark and the stench of a rotting carcass. Life and death were hidden all around her. She shook at the thought of all the creepy things burrowing out of sight—insects, worms, salamanders, slugs, and snakes. The glow of golden eyes ahead meant they were watching her, those animals of the forest, rodents, birds, raccoons, and coyotes. She had been to this place in her dreams many times before.

She fought her fear and confusion. Horrified by the wildness raging inside her, pushing her deeper into this nightmare, Vicki knew she was running away from something evil. She stopped and rested on a log. Her sides hurt, and her feet were bruised from slamming into trees across the trail.

Why did she think escaping through this canopy of light and dark woods was the answer? Everything was closing in on her. It wasn't safe here. Another shot rang out, echoing, not easily revealing where it was coming from.

Tears mixed with her dripping nose, and her eyes stung from the dusty spores flying from everything she touched. She wiped her face and brushed back her hair. Where to go now? Left or right?

Chapter Thirty-Seven

David

Once the house came into view, David knew Vicki was close by. He pulled into the driveway behind the white Maserati and jumped out of the truck. Ben's car was right behind. David stood, searching for a path on the side of the road into the forest until he found one. "She's in the woods. I'm going after her. You stay here and wait for the police," David told Ben.

"You don't have a weapon. I'm going with you!" Ben yelled.

"Stay. I can handle it." He'd figure out what to do when the time came.

David entered into the darkness beneath the trees and then heard a gunshot. He scanned the woods for where the noise had come from. The width and depth of trees went on for miles.

Strokes of Desperation

She went north.

He took off running, leaping over downed logs and branches. It was a broken forest of obstacles. The light coming in from holes in the ceiling of outstretched evergreens played tricks on his eyes. He'd have to depend on his gut to guide him through this maze. Vicki had gotten a head start, but that may not be to her advantage. The woman who lived here was probably familiar with all the trails and deer paths. She'd know the shortcuts and could circle Vicki like an eagle going after a fish in a pond.

Pushing branches aside, he froze when he realized there was no clear path ahead. He'd need to double back. It would cost him valuable time. *Shit.* How long could Vicki keep running before exhaustion took over?

It was a maze in there. At the intersection of two paths, he started to follow one, then immediately knew it was wrong. He turned and went the other way. This was a network of confusing choices. He soon found several matted-down animal trails that led to dead ends. Looking out past the ferns and saplings that littered the immediate area, his vision was blocked by the trunks of tall evergreens in every direction. The only compass he had was his intuition.

The smell of a dead animal rotting nearby made him look to the side. Crows sat pulling out bits of what a coyote had left behind. It was easy to forget that these woods had their own cycle of life, dependent on the survival of the fittest.

He continued down the path, deeper into the woods, until he came upon a giant trunk that had toppled in a windstorm. He scurried up on top of the downed tree, where its giant roots reached out like sea coral, and then looked around. Another shot rang out.

Concentrate.

Ahead, a shape flickered through the trees. He could've mistaken it for a deer, except the figure suddenly stopped, and the sound of a gun went off again. To his side, a flutter of wings sent a bird into the air. His pulse was racing. He needed to be quiet if he was going to sneak up on the woman.

His senses were on high alert. The forest was green with lush vegetation and moss. A snake slithered across the dirt. Sweat was dripping down his neck. He batted away a pesky fly. Willing himself not to make a sound, he got closer to Christine. She was taking a stance with the gun held out in front of her. He intuitively knew Christine had a clear shot at Vicki, and it would only be a matter of seconds before she pulled the trigger. He threw a stick at her.

"Drop the gun, Christine!"

She swung her weapon toward him. He ducked for cover. A chunk of wood blew in the air from the tree next to him. When he peeked from behind his protection, she wasn't there. He could feel her, though. She knew where he was, and he didn't have a gun.

At the snap of a twig, he turned to find her fifteen feet away with the barrel pointed at his chest. Making her way closer, she stepped around a thicket of snarled wood and a hollowed-out tree. Christine stood on a log, smiling. "Well, who do we have here?"

A low growl came from behind her, and she glanced back. A skinny, mangy-looking coyote was crawling out from a den, baring its teeth. Several pups whimpered behind it.

While Christine was distracted, David picked up a moss-covered branch and threw it, knocking her off balance. She fell backward onto the wet leaves. The coyote growled and lunged at her from behind. David threw a rock and yelled. The animal stopped and looked over at him. Christine sat up and pointed the gun at him, and he jumped to the side the instant she pulled the trigger.

The coyote ran from the scene with its pups in tow. In the confusion, David smacked Christine's gun-wielding hand with a branch. She released it, and David jumped forward, kicking it away. It rolled under a log.

Christine got to her feet. They stood eye to eye. She spun around with her leg out and kicked the branch from his hand. He could tell by her posture that she had studied martial arts, but so had he.

In a fury of hands and legs, he blocked her moves. She twisted around, grabbed a spear-like piece of wood from the ground, and lunged for him. He quickly stepped aside, reaching for the wood as her body propelled forward. They struggled for control, but he was stronger than her and ripped it away.

She tripped over a rock, giving him the opportunity to restrain her. He reached down and yanked her up, then twisted her arm behind her back. Sweat was pouring down the sides of his head, and he was breathing hard.

A beam from a flashlight lit up the trees nearby.

"Over here!" David yelled.

Ben and a police officer came running up the path. The officer pulled out his gun.

"She's all yours," David told them, shoving Christine toward them, then he nodded at Ben and took off through the woods again, searching for Vicki.

Chapter Thirty-Eight

Vicki

A flashlight's beam pierced the forest, creating a glow in the trees around Vicki. She ducked down so no one would see her. Paralyzed, not knowing what to do, she closed her eyes. In her mind, she was still running. The woods flew past on fast forward, making her dizzy. Forced to open her eyes again, she prayed. She didn't know where she was, where the road was, or how far she was from Anthony's house. Why was she being hunted? Or were they hunting Catori? Was this just another dream of jumbled-up images? She was going insane. That was the only answer.

She pushed her tired body up, then walked across a log that stretched to a pile of gray. Reaching a snarl of exposed roots, she turned back, then jumped, landing on her rump in the dirt. Sitting quietly, she listened. In the distance, she heard voices but couldn't make out what they were saying other than occasionally yelling her name.

Sitting in the dampness, wondering when she would wake up from this nightmare, Vicki rocked back and forth. *I just want my old life back. I want you out of my head, Catori.*

She reached up and yanked furiously at the necklace, not caring as it bit into her skin. She pulled and wrestled with the bauble's chain until it finally broke and released the wooden piece into her palm. Standing, Vicki hurled the necklace high in the air, watching as it fell back down through an opening in a split tree.

Twigs broke nearby. Vicki dropped to her knees, huddling on the ground in fear.

"Vicki are you all right?" the familiar voice asked.

She leaped up into David's arms, clinging to him. He held her tight. Tears flowed down her face. Adrenaline was still racing through her.

"I've got you. You're safe now. Nobody's going to hurt you."

Through hiccup-filled sobs, she asked, "How did you know where to find me?"

"I just knew where to look. I'm so glad you weren't hurt."

DAVID LED her back through the woods to the road and down to the place where she had escaped. A police car was sitting in the driveway. Christine had her head down and was in handcuffs. An aid car pulled up with its red lights flashing. Someone jumped out, opened the back door, and Anthony was wheeled out on a gurney. Ben, who was talking to an officer, looked up and nodded at David. Another officer walked out of the house with the computer that Vicki had seen downstairs in the secret room.

"Vicki, are you okay?" Ben asked, coming over to her like a momma bear.

Okay? She was just starting to let what had happened seep into her mind. It had all seemed unreal. Looking at the activity around her, she wondered if what she'd experienced had been a nightmare. It must have been real because there had never been police cars before.

Vicki pushed back her hair, then tilted her head back and closed her eyes.

"I know now."

"What?" Ben asked.

"I know what happened to Catori." No one had told her what had happened. She just knew. Perhaps Catori had been trying to tell her all along. Their stories had intertwined, and it was hard to distinguish whose was whose.

"I'm listening. Tell me what you know," Ben replied.

"She's in the woods. Her body is inside the base of an old tree."

"Do you know who was responsible for her death?"

"Yes. Everyone."

"Excuse me?" Ben angled his head to the side.

"Catori was running away from life on the reservation, her father, her boyfriend, Christine, and Anthony. She wanted to be free, to find a better life somewhere else. Both Christine and Anthony promised her they would help her. It was a lie. He did awful things to her. She tried to escape by running through the woods."

Vicki opened her eyes and wiped away a tear. "Catori

fell inside a tree and was stabbed by a piece of wood. Her spirit flew off, and took refuge in the necklace I found. I became her conduit, painting her back to life. Catori wanted me to know her story, but our pain got all tangled up in memories. She wanted revenge against Anthony and was using me. She also wanted me to bring her necklace to the place where she died."

"Where is the necklace?"

"It's with her in the bowels of the tree."

Chapter Thirty-Nine

David

After Vicki gave her statement to the police for their report, David led her over to his truck, opening the passenger door for her. He worried that some part of Vicki was now lost along with the necklace in the rotting tree. Would she fully recover from her harrowing ordeal, or had the cursed necklace somehow stolen a piece of her soul, taking her most cherished memories with it?

Searching for even a flicker of warmth between them, he came up only with the faintest glow. Her hand was icy cold when he helped her into the truck, and now she sat quietly and withdrawn beside him. He glanced over at her as he pulled onto the road. Her clothes were still muddy from her escape, and her face was streaked with little paths where tears had fallen. Dark bruises covered her arms and legs where she had struggled, and her dress was badly torn

Strokes of Desperation

from the branches as she fled through the woods. Her long brown hair was a tangled mess around her shoulders. She looked almost like a woodland nymph who had been cast out from the forest.

While traveling in heavy silence down the dark road, they both avoided looking back at the looming shadows behind them that hid the evil acts that had taken place on that cursed property.

A chill crept over David as he drove. Suddenly, an animal darted across the road ahead, and he slammed on the brakes just in time to watch a deer disappear into the trees. He felt his heart racing, and a disturbing thought came to him. Could there be souls of other lost women wandering in these woods, unable to find escape even in death? He let out a weary sigh. As much as he wanted to, he knew it was not his destiny to find them or free their spirits. That task would fall to the police now that this evil place had been brought to light. His only mission now was to protect and care for the living woman beside him.

David looked over again at Vicki. She sat with her eyes closed, retreating deep into herself. Ever since the storm had brought that rotting tree crashing down onto her house, it was as if she had been locked in battle with her own private demons, and he had been forced to stand helplessly by, watching her struggle. She was just so stubbornly independent, determined to make it through on her own even as she endured a kind of personal hell.

Alone with his swirling thoughts as he drove, David wondered if Vicki had any idea just how much she meant to him. More than anything, he wanted to be the one to pull her back from the brink of devastation. He wanted to be her rescuer, her hero. His intuition enabled him to stop

Christine from killing Vicki tonight, but was that enough? Could he ever truly free her from the demons that haunted her?

As he drove down the winding county road toward home, David glanced again at Vicki's fragile form in the passenger seat beside him. Right now, all he wanted to do was take her in his arms, hold her close, and wash away all the pain she had suffered. To somehow replace all of those traumatic memories with hope for brighter days ahead.

Over their time together, he had grown to truly love her. If only she could look at him with that same love shining in her eyes, he would do everything in his power to show her that life could still be rich and beautiful.

Vicki stirred slightly in her seat, turning to look out the window into the dark night. David studied her profile, bathed in the dim light from the moon above. Even with the bruises and disheveled hair, she was still so beautiful to him. He ached to reach out to her but hesitated, unsure if his touch would be welcomed right now.

"Thank you for coming," Vicki said softly, her voice raspy. David glanced over again, surprised to hear her speak after so long in silence.

"I knew you were in trouble," he replied gently. "I'm just sorry it took me so long to get there."

Vicki just nodded, her eyes glistening with fresh tears. She continued staring out into the darkness as the truck made its way down the rural roads.

David's mind raced as he drove. He remembered their first meeting - was it only a few months ago? She had teased him when he asked about bringing in his driftwood tables for her to sell. "Rejects from the sea," she called them. When he sliced his finger on a nail, he forgot to hammer down on the underside of one table, she pulled out a first aid kit and insisted she clean his wound and put the bandage on. It was only a tiny prick, but it bled like it was worse than it was. He didn't think it warranted the fuss she was making, but he was enjoying the attention. When her hand touched his skin, he felt something, a pleasant sensation. That was his first clue that there was something there between them. She must have felt it too because she gave him a curious look, then backed away.

Then, the night of the storm, he got the opportunity to hold her and never wanted to let go. Protecting her became his mission, though he struggled with keeping her safe. She had been wary of him at first, stubbornly insisting she could handle things herself. But he'd had seen the strain in her eyes, the sleepless nights haunting her. He knew where to find her when she was lost. Something grew over time between them—a connection that went beyond her need for a hug. He had found himself wanting to know her, to understand her past hurts. And he thought she had started to let him in, little by little. Until the ghost in the paintings stirred up the demons again. And she turned to that slimebag Anthony and his lies, believing he could make her dreams come true. Afraid and under the spell of Catori, she lost sight of who she was—insisting she could endure her nightmares alone.

David sighed, focusing on the road ahead. Glancing over at Vicki, he longed to see her flash that defiant, playful smile he had come to love. To see the light dance in her eyes once more. But those parts of her seemed muted now, faded like a damaged photograph. He tightened his grip on the steering wheel and renewed his vow to help Vicki reclaim everything this evil had tried to rob from her.

Chapter Forty

Vicki

Vicki sat quietly as David drove her to his house and parked in the driveway. She was exhausted from all that had happened in the last two months—tired of trying to manage everything on her own. She was drained from reliving all her nightmares. But for some reason, she knew that by facing them, she had gained power over them. A quiet peace was beginning to settle within her in their place.

When the truck stopped next to his house, she turned to David. "You always seem to show up when—"

"You need a hug." David's sad face now held a half-smile. He pulled her over to him and wrapped his arms around her, then kissed the top of her head.

She looked up at him. She had been falling in love with him but didn't want to admit it. "I'm sorry for being such a crazy lady. At least now you can go back to your own life and not worry about me anymore."

"Oh, I don't think so." His blue eyes twinkled as he looked at her. "We need to talk."

"About what?" She turned her body to face him.

He tucked a strand of hair behind her ear. "About why you won't let me help you."

"Why do you want to help someone like me?"

He picked up her hand. "Because I have feelings for you, and it hurts me to see you suffer."

"No, don't say that." She frowned and withdrew her hand and set it in her lap. "You're a nice guy. Nice guys don't belong with girls like me. They should be with girls who come from good families and have decent jobs." She wasn't worthy of a man like him. She was ashamed. Men had used her for pleasure. He must have known that.

"Who says?"

"David, trust me. You don't want me." She choked back a sob and gazed out the window.

He placed his hand on top of hers and squeezed it. "Trust goes both ways. You need to trust me too."

"I do, it's just that—" Before he came along, she'd never wanted anyone to get that close to her.

"You're afraid of me because you've been hurt."

Vicki nodded her head. She wanted to believe that he wasn't just putting on an act and wouldn't break her heart once she let her guard down. She wanted him to genuinely love her, not just say the words.

"I'm not going to use you and toss you aside if that's what you think. I promise." He touched her chin. "I want to show you how special you are, that you deserve love and respect."

Her eyes filled. She wanted to feel loved more than anything—especially by him.

He placed his lips on hers. She brought her arms up, pulling him toward her, letting go of her resistance, losing herself in him as he continued kissing her. He was taking her deeper into a place of comfort and desire. Her troubles washed away like swirls of paint from a dirty brush soaking in clean water. He was freeing her from the anxiety that had clung to her, unlocking the door to her feelings that she had kept shut for so long. He made her feel accepted, not for what she could do for him, but because he cared for her. She craved the love he was showing her. A tear slipped from the corner of her eye.

Neither of them wanted the kiss to end. Breaking away, they were both breathing heavily, trying to regain their composure.

"Ahh. I've wanted to do that for a long time," David said softly, grinning, stroking the side of her cheek with his thumb. His eyes danced as they looked deeply into hers.

So had she, but she wouldn't allow herself to go there.

His face took on a serious look. He put his hands on her shoulders and looked her in the eyes. "But if we're to be together, I need you to promise me that you'll be monogamous. This means no flirting around with other men. I'll do anything for you if I know I can trust you. I want you always to be honest with me and tell me if I ever make you unhappy. Just don't play games. Do you think you can do that?"

Vicki swallowed, then let out a sigh. He was talking about wanting a committed, loving relationship with her. Was she ready for that? *God, yes.* "I don't know what to say."

Strokes of Desperation

"Say yes, David. I want to be in a relationship with you." He watched her. "And we'll see where it goes from there."

"Okay." She smiled.

"Okay, what?" he said playfully.

She repeated his words. "Yes, David. I want to be in a relationship with you and won't mess around with anyone else."

He grinned and bent down for another kiss.

Vicki shook her head. "I'm tired and dirty. Can you take me back to Jenny's now?"

"Until your house is ready, I'd like you to stay with me."

Her mouth dropped open. "Here? With you?"

"I know you've been through a lot, and I just want to ease your burden. With me, you can relax and not have to worry about how you're going to survive. I have space in my warehouse if you want to paint. We'll get you creating something you can be proud of. That way, you'll be ready to move into your house and open your gallery again soon."

This new relationship with David was going to take some getting used to. Then she thought about what was waiting for her at Jenny's house—the paintings, the crazy dreams. Were they really over? She was tired of all of it. He was offering her refuge from all that haunted her, a place to help her heal from her wounds.

"I can't believe you would do that for me."

"In case you thought I wanted something in return, I'm not expecting you to sleep with me while you're here. I don't want to pressure you into doing anything that doesn't feel genuine. But I'll be more than happy to wrap myself around you and keep you safe at night," he teased. "And while we're hugging, you can tell me if there is anything else you'd like me to do to make you feel better." He kissed her hand.

"Oh, David." Vicki shook her head. Why had it taken her so long to recognize this remarkable man?

Epilogue

David would be arriving soon, so she'd need to get things in order to close for the day. Vicki looked out the window at the clouds off in the distance, and a chill cascaded down her back. She never wanted to go through a storm as bad as the one that had caused the tree to crash through her roof ever again.

Vicki strolled around the shop area of her house. Many of the original artists had brought their items back for her to sell. In the glass case were handmade earrings and necklaces. Hand-knitted scarves and hats hung from a coat rack. A new display of her painted sailboats and seagulls hung from the wall. In one corner was a gray table made from driftwood.

Vicki had put a sign in the window announcing children's art classes, which she taught on Sunday afternoons to tourists and local kids. She'd even created a special section on the wall where each child's artwork was matted and displayed.

She had returned to painting what she knew—boats

and sea life—and added portraits of people on the beach enjoying themselves.

"I bought a boat!"

Vicki turned to find the young man she had sold the sailboat painting to on the day of the storm. He was bursting with pride and enthusiasm, coming toward her. He reached into his pocket to pull out his phone and showed Vicki a photo of his new boat—a *San Juan 24*.

She smiled. "I thought your dream was for a larger sailboat. One you could sail around the world in."

He smiled. "Ah, I think a small boat is just fine. I don't need to have the biggest boat on the dock. I'm happy as long as I can take her out for a sail."

"Sometimes one can lose sight of the value of the little things in life when they run after big dreams," Vicki admitted to him and to herself.

"Yeah, like love and friendship," he said. "I got engaged, too."

"Congratulations. Yes, like love and friendship," Vicki replied with a grin.

She waved goodbye to the young man, locked the doors and went outside. Vicki pulled her sweater around her neck and walked to Jenny's shop to wait for David.

"Hi, Vicki," Jenny called when the door opened.

Vicki went over and gave her friend a hug. "Thanks for putting up with me for as long as you have—and storing my paintings."

"I'm just glad everything worked out for you—and David." She smiled.

They heard a commotion from the other room and went to investigate. Vicki walked into the kitchen area to find David coming in the back door. His hair was tousled.

He ran his fingers through it to smooth it back down and came over to Vicki, smiling.

"It's okay to kiss her." Jenny giggled.

He stepped forward and gave Vicki a quick kiss on the cheek. "You ready?"

"Yes."

"Then let's get to it." He trotted up the stairs, and Vicki followed.

When she opened the door to the room she had used as her studio, she immediately saw all the hurt and pain she and Catori had shared. Vicki sighed. She'd made peace with her past and was ready to move on.

She and David began picking up paintings and carrying them downstairs and out the back door, repeating the process until the room was empty.

"I think that's the last one." David closed up the back of his truck. Vicki looked at the pile of paintings, then crawled into the passenger seat.

Once they arrived at David's, they carried the canvases and laid them on the sand next to the fire pit. David stacked the paintings in the center and lit the kindling underneath. Slowly, a plume of smoke snaked up, flames ate the edges, and the pictures collapsed into the hungry bonfire.

Vicki watched tearfully as Catori's images shriveled and curled, then melted into dark smoke that billowed up into the sky.

She laid her head on David's chest, and he wrapped his arms around her. Her memories of abuse crumbled into ashes, along with the story she had painted of the girl in the woods.

IF YOU ENJOYED this book please leave a review. Your opinion maters. Readers read reviews and it helps them decide if this book is something they would like to read.

HERE IS a sample from Taken from the Sea another book in the Cook's Cove collection. It is a stand alone.

The sun drops, and the incoming tide now pushes at the dock. The salty scent of the sea mingles with the evening breeze as Colleen steps aboard Paradise, her Erin Citation thirty-four-foot sailboat. Undoing the ropes and pulling in the buoys, her body adjusts to the boat's movement. She makes her way to the stern and starts the engine. With steady hands on the wheel, she skillfully steers away from the marina. She guides Paradise westward through the cover of night, where she last saw the sun sink below the horizon. Glancing back, she spies the faint glow of headlights as a car pulls into the marina parking lot. *Did someone follow her there?*

Strokes of Desperation

With worry on her mind and troubles stalking her, the allure of the sea calls to Colleen. It's the only place she's free. The night's cool wind brushes her face as she stands at the wheel, steering the boat to her sacred place. Her ebony hair billows behind her like untamed strands of silk as the wind runs its fingers through it. Above her, the night sky twinkles with a tapestry of stars, and the face of the moon looks down upon her.

As she approaches the tiny island, ripples splash against the hull. She kills the engine and drops the anchor. Here, in this peaceful sanctuary, she hopes to remain hidden. Tonight, she'll sleep onboard her boat. At first light, she'll search for a place to hide.

Thoughts race through her mind as she contemplates her options. She could stop at one of the San Juan islands and get supplies, leave Puget Sound, head for the open sea, and sail down the coast to Oregon. After that, she could stock up and maybe head for Hawaii.

She frowns. As much as she wants to leave, running away from her life isn't the answer. Besides, she owes it to her father to return and participate in his business, even if her role is minor. Contacting the police is the best option. They can solve the mystery.

Colleen grabs a bottle of wine from the refrigerator and pulls out the cork, filling her glass. Looking up at the night sky, she stares into space. Soon, her body relaxes, and she lets go of her troubles.

Pouring another glass of wine, listening. In the distance, a strange sound travels in waves on the wind. It's a song, or at least she thinks it is. Her mind stirs. She's heard it before. However, she can't place where or when.

After she finishes her drink, she heads below deck to her

bunk and crawls in. The gentle rhythm of the waves against the boat rocks her to sleep.

AT DAWN, seals climb onto the deck and nudge open the hatch. A low growl pulls her from sleep. They tug at her blanket, letting the cool air touch her skin. Colleen turns and then sits up. Big, dark eyes stare at her. They smell of the sea—salt and fish. The large creatures wiggle and use their flippers to go back upstairs.

Colleen climbs out of her bunk. Discarding her nightshirt, she pulls on her wetsuit and zips it up. Its gray, spotted design resembled the sleek skin of a seal, allowing her to mingle with these marvelous creatures underwater. On the deck, she tucks her hair securely inside the cap. The seals slip into the water one by one, their heads bobbing, watching as if calling for her to join them. Colleen adjusts her diving tank, pulls down her face mask, puts her legs over the side, the mouthpiece in, and jumps.

Beneath the waves, Colleen enjoys a sense of liberation from being one with the creatures that surround her. She follows their lead away from the boat to the nearby refuge island. Now, she's only a shadow in the water.

As she approaches the shallow pebbles below, she pushes toward the surface. Breaking free from the depth, she looks at the island. Spotting a secluded spot along the shore, she swims toward it. This is her secret place, where she escapes from all the stresses of the world. Here, she can be alone.

Emerging from the sea, she steps onto the sand, her feet sinking into the warm softness. She removes her face mask and sets her tank on the sand, leaving them at the water's edge. The rising sun casts a glow on the gray rocks where small groups of seals are resting. Their bark welcomes her. Walking farther up the beach, she removes her hood and shakes out her long hair, allowing it to cascade down her back, combing it with her fingers. She unzips the front of her suit and sheds it, discarding it on the sand. Without the confinement of clothing, she climbs to a flat, worn rock, sets her elbows on the hard surface behind her, and leans back, letting the sun caress her bare body.

The warmth feels good. Colleen pushes strands of her hair off her chest and flicks them over her shoulder. The surrounding seals shift, readjusting as they return to their spots, grunting at one another. Thin clouds traverse the sky overhead while gray seagulls ride the wind like kites in flight. Breathing in the salt-tinged air, she tastes the sea on her lips. The rhythmic lapping of the tide becomes her heartbeat, its ebb and flow resonating within her soul. At this moment, in this sliver of paradise, she's free from the expectations of her mother and sister and her thoughts about her father, Eric, and the men following her. All her worries and troubles dissipate in the gentle breeze, leaving a profound sense of peace within her. She closes her eyes.

Stretching her arms, the mood shifts around her, and a sudden commotion disrupts her tranquility. The seals, once calm, now grunt and bark, their bodies scattering across the rocks. Colleen's eyes snap open, her senses heightened by their confusion. In a split second, her instincts kick in, propelling her into action.

A woven net sails through the air, crossing her line of vision. *What the heck?* She rolls to the side, dodging it before it lands. Springing to her feet, adrenaline surges through her. Sensing her urgency, the seals circle her, forming a protective barrier.

A voice cuts through the barking chaos. "No, you don't. You ain't getting away from me!"

Alarmed, Colleen jumps from the rocks and runs toward the shore, where she left her scuba equipment. Fumbling with her wet suit, she pulls it up over her body, zips it closed, and tucks her hair in the cap.

From behind a boulder, a man charges toward her with his arms outstretched. As he reaches for her, she picks up a stick and swings it, smashing it against his face. He curses, and his hand goes up to the blood dripping from his nose.

Raising her foot, Colleen kicks him in the chest, sending him tumbling over the seals behind him. As he struggles to regain his balance, the seals move to create a wiggling obstacle course for him to maneuver around. Sprinting to the beach, she quickly fastens on her tank and breathing apparatus. She runs to the incoming tide and dives head first, slicing through the water with effortless grace.

With adrenaline flowing through her, Colleen propels herself through the murky depths, scattering schools of fish in her wake. Glancing at the light of the surface, she spots Paradise and heaves herself over the railing.

Onboard, she removes her mask and tank, letting them fall to the deck with a clatter. The chain of the necklace Eric gave her snaps. The delicate seal pendant bounces on the bow before slipping from her grasp, then plunges into the water below. She sighs, retrieving it is out of the question.

Shielding her eyes from the glaring sun, she scans her surroundings to see if any boats are nearby. She spots two: a sleek black cruising boat and a fishing boat. Not knowing if she is being pursued or which vessel holds the man who tried to capture her, she cranks up her anchor and runs to the back to start the engine. Her gut is telling her she is in danger, and she can't just sit out there and wait to find out why.

Gripping the wheel tightly, her only focus is to get the hell out of there. The wind whips through her hair, and the ocean spray mists her face. Aiming for an inhabited island, she travels as fast as her engine will carry her.

There, she can dock and find shelter. Call someone to let them know what is happening before her pursuers catch up with her.

But her boat is slowing down. Suddenly, the motor goes silent. *Shit.* She was in such a hurry to leave the marina in Cook's Cove that she forgot to check her fuel supply.

Quickly, she hoists the mainsail; it flaps lifelessly in the air, so she drops it. The sound of an approaching motor is growing louder. She searches the horizon. Several boats are hovering near the island's shore, but there isn't enough wind to escape. Panicking, she glances around for her phone. She picks it up, but it slips from her hand, and flies over the side into the water. She has to decide—stay and face who is chasing her or jump.

Wearing nothing but her wetsuit, Colleen takes a deep breath and dives over the side into the water, leaving her face mask and the tank behind. There's no turning back now.

Colleen begins to swim. *Don't panic*, she tells herself. Each stroke propels her forward, her limbs slicing through the currents with precision. The shore seems unreachable, but she refuses to let doubt detour her.

As she swims, her muscles strain under her exhaustion.

The adrenaline that propelled her into the water is now turning against her, causing her muscles to tighten with each stroke.

Just when she thinks her strength is about to give out, an orange float splashes in front of her. She grabs it, clinging on as it pulls her toward a boat. Almost to its side, she recognizes who is waiting for her on deck. She freezes with fear, letting go of the orange object, and dives beneath the surface.

FOR INFORMATION about other book by Judy Leslie go to www.judy-leslie.com

Acknowledgments

I would like to thank my husband Ralph and my friends for their support. Especially the ladies in my book club for not getting upset with me when I haven't read the month's book. A special thanks goes to the editors that have helped make my stories better and my cover designer for her wonderful designs.

My house hasn't been as tidy and my meals haven't been fancy while I've been sitting at my computer dreaming up stories. But my family understands in order to create it takes time. I am thankful for everyone's support and understanding. Love you all!

Judy Leslie

About the Author

Who doesn't love a mystery? Throw in a bit of suspense and a romance and you're off on an adventure. Nothing like curling up with a good book on a rainy day or before you drop off to bed at night. Especially if there is a little strange activity lurking in the background.

The best way to describe her Cook's Cove collection is that they are mysteries with a romance containing emotional elements found in woman's fiction. Several of these stories lean towards the sweet with heat romance rather than spicy, but they also contain some darker elements.

Judy Leslie lives in the Pacific Northwest and splits her time between living in a city on the water and a cabin in the mountains.

She also writes contemporary small town romances that take place in the mountain town of Leavenworth, Washington. Visit her website for more info about upcoming books www.judy-leslie.com

Made in the USA
Monee, IL
04 August 2025